The Dead Beneath Us

The Chichester Crime Mysteries

Matthew J. Evans

ISBN: 978-1-7394834-0-1

Disclaimer

The Dead Beneath Us is a work of fiction. Names, characters, businesses, schools, police operations, criminal cases, police warrant numbers are a product of the author's imagination or used in a fictitious manner. Any resemblance to actual persons alive or dead, or actual events is purely coincidental.

For Albie.

Chapter One

Monday, 24th April.

The school was a labyrinth of dark corners, forgotten rooms, and clandestine passageways, all of which would have made it easy to hide a body and for it never to be found.

The police had already searched every room, dormitory, and inch of the cellars and loft spaces, but Charles Brady, the Head of Mathematics, was still missing.

Cotisham, a private school for boys, was once a Tudor palace and later a country manor with grand halls and bustling kitchens, the ancestral home of the now-extinct Aversham family. The prestigious school had earned a reputation for academic excellence, and a place there was highly coveted.

Set within acres of fields and woodland, the house shrouded in downland flint and crowned with crenellations and tall chimneys. A short distance away stood Aversham's Folly, a tall brick tower supported by two cylindrical columns on either side. Along with the pond, the tower was among the last places on the school grounds to be searched.

At ground level, the folly was overrun with brambles and nettles, fallen bricks, and other debris, which made the path to the foot of the steps difficult to walk on. But PC Frend had decided that it was safe to go up. It was dry in there—the stretch of warm spring weather had seen to that—and the brickwork appeared solid enough even for Frend's larger-than-life frame and size-ten feet.

A rasping clamour of rooks called to one another, mocking him from the treetops, putting Frend on edge. An earthy sweetness hung in the air, mingling with something dark and sour.

Frend looked at Andrew Winston, the young deputy head, who had waited for him. "I'd better have a look."

"You're wasting your time, constable," said Winston. "He wouldn't have gone up there."

"Maybe, but it's best to be sure."

Frend took one careful step at a time until his confidence in the brick structure grew. The steps had a steep rise, and with the weight of his stab vest and utility belt, a wash of sweat soon formed on his brow and under his police shirt.

He had been told the tower was off-limits to the students, but the graffiti and the messages scratched into the surrounding walls told a different story. Empty bottles littered the floor, along with charred branches and cigarette ends—things that teenage boys did no matter how wealthy their parents were.

He reached the first level and looked out of the open archway onto the vast grounds below. Lord Aversham's Folly, although partly concealed by trees, still captured a view of the manor house about three hundred yards away. The tower rose above the Sussex countryside, protruding from an emerging spring canopy.

Below him, Frend saw the deputy headmaster looking up at him, standing among the haze of bluebells. Frend caught his breath for a moment and continued his journey up. The next flight of steps was darker and more enclosed. That sour, rotting odour was coming from above him, and he recognised it now. His heart sank.

He'd seen death many times before. Sometimes it was an ordered and planned end, and other times it was cold, sudden, and despairing, with no time for goodbyes or to make amends. Some bodies were fresh and warm, but others were foetid and unrecognisable.

Frend steeled himself as he came onto the second level and looked at the concrete platform, but there was nothing apart from crumbling bricks and mortar. Now the stench was more pungent. It seemed to be coming from the very top. He reached for the radio clipped to his stab vest.

"Control from Charlie-Whisky-one-zero-one."

"Go ahead, Charlie-Whisky-one-zero-one," the control room responded.

"How long until the drone unit gets here?"

"They said another thirty minutes—coming from Shoreham."

Frend sighed. "Roger. We'll need the drone to get some shots over the old folly."

"One-zero-one, what have you got?"

"Something unpleasant, by the smell of it. I'll update you."

"Roger."

Frend knew he had to see what was up there for himself. Perhaps he should have waited for the skipper, but he was only twenty feet from the final level. He activated his body-worn video camera, and the beeps told him it was recording. Each subsequent step was harder than the last, and the rancid smell grew stronger. There was a sense of inevitability about the climb now. One more step, and then another. Sweat dripped into his eyes, and he cursed as they stung. Something dark and buzzing struck his cheek. A fly. He pressed the back of his wrist into his nose as the blood pounded in his ears. Frend was a few steps away from turning the final corner onto the third platform. The stench was now almost unbearable. The air was thick with blowflies. He took the next step. A scuffed brown brogue came into view, followed by a grey trouser leg and a black curled hand. Then he saw something else, and the acid contents of his stomach hit the back of his throat. Frend backed away and headed down again to fill his lungs with less putrid air. He wiped his forehead—it was okay; he wouldn't throw up. Frend pressed the button on his radio, and his burning throat made him cough.

"Control from Charlie-Whisky-one-zero-one."

"Go ahead, one-zero-one."

"I think I've found what's left of our misper, Mr Brady. Could you let supervision know? We're going to need CID and SOCO here."

Frend couldn't stop the heave of his stomach when it came, and he emptied himself onto the concrete slab around his feet.

Detective Sergeant Emily Summers was sitting at her desk in Chichester Police Station, reading the incident log about the job that had come in from Cotisham School. The last update was one minute ago, and they were calling for CID to attend. Soon, the telephones would be ringing.

Summers was in her early thirties, petite, blonde, and fiery, with a sharp and creative mind. Her desk was in the corner of a long, open-plan office on the first floor, and it was her territory while she was on duty. There were six other desks, back-to-back, in front of hers, and her boss's office was behind her, like a large fish tank with Venetian blinds. There were desks beyond the

Major Crimes core team, filled by civilian staff and seconded officers.

From the initial account of the Cotisham job, it looked like this would be Summers's first murder inquiry with the team, and she needed this to work well for her. She was eager to tell the DCI, but he was talking on the phone in his office, unaware of the unfolding events. She watched him for a moment, hoping to catch his eye. The DCI seemed aloof and strange. Summers wondered if it had something to do with his Romanian culture or if he was self-conscious of the scar on his face.

She had four DCs she could send straight away, and another four civilian investigators could be diverted if needed. DCs Burgess and Booker were sitting a few feet away. Summers wracked her brain to remember their first names. Was it Sarah and Jared? She'd only been there a few days, and there was so much to remember.

This latest move was not going as well as she had hoped. The team she had joined was close-knit and wary of outsiders. The previous DS had moved away, and the team had already made it known to Summers that he was a hard act to follow. So Summers put her foot down early on to let them know she was capable enough to do this job.

Summers retied her ponytail as she watched Burgess and Booker talking and looking at Booker's computer screen.

"Sergeant?" said Booker, looking up from his screen. "Have you seen the Cotisham School job?"

"I prefer, Sarge, if you don't mind, Jared. Yes, I'm just reading it now."

"It's Gareth, Sarge. Do you want us to go down there?"

"Just wait. I haven't finished yet." From the corner of her eye, she saw the slight shake of Booker's head. He was in his mid-twenties, slim, and had a handsome face. His brown hair had an annoying, perfect bounce, and he'd grown a short beard and a moustache that Summers thought he'd look better without.

Summers's personal mobile pinged. It was her partner, Anthony, texting her again. She didn't want to read it, not after last night. Her hand went to the bruise on her shoulder.

She looked up at the DCI's office. He had come off his phone now.

"Where are the others?" she asked Burgess, an elegant black woman with colourful, beaded dreadlocks.

"In the kitchen getting a drink, Sarge."

Summers got up and knocked on the DCI's door before entering.

"Boss?" she said, edging into his office.

"Emily," he said as he pulled at his shirt sleeves. Summers wondered if it was a habit he had to hide the burn marks on his wrists.

"A job has come in. That misper from Cotisham. It looks like it's turned into a suspicious death."

The DCI looked up from his screen and studied Summers for a moment. "Okay. You're attending with the team?"

"Yes, boss. The response sergeant is on scene, and SOCO is on the way."

"Very well."

His response was stilted, and Summers was waiting for him to continue. "Right then. I'll get down there, sir."

"Fine. I'll monitor the log from here. Keep me updated."

"Fine. I mean, yes, boss." She was hoping for something more urgent from him.

Dinescu nodded and continued with what he was doing.

Summers closed the door behind her and shook her head. This place was nothing like the last major crimes team she was with in Surrey. Were they all half asleep in rural Sussex?

The others had returned from the kitchen with their drinks,

and Summers held out her arms as if she were herding them together.

"The Cotisham misper has turned into a sus death. It looks like Charles Brady's been found with a hole in his chest. Can we all get down there now and RV outside the school?"

The other two, whom Summers had forgotten the names of, looked at their hot drinks and then at each other.

"We'll have to find another pool car," said Booker.

"Why?" asked Summers. "Can't you share?"

"Four in a car?"

"Well, just find another car. It can't be that difficult!"

"You'd be surprised. And no one wants the silver Focus."

"The Astra's back from the workshops," said Burgess.

Summers sighed. "This is a very boring conversation, Jared. Just sort it."

"Yes, Sarge," he said.

And as Summers walked out into the corridor, she slapped her forehead. "Shit! Gareth." But it was too late.

Chapter Two

The silver Ford Focus followed the winding Midhurst road, hugging the curves of the South Downs. It cut through a thick crown of trees and descended into a landscape of tilled farmland. A dense hedgerow appeared on one side of the car, and a weathered, flint-encrusted wall marked the boundary of the Cotisham Estate on the other.

Detective Chief Inspector Beniamin Dinescu decreased his speed as he followed the blur of the boundary wall, looking for the school entrance. He came to a flint gatehouse with a tall brick pillar on either side, standing guard like blind sentries. The black iron gates were open, and Dinescu entered the estate. He followed the narrow tarmac road, cracked by the erupting roots of overarching trees and glossy-leaved rhododendrons. He passed a sign warning of impending children, and then the road widened, the trees dispersed, and the car swung onto a pea-shingle drive that circled the front of Cotisham House. Two police vans were already there, and he parked his car beside them. The police search advisor was briefing the search officers, and she raised her hand when she recognised Dinescu.

The car door swung open, and DCI Dinescu stepped out,

stretching his long back and rotating his broad shoulders. He listened in to the search team briefing. After a few minutes, he felt the strengthening morning light warming his bald head. The left side of his face, from his temple to his cheek, bore a burn scar that was raised and discoloured. The edges were puckered, while the skin around the scar was smooth and unmarked, making the disfigurement stand out.

Dinescu stepped away from the briefing, scrunching the shingle beneath his tan brogues. He turned to survey the surrounding scene. There was something about the house that made his skin crawl. It was imposing and austere, with long, sharp lines and angular bay windows. Two thin, hexagonal turrets were set into the corners of the southern aspect, one capped with a weathervane. Tall, rectangular chimney stacks, darkened by years of use, rose from the leaded roof. Dinescu imagined the cavernous stone fireplaces beneath them, belching smoke through the wide brick flues. Below the stacks was a line of square attic windows peering down at him. Dinescu shuddered. What kind of parent would send their child away to this place?

The house was surrounded by fields that dipped and rose with the Sussex countryside, effusing a faint smell of manure and cut grass. Ahead was an area of woodland with oaks and coppiced sweet chestnuts, and in front of it was a large pond encircled by a wire fence. Several off-road police vehicles and SOCO vans were gathered there like thirsty savannah beasts surrounding a watering hole.

Set inside the wood, a short distance away, the folly's tower poked its red-brick ramparts above the treetops like a giant walking through the woods. That was Dinescu's destination. Taking a deep breath, he tugged down the cuffs of his blue shirt, adjusted his tie, and made his way across the field towards the trees.

A little further on, two young PCSOs were talking in the shade, their hands tucked inside the armholes of their stab vests. When they saw Dinescu, they approached the line of police tape they were protecting to meet him.

"Good morning. I'm DCI Dinescu, the senior investigating officer. I'm here to view the crime scene and see DS Summers. Is she here?"

One glanced at the warrant card on Dinescu's lanyard, looked twice at his face, and then averted his eyes. "Yes, sir," he said. "DS Summers is already here."

Dinescu tensed his jaw.

"How long have you been here?" he asked the PCSO.

"A couple of hours, sir. We've had a few curious teachers ask questions, but it's not like we know anything."

"Often the best way. Sign me into the scene, please."

Dinescu ducked under the tape and continued towards the folly. He sensed the PCSOs were both watching him as he went.

The sound of murmuring voices from somewhere ahead led him through the trees towards the base of the tower and a line of red and white police tape: the inner cordon. A PC was standing outside of the cordon, watching Dinescu approach.

Again, he showed his warrant card. "I'm DCI Dinescu. I'm here to meet with DS Summers. I'm not going inside."

"Thank you, sir," said the PC.

Dinescu could hear the voices again. They were coming from the tower above him. He could now smell something dead and rotten hanging in the air and drifting through the trees.

He spotted DS Emily Summers. She was wearing protective clothing, gesticulating, and pointing at the crime scene manager, who was shaking his head.

Dinescu sighed. "Emily. Come over here."

When Summers saw him, she glanced away, and he saw the

tail end of a smirk. She nodded to him and tucked her blonde hair back inside her hood. Despite the glowing recommendation from the Chief Superintendent, it would be some time before Dinescu felt comfortable working with her.

As she approached, he saw she had lost the colour in her cheeks.

"Hello, boss. Did you see the search team is here?"

"I did, thanks. You look pale."

"I'm fine." She tempered her curt response. "I've just seen the body—not something I want to look at again in a hurry. He's right at the top of the tower. He's been shot in the chest—blown his insides out."

"The call log mentioned a shotgun."

"Looks like it was, sir. Close range." She screwed up her face as she remembered what she saw. "He's black and full of maggots now."

"Any chance he did this to himself?"

Summers brushed off his question with a snort. "I'm no expert, but he would have needed very long arms."

Dinescu didn't look amused. "It's too early for sarcasm, Emily."

Summers looked away. "There's no gun with him, sir."

"Could it have fallen from the tower?"

She shrugged. "Possibly, but nothing has been found so far."

"How certain are we that it's Charles Brady?"

"Pretty much, sir. The wallet in his jacket contains a driving licence and bank cards. His wristwatch has his name engraved, and his clothes match exactly what he was last seen wearing."

"Who's the pathologist?

Emily looked up at the top of the tower. "Luckily, it's Doctor Dufour, an expert on gunshot wounds. His initial thoughts are that Brady was shot from about four to six feet away."

"I've spoken to the coroner, and the postmortem is authorised. Did Doctor Dufour say when he could do it?"

"Tomorrow, first thing."

Dinescu ran his bottom lip under his top teeth as he thought. "You were talking with the crime scene manager. Does he want to see me?"

"No, sir. I've spoken to him and told you everything we know so far. It's all in hand. He said he'd contact you with any further updates."

Dinescu was watching a pair of SOCOs searching on their knees close to the base of the folly.

"Okay, I'll leave you to finish up. I'm heading over to the school."

"I don't think they need me here, and I'm done. The pathologist is up with the body now, trying to figure out how to bring it down without it falling apart. They've been poking around, and the stench is getting a bit much now. I'll come with you if you don't mind."

Summers stepped under the inner cordon tape, removed her stained coverall, blue gloves, and shoe covers, and ditched them into a hazardous waste bag. She looked relieved to be free of it all. Dinescu had already begun to stride away, and Summers had to hurry to catch him up.

Dinescu glanced over his shoulder at the approaching DS. "Where are Sarah and Gareth?" Summers looked at him with a blank expression. "Sarah Burgess and Gareth Booker."

"Ah, yes. They're talking to the staff inside the school, and DC Ross Taylor is somewhere around here, too. He keeps making himself scarce."

"I don't believe that. He's likely to be following a lead." Dinescu slowed his walking pace for Summers. "So, Brady was last seen a week ago. That was the first day back after the Easter break. Do we know if he went home that Monday?"

"That's unknown, sir. Enquiries were made with the neighbours when he was first reported as a misper. None of them said they'd seen him. He lived on his own, according to his colleagues. The headmaster told me that Brady's VW Golf hadn't moved from the car park. When he went missing, he took Brady's keys from his office, and the office was secured. I've seized them."

"You have been busy. Next of kin?"

"His mother. She lives in a nursing home in West Wittering. DC Chester Kirby has gone down there."

Summers was still a little out of breath, so Dinescu relented his pace a little more. "Good. Chester will be good at that. It will be helpful to get a time of death soon."

"The pathologist said the maggots should give us that."

They'd walked through the trees and were back in the sunshine. Dinescu stopped and looked up at the top of the folly poking out of the treetops.

"Why do you think Brady was up there, Emily?"

"Beats me. But you'd have thought someone would have heard the shot. The tower is only a few hundred yards from the school."

Dinescu agreed. "Have we got the first accounts from the school staff?"

"Yes, sir. They haven't exactly been forthcoming with information. The head is nice but a bit of a wet fish—just telling us the bare minimum."

They signed out of the crime scene and headed towards the house.

Dinescu looked over at Summers. "What sort of school did you go to?"

"A girls' school in Portsmouth. Nothing like this. It costs a fortune to send your kids here—more than my salary. They don't know they've got it made. I met some of the hormonal teenagers when I arrived. Boys are all the same, even private school boys."

"It's a tough age for anyone, and girls are a mystery when you're a teenager. Well, they were to me."

They continued onto the driveway, and Summers brought out her personal mobile, buzzing in her hand. She cancelled an incoming call and groaned in exasperation, shaking her head.

"Men are a total mystery to me, too."

They reached the front of the school and passed through a heavy oak door inset in Gothic-styled stone. The entrance hall was bleak, musty, and unwelcoming. The main assembly hall was to their right, with grey plastic chairs stacked against the walls and a covered grand piano at the far end.

They looked at the sign above them on the wall. The school motto, *Nurture to Achieve*, was emblazoned in gold on dark mahogany panelling. Aside from the main hall, three heavy oak doors led out of the hallway, and a wide stone staircase rose before them. One door was labelled *Reception* on a brass plaque in faded black lettering.

They heard far-off young voices calling to each other, reverberating around them like lost souls. Doors slammed, and feet were running somewhere. Dinescu shuddered.

"This place gives me the creeps," said Summers. "I wouldn't send my kids here. Not that I have any."

Dinescu tried the reception door, but it was locked. He shrugged at Summers and walked to the bottom of the stairs to look up into the darkness above. "Perhaps we should go up."

"Do we have to, boss?

He was about to answer when a door creaked open. A woman in white-framed glasses and bleached, spiky hair appeared. She wore a red quilted jacket with matching lipstick, and a short plaid skirt covered her thick black tights.

Summers smiled and stepped forward. "This is DCI Dinescu, and I'm DS Summers. We're looking for our colleagues."

"Ah, yes," said the woman. "I've been sent out to find you. I'll take you to them now. I'm Celia, Doctor Greenway's PA."

They followed Celia back through the door and were now in a long, gloomy passageway. Celia's heels clicked and clacked on the uneven stone floor. It was cold in there, and Dinescu was looking at Celia's thick tights.

"It's always cold in here," she said as if she had read his mind.

"I wish I'd brought my jacket," said Summers. "It must cost a fortune to heat this place."

"You wouldn't believe it if I told you."

"I think I would," said Dinescu.

"They're in the dining hall taking statements or whatever it is you do. We'll need to move you soon. It's almost time for the boys to have their lunch."

A smell like stew and custard wafted over them from somewhere. Celia made a sharp turn, and they entered the large dining hall—much warmer than the corridor—with a tall ceiling and three rows of long tables. Along three walls were leaded windows, the tops of which were stained glass. On one wall was a great fireplace with a heavy marble mantelpiece and a shining copper dinner gong below.

Celia pointed to the far end of the hall. "I'll leave you to it."

Detective Constables Gareth Booker and Sarah Burgess were sitting at the end of a table. Burgess, her long, beaded dreadlocks clattering on the tabletop, was conversing with a man in his late fifties who had silver hair and matching framed glasses. He looked gangly in his ill-fitting charcoal-grey suit.

Dinescu recognised him from the school's website. Greenway looked up in surprise when Dinescu stood beside him.

"Doctor Greenway, I'm Detective Chief Inspector Benjamin Dinescu. I'm the senior investigating officer. This is Detective Sergeant Emily Summers."

Greenway nodded. His face was ashen and wrinkled. "I've just given my statement to these officers. Probably no help at all, but..."

"I'm sorry for your loss, Doctor Greenway. It must be a terrible time for you all."

"Completely unexpected. We're all in shock." Greenway's eyes wandered over Dinescu's face. "We had no idea Mr Brady was feeling so desperate. May I ask why you are leading this investigation? Surely, it's cut and dried?"

Dinescu looked at Burgess, who shook her head. Greenway hadn't been told. Dinescu sat beside Greenway, who swivelled to face him.

"Doctor Greenway—"

"Call me Eric."

Dinescu nodded. "Eric, we've had to withhold a few details about how Charles Brady was discovered. But I can share more information with you now."

"What is it?"

"We suspect he was murdered."

It took a few seconds to sink in.

"Murdered! Oh, God, no! How? We assumed that..."

"It's unlikely he could have inflicted the injuries he suffered on himself. We need to confirm this, but he was shot from close range. Possibly with a shotgun."

"Shot!" Greenway put his head in his hands.

"I was wondering, being as we're in the countryside, if your school owns a shotgun, Eric?"

"We have six double-barrelled shotguns at the school for

16

clay pigeon shooting. We run a club for the older boys. The guns are kept in a cabinet in my office."

Dinescu glanced over at Booker.

"Perhaps we could check, Doctor Greenway?" said Booker, running his thumb and forefinger down his moustache and beard.

The headmaster agreed. "There's a book we sign when the guns are taken out. It's all above board. All keyholders are licensed, and my PA looks after my key." He looked at Dinescu and frowned. "Will we need to close the school?"

"I think the safety of your boys and staff is paramount," said Dinescu. "How easy will it be for your boarders to return home?"

"Home? I doubt we could send any of them home without causing severe disruption to their families. We have sixty full-time boarders, Chief Inspector. Twenty of them are from over-seas—France, Kenya, Japan, and the USA. It won't be at all practical. The other forty have homes in the UK. Some of them are hundreds of miles away."

"How many day students are there?"

"A hundred and eighty."

"I suggest you send the day students home until we can assess their safety. Perhaps contact the parents of the boarders to see what they want to do. We will need to know who is staying."

Greenway shook his head. "I don't want the word *murder* to get out. It will panic the parents. Covid was bad enough—it almost ruined us. We can't afford them to pull their boys from the school."

"I appreciate this is very challenging, Eric, but until we are certain no one else is in danger, we must take reasonable steps to reduce the risk."

Greenway's shoulders rolled forward. "Of course. What's happening now?"

"A police search advisor is now on the school grounds. I've already spoken to her and agreed on a search strategy regarding the murder weapon. We have officers searching for it now."

DC Sarah Burgess leaned closer and engaged Greenway with her soft Caribbean accent. "We don't want your boys to be alarmed, Doctor Greenway. There will be a police presence here for several days. Hopefully, that will give them and their parents some reassurance."

"Some may see it as an excuse to withdraw their children. But I'm grateful for any support you can afford us."

Dinescu sat forward with Burgess. "Perhaps my colleagues have already asked you this, but do you know of any reason why Mr Brady would have been in the tower last Monday or any day?"

"None whatsoever, and it's off-limits to the boys, with severe consequences if they're caught."

"Do the staff use the tower for anything?"

"We ask them not to. So, not as far as I'm aware."

Dinescu tugged down his sleeves and thought for a moment.

"Do you know if Mr Brady had any recent fallings-out with anyone?"

"There were a couple of issues. One was all over a simple misunderstanding, and the other was a problem with a student. My deputy deals with things like that. Andrew said there was nothing to be concerned about. And Mr Brady was well-liked by all the staff."

"What was your opinion of Mr Brady?"

"A nice chap. Quiet, but achieved good results in the maths department. He'd turned it around in the short time he'd been here." Greenway glanced at his watch. "Sorry. I need to call a staff meeting and then an assembly. I've sent the boys to their rooms and their tutor groups. Talk to my PA and get the keys for the gun cabinet from her. If there's nothing more?"

"Thanks, Eric."

"Sarge, we'll seize the shotguns now," said Booker.

Summers agreed. "As soon as, then meet us back by the cars."

Greenway stood, muttering something under his breath. With his head down and lost in thought, he left the hall. There was a sudden clatter of shutters rising, which startled Dinescu. The kitchen serving staff were watching them.

"That's a hint for us to go," said Dinescu.

"I agree, boss," said Summers. "I don't fancy school dinners, but I am getting hungry. I've got a cheese sandwich with my name on it back at the office."

"Just cheese?"

"Yes, boss. I love cheese."

Several boys in light blue polo shirts and dark blue fleeces peered around a pillar at them from the shadows. Dinescu felt sorry for them. An unwelcome intrusion had roiled their ordered lives.

A movement above caught his eye. Along the top of one side of the dining hall was a line of dark ironwork. A shadow slid along behind it and then disappeared out of view. Dinescu wondered if his mind was playing tricks on him or if the house itself was keeping an eye on them.

Chapter Three

Ruth had been muttering to herself all morning. She had sat in the same chair facing the window every day, year after year, as her memories drifted further away. Her powdery eyes stared out at the view of the beach, and she was lost in another time and place, which was more real to her than Ocean View Nursing Home.

Her skin was mottled and bruised, her skeletal frame concealed by a baggy blouse and purple cardigan, bobbled and worn-through around the elbows.

She liked her daily routine, so when Clare, the nail girl, came in on Monday mornings, she was an unwelcome interruption.

She stuffed the remains of a custard cream into her mouth as Clare pulled up a chair in front of her. Ruth looked away when she heard someone calling. It was Gerald begging her, telling her he loved her, that he'd give her anything she wanted. But his promises were only a means to an end. She should have known.

Now it was Clare she could see—pretty Clare, holding her right hand. Ruth didn't like the fuss over her nails. It was her daughters who insisted that she have a weekly manicure. She had overheard her eldest say it was what she would have wanted when she was well.

"Hello, Ruth!" Clare was bright and friendly as if she were talking to a child. She was from Derby, and her voice was young and sweet. "How are you, my love?"

Ruth looked at Clare's belly and noticed the telltale bump. Her eyes drifted towards her face. She didn't recognise her at first. Was it the other girl, the stuck-up one? She couldn't bear her—always mithering, not like Liv.

"Go away! I don't want you. Not you."

"You don't mean that. I've come especially."

Ruth didn't answer. She looked back out of the window and ran her tongue over her biscuit-encrusted lips.

"It's a lovely day again, Ruth. The warm weather will be here soon. I can't say I'm looking forward to it getting too hot." Clare opened a packet of wipes and cleaned Ruth's fingertips and nails, removing the biscuit pieces lodged there.

"Where's Liv?" asked Ruth.

"Liv?"

"Yes! Where's Liv?"

"I'm so sorry. I don't know who Liv is."

"Bitch!"

Clare ignored it. "Do you want your usual red?"

"Tell Liv it had to be done—the dead girl. It's in the letter."

Clare's eyes widened, and she held her breath for a moment.

"What did you say?"

"Whore!"

Clare dropped Ruth's hand. "That's not very kind."

A male carer in a maroon shirt knelt beside Clare. "Don't mind her. She's grumpy this morning. She couldn't have her usual porridge for breakfast, which always puts her in a bad mood."

Clare smiled back at him. "That's okay. I'm used to it. The things I hear sometimes."

"Listen!" Ruth jutted her head forward. "Tell Liv I killed the girl. The pretty blonde one, like you. Stupid bitch, she was. It was dark, and I had to see if she was dead. I put it all in the letter. The letter! Read the letter!"

Clare bit her lip and looked at the carer.

"Don't worry," he said. "She says it from time to time. Her daughters know about it. Most likely something she heard on TV."

The carer was called away, and Clare continued with the nails.

"So it's the same as last time, Ruth."

Ruth watched Clare select the varnish from her box and unscrew the lid.

"Yes, please. Sorry, dear."

Clare smiled. "That's okay." She cradled Ruth's hand. It was warm and clammy.

"Thank you, dear."

Clare brushed on the nail varnish in long lines, and Ruth kept her hand still.

"That's one hand done," she said, placing Ruth's hand on the arm of the chair. "Now leave that one there, and let's have your left." Ruth tried to sit forward. "No. Best to stay still, my love."

"Clare. Please!" There was desperation on Ruth's face. "Tell Liv I saw the pretty blonde girl. She was dead. I think I killed her. But..." She looked down and shook her head. "It couldn't have been me, could it? Not me. The little chicken was so pretty, like you."

Ruth pulled back her hands and folded her arms over her chest.

"Ruth, no! It's not dry yet."

"Bitch!" she screamed, spitting the contents of her mouth over Clare. "*You* killed her. It was you! You buried her!"

Clare stood in panic and gathered her things. The carer stood beside her and held her arm.

"Best leave it today. She'll soon forget this."

Clare gave an uncertain smile. "Sure. I'll try again next Monday."

Detective Constable Chester Kirby signed in at the main door of Ocean View Nursing Home. He looked around for someone to help him and heard loud music coming from somewhere. Someone was singing too close into a microphone. A short woman in an apron appeared carrying a bucket and mop, ready to wash the flecked linoleum floor.

"I'm looking for Irene Brady," said Kirby. "I believe she's a resident here."

"Try the small lounge on the left," said the woman. "She prefers the quiet, and I don't blame her." She rolled her eyes and sank the mop head into the bucket. "Mind the wet floor on your way out."

Kirby smiled and nodded.

He was directed to a communal lounge, bright and south-facing, with blue high-back chairs and a large TV on the wall, which was left on with nobody watching. A much larger room was opposite the entrance, with some sing-along entertainment bellowing to a backing track.

The smell of the place reminded Kirby of his grandmother, who had spent the last days of her life in a place like this. A twinge of regret struck him. He smoothed down his ginger hair and looked around for anyone who could be Charles Brady's mother.

Only a handful of residents were in the lounge, all asleep except for an elderly woman in a baggy purple cardigan sitting facing the window. A young pregnant woman and a male carer were walking away from her, talking together. As they passed Kirby, they saw the police lanyard around his neck and the young woman glanced back at the elderly resident looking out the window.

Kirby stopped the carer. "Is Irene Brady here?"

The carer inclined his head. "No, Irene is in her room. Can I help?"

"I have some news I need to give her."

"One minute, please." He exchanged a few words with the woman.

"I'll be back next Monday," she said to the carer and left.

Kirby lifted his warrant card on his lanyard. "I didn't introduce myself. I'm DC Kirby from Chichester CID. I'm afraid it's bad news. Will Irene be okay to talk to me?"

The carer shook his head. "I'm sorry. Irene isn't able to engage with you. You can try, but she won't understand you. She's very ill."

Kirby lowered his voice. "Irene's son has died, and we believe she's his next of kin. Do you know of anyone else in the family?"

"Oh, goodness!" He put his hand over his mouth. "I'm so sorry to hear that. I've known Irene for many years. It was only Charles who visited her. I don't know of anyone else."

"Do you think it would do her harm to tell her?"

"I don't know. She wouldn't understand it. I can talk to her on your behalf if you prefer."

"Thank you," said Kirby.

The elderly woman in the chair muttered something about a letter, and the carer ushered Kirby away. "Let's go into the office so we can talk. Ruth doesn't like seeing people she doesn't know."

Kirby followed the carer out of the lounge and into a small, stifling office on the ground floor. He declined a seat but waited for the carer to find his reading glasses, clean them, and look through Irene's file.

"There's no one else on Irene Brady's file," said the carer. "Charles was a loving son. He was very protective of his mother. He didn't like her being in the main lounge with some of the other ladies. Even had a falling out over it."

"What about?"

"Nothing, really. One of the residents got a bit loud and said some things that upset his mother. It happens from time to time. Ends up in fights sometimes."

"If there's no one else on your list as family, I'll leave it to you to talk to Irene. I will ask you to sign a note to that effect."

"Sure. Charles was a nice man. I'm very sad to hear he's dead. How, may I ask, did he die?"

"He was found dead at the school where he worked. I can't say much more than that at the moment."

"Oh. I've heard a lot about that school," the carer said. "Leave it to me. Good luck finding Charles's relatives."

Chapter Four

Cameron Hyde was the school caretaker, gardener, and general drudge. A list of recurring jobs, requests, and complaints from staff drove his work to keep the building and grounds together. If he couldn't fix something, he would call upon his crew of contractors, including his father and his father's friends. Cameron was in his late twenties, handsome-faced, with a strong jaw like his father's and long, sandy-coloured hair.

Cameron was troubled, and his eyes were red after a sleepless night. He was walking back from the boiler room at the rear of the school. The police had left it unlocked after the recent searches, and the students would have had a field day in there if they had known. He walked along the side of the Tudor house, where he could see the folly tower and the police officers forming lines to begin their search. About two dozen or more of them were dressed in black with baseball caps and carrying long sticks to poke the undergrowth. They'd have a job going through the woods, thought Cameron. It was overgrown with brambles in some places, and rabbit holes were everywhere.

He kicked at the stones on the path beneath his feet, breaking the stem of a dandelion clock and causing the seeds to fly away in the breeze. It brought back a memory of when he was a child, blowing the delicate parachutes into the air. They looked so fragile as they floated away, but now he knew dandelions were hardy, deep-rooted buggers and hard to kill. They reminded him of some people he knew.

But that day, the question that bothered him the most was, what if the police found what he had lost? He'd been searching for days and was about to turn out his workshop.

He couldn't stay back any longer. His heart quickened as adrenaline narrowed his vision and churned his stomach. He didn't think it would do any harm to ask them. He would volunteer his services, and he had to be subtle. He saw the two younger officers standing beside the police tape. They looked approachable—he'd ask them.

He dug his hands into his Barbour coat and walked towards them. A few moments later, he heard footsteps running behind him and someone out of breath.

"I wouldn't, mate," said the voice. A strong hand grabbed his shoulder.

He turned to see Archie Faulkner, one of the contractors and his father's lifelong friend. He was in his early fifties, a builder-decorator with a matching physique. He did the building jobs around the school that Cameron couldn't, and he had known the school for many years. The sun reflected off his round head, and his face flushed after his short jog.

"Archie. What's up?"

"Have you found it yet?"

"No. I was going to offer to help search—"

"Don't be bloody stupid! Do you know how that would look? Keep your head down, mate. Why draw attention to yourself?"

Cameron stopped and considered what Archie had said.

Although Archie was close to his father, Cameron was wary of him.

"You're right."

Archie grinned, revealing his gold tooth. "Now, a birdie told me you have a rat problem."

Cameron was puzzled for a second but then remembered. "Oh, yes! Chef was saying they've got rats outside the kitchen. I was going to shoot them, but..."

"Bloody messy, mate. An air rifle would have been better. Or better still, try poison."

"That's what I was going to ask you. I've run out."

"Leave it to me. Now, let's go over to your workshop, and you can make me a cuppa. I can tell you all you need to know about that ugly bald detective and his gorgeous sidekick."

Cameron wondered if Archie had stopped him from making a big mistake. "What was I thinking, Archie?"

"God knows, mate." He gave a wheezy laugh. "You're as daft as your dad sometimes. Or was it your woman's idea?"

But Leah didn't know—he hadn't told her. Leah was his partner and an art teacher at the school. It was where they first met two years ago. He'd fallen for her the moment he saw her. She was a slim brunette with the sweetest, bluest eyes he'd ever seen and a figure he struggled to keep his hands off. She had something about her that attracted men, like the proverbial honeypot. She wasn't flirtatious but could draw men in with her disarming smile and compelling eyes. The problem for Cameron was that several of the older boys at the school and some of the teachers thought the same.

Cameron wondered if his impulsive decision was because of his argument with Leah that morning. It had rattled him. Leah had been wary of Cameron since an incident after the New Year's party in January. He had put his foot down and taught Charles Brady a lesson. Now she was distant, almost as if they had become strangers. What more could he do? He'd bought her that new car, the flowers, and even booked a holiday in Greece. But it was like she didn't want him to touch her. Was there someone else? It felt like it. And now that Brady was dead, what would she think?

Sarah Burgess and Gareth Booker followed Celia, the PA, through the school corridors. It reminded Sarah that she would soon need to start looking at schools for her four-year-old daughter, Rosie. She couldn't imagine why a mother would want to send their child away to school. It was so far from her own childhood experience that she could barely imagine it. Paying vast amounts of money to send your child to a dark and colourless place like Cotisham seemed like insanity.

Sarah's sister, Marie, helped her look after Rosie. She picked her up from nursery and gave her tea—she was like a second mother. Marie had her own children and said having Rosie was no bother. The hard fact was that Sarah had to work to afford to pay for everything. Fuel prices had gone through the roof, as had food. She was often tempted to throw it all in and live off benefits and her survivor's pension. But life was enough of a struggle, and losing her wage would be too much.

Celia showed Sarah and Gareth into Greenway's office, and Sarah was taken aback by the oppressive dark brown furniture. Celia's distinctive perfume hung in the air, and Sarah wondered if she had been spraying everything beforehand. What was she trying to hide? Cannabis? Alcohol? Perhaps she had a secret spliff and a drink for lunch every day.

The room was a traditional headteacher's study with brown leather-bound books stacked in floor-to-ceiling bookcases. Greenway's desk was a grand old antique in chunky, polished oak. Sarah thought it was everything a headteacher's desk could have been a hundred years ago. His chair, with carved scrolled arms and a worn leather seat, had been left facing the leaded glass windows. It was a perfect match for the table, and Sarah wondered how comfortable it was.

It was apparent now that Sarah irritated Celia as she looked around. Her hand had been rubbing her neck, causing a sore-looking welt. She kept huffing at the detectives, fidgeting with her keys, and checking her watch.

Celia pointed. "The gun cabinet is over *there*."

The cabinet was also in dark oak and had been fitted into a recess in the wall opposite the window. Celia produced a long key and handed it to Booker.

"Who else has a key?" asked Booker.

"I have Doctor Greenway's key. Mr Hyde—the caretaker, and Mr Roberts have the other two. I can't trust Doctor Greenway with his. He'll lose it within thirty seconds." Celia picked up a notebook with a label stuck to the front. "And this is the book everyone has to sign. Only the three keyholders are legally allowed to take out the guns. But you'd know more about that than I do."

"Thank you, Celia," said Sarah. "Strictly speaking, Doctor Greenway should be the one who looks after his key. He shouldn't be giving it to you."

"You'd better tell him that yourself."

Celia turned up her nose, and Booker inserted the key and unlocked the door. The gun cabinet smelled of oil and metal, and the shotguns were inserted into slots.

"Five guns?" asked Booker.

"Six," corrected Celia. She looked into the cabinet, and Sarah saw a question as it formed on her face. "I don't understand."

She picked up the notebook and leafed through the pages.

"Should there be six guns in here?" asked Booker, knowing the answer already.

"Well, according to the book, there should be six. Where is it? There's one missing."

Booker photographed the five shotguns in situ and checked the book for himself. "No one has booked a gun out."

"No. There must be a mistake."

"Can you find the cases for us? The chief inspector wants us to seize the guns. We've got to consider the safety of the students and staff. You'll get a receipt for them."

"Very well, but the boys won't be best pleased."

Booker shrugged. "And can you check with the two key holders to see if either of them has borrowed the missing gun?"

"Add it to my to-do list, shall I?" Her sarcasm had a bite.

Sarah and Booker had got the message. They had outstayed their welcome. Celia reached into a drawer below the gun cabinet for the soft cases. "There are only five cases here. So, someone must have just forgotten to write it in the book."

"Let's hope it's as simple as that, Celia."

She rechecked her watch. "Look, I have to go to a staff meeting now."

The detectives followed her out of the door, which she locked, and Sarah watched her ascend the staircase.

"She's a strange one," she said.

"She doesn't like her domain being interfered with," said Booker. "She even sprayed her perfume everywhere to mark her territory."

"Funny thing, don't you think? Summers is trying to do the same thing." Sarah lowered her voice as if Summers could hear her. "I had a cat that used to piss on the bed when my husband came home from his tour of duty. It was most weird. I wonder if that's why she's been pissing on us."

"Quite. Let's find the boss. A missing gun doesn't bode well."

The staffroom was on the floor above the school's main entrance and had a view of the recent comings and goings in the car park and the folly in the distance. The room had changed little over the years. It still had the decades-old leafy-patterned wallpaper in olive green, touched up and re-glued in places. The ceiling had a permanent nicotine stain and an ugly central rose resembling an inverted iced cake. Hanging from the rose was a yellowing chandelier that had lost several of its glass icicles over the years after being repeatedly caught by the tops of Christmas trees. The room was adequate, with an assortment of armchairs, sofas, and stools and a large, brown table with years of ingrained coffee cup smudges.

The teaching staff had gathered at one end of the room, looking out of the steamy window. They were all watching the detectives meeting in the car park below them. The staff were bewildered by the news, and it was a while before anyone could speak.

"Poor old Charles," said Olivia Grainger, otherwise known as Matron. She was a sturdy woman, somewhere in her early to mid-forties. She studied the scene with her deep brown eyes buried beneath a scowl that had been perfected over many years. Despite that, Olivia Grainger had a certain beauty that used to catch men unawares and had led to two broken marriages.

"Why shoot himself?" said a flushed David Roberts, still in his tracksuit from the five-a-side football lesson.

Andrew Winston, the deputy head, walked up behind them to see what they were watching. "Made an awful mess. Didn't see it myself, but that poor bugger of a policeman went as white as a sheet."

"Why didn't he just jump?" said Roberts. "Would have saved—"

"David!" said Celia, who had arrived with Winston. "I don't think that's appropriate, do you?"

"Well, it's true." Roberts stroked his thick ginger moustache and sighed. "I liked the man. He was a bit of a loner, but it takes all sorts."

"Never had the time to get to know him," said Matron. "Such a tragedy. Perhaps Charles had something on his mind that was worrying him, or someone had broken his heart."

Glances were directed towards Leah Turnbull in her paint-covered overalls, but she ignored the looks and watched the tall, bald detective put the gun cases into the back of a car.

"What's that on his face?" said Roberts.

"A scar, by the looks of it," said Celia. "He's quite scary. I wouldn't like to meet him in a dark alley."

"Why would you be walking around dark alleys, Celia?" quipped Roberts. "Unless you have a sideline you haven't told us about."

Celia shook her head and frowned.

"Why have they taken the guns?" asked Leah.

"Routine," said Winston, looking for a moment at Celia. "Just to give you all a heads-up—there's one missing."

"Missing?" said Grainger. "Surely it was with Charles if he'd...?"

"Nope. It wasn't there."

"But how?"

They all shifted to look at Winston.

"Work it out yourselves. Eric will be up here shortly for the staff meeting."

33

"Gosh! Look at the time!" said Grainger. "I've got to get the boarders moving." She turned and left the staffroom in a hurry.

A long, electronic tone came from the table behind them, where a man was doing something technical with a lamp plug. Everyone knew him as Mac, and he appeared now and then to do PAT testing of their electrical equipment at the most unhelpful times. He was useful when a lightbulb needed changing unless you were short on time and couldn't stand to gossip.

"Have you done yet, Mac?" asked Winston. "We've got a meeting in here in a few minutes."

"Not long. But don't mind me, Andrew." He tapped the side of his index finger against his lips. "I'll be as quiet as a church mouse." But then he gave a full-throated, chesty cough.

"It's confidential. You need to leave."

"Confidential? Ha!" Mac scratched his grey mop of hair. "Nothing goes on here that I don't know about. I've known this school since I was a nipper. I won't be telling any secrets, don't you worry."

"No, Mac. You need to go now. You can continue later."

There was a loud harrumph, and Mac dropped his tools into the toolbox, clattering them as he packed away.

"Is Eric okay, Celia?" asked one of the female learning support assistants. "Must be a shock for him, all this."

Celia shook her head. "He's bearing up. He has some difficult decisions to make." She moved closer to the glass and looked at the folly in the distance. "What I don't get is why didn't we know. Charles has been there all week, and his car was still parked outside the front."

The paunchy music teacher in tweed tutted. "Oh, for goodness' sake, Celia! How could we have known? He's always seemed cheerful—quiet but good-natured."

"Did he have anyone?"

"Divorced, I think," said Roberts. He then lowered his voice. "But saying that, one of the lads said he'd seen Charles taking a blonde woman to his office."

"What, here?" said the music teacher.

Roberts gave a wry smile. "That's what he said. Charles took her to his room, and they... *talked.*"

"David!" Celia scolded him again. "Stop it at once! Which boy said this?"

"Daniel Curtis," replied Roberts. "He wouldn't say who she was."

Celia shook her head and tutted. "Well, I know for a fact that isn't true! You know what Curtis is like. He has a puerile imagination."

"That's true," said the music teacher. "He does it for attention."

Mac coughed again and muttered something under his breath. Winston scowled at him, and Mac rattled his toolbox and left.

"Curtis creeps around the school talking to himself," said Celia. "No wonder he doesn't have friends. I'm sure Charles Brady wouldn't have done anything like *that* in the school."

Roberts gave the music teacher a wink. "Of course not, Celia. How could I even suggest it?"

"I think that's enough now," said Leah Turnbull. "We know nothing about what's happened."

Celia agreed. "Quite right, Leah. What do any of us know?"

Chapter Five

The dormitories in Cotisham School were split between two floors. There were ten rooms on each floor, with up to three boys per room. There was enough wardrobe and desk space for each student, with the older boys having the larger rooms. They were cleaned at the start of each term and comfortable enough all year round.

A group of year sevens were dashing between each other's rooms, shouting and laughing. They took turns going into the common room to look out of the large bay window and watch the police officers with long sticks heading towards the woodland. That stirred up a lot of nervous excitement among them. A whisper went up that someone had spotted Matron coming up the main staircase. There was a mad rush back to their rooms, and doors slammed closed behind them.

Daniel Curtis, a lanky, black-haired eighteen-year-old, entered a sweaty Room Alpha on the first floor. One-Alpha was its official name. He closed the door behind him without making a sound and watched the two young men silhouetted against the open window. He shared the room with Ethan Bishop and Harry Price, who were just in from playing football on the five-a-side pitch. Daniel was unhappy with the sharing arrangement thrust upon him when he turned sixteen. Ethan was a bully, and Harry went along with it. They took pleasure in tormenting and ridiculing him. They were always getting into trouble and often dragged Daniel down with them. So, he was a loner by choice, and sharing a room caused him considerable anxiety, manifesting itself in a nervous tic that isolated him even more. But Daniel had no one else. He was invisible and walked the corridors to lessons as if he were a phantom haunting the school.

This was their last year at Cotisham, but out of the three of them, only Harry had the prospect of going to university. Harry, with his black curls and a face that could charm anyone, wanted to study for a computer science degree, and university couldn't come soon enough for him. If all went well, he'd be at the University of East Anglia in September. His father had other plans for him—a career in the army—but that was the last thing Harry wanted. Daniel knew Harry hated his father and was scared of him. He'd told them he'd rather be dead than join the army, which scared Daniel because he knew he'd meant it.

He had met Harry's parents once, on the last school sports day. Harry looked like his mother, and he was a different person when his father was around. Cold, subdued, and distant. Despite how Harry treated him when Ethan was around, Daniel cared for Harry.

Daniel knew Ethan was gifted, despite being so conflicted. He excelled at almost everything he put his hand to, but he didn't want to do what others wanted. His natural blue-eyed good looks and gift of the gab were all the talent he said he needed. He boasted that he would run away as far from home as possible, get a modelling job or work in London's West End theatres. Daniel wished he had the balls to do that—to run away —but he didn't and most likely never would.

Daniel's life was already mapped out by his family. He was

expected to work for his older brother on the farm. It was all his parents thought he was good for. They thought he wasn't as bright as the others, but he was clever and observant. He was a people-watcher and understood what was going on around him. Despite his desire to follow a creative path in life, going to farming college to learn farm management was on the cards for Daniel after a gap year working for the family business.

Daniel watched Harry and Ethan in silence. His roommates hadn't heard him come in, as he was light on his feet. He was good at remaining still. He knew how to move around the passageways of the school unseen, and he'd been scouting to find out what was going on in the woods with the police.

As Ethan and Harry watched the four detectives, Daniel moved closer so he could see out of the window. The detectives were talking by their cars, and Daniel saw that two were carrying long brown cases.

"What I wouldn't do for a piece of her," said Ethan as he looked at the blonde detective.

"She wouldn't look at you twice," said Harry.

"She can come and tuck me in anytime." Ethan squinted to see them leaning the cases against one of the cars. "Something's happened. They're taking the guns away."

Harry caught something in the reflection of the glass and flinched. He turned and saw Daniel moving behind them. He had started hopping from one foot to the other, something else he did when he was nervous. "Dan! You scared the shit out of me. What did you find out?"

"It's Brady."

Harry and Ethan glanced at each other. Daniel looked smug, knowing something they didn't.

"What about Brady?" said Ethan. "Has he been arrested?"

"Nope. Not that."

"Get on with it, Dan! What about Brady?"

"They've found him! Brady's dead. That's why the police are here."

Ethan dropped back onto Harry's bed.

"How do you know?" said Harry.

"I just know. Anyway, I overheard Greenway in his office. Brady's been murdered!"

"You *are* joking, Dan?"

"No! I'm not. The police told Greenway."

"That's bloody brilliant," said Ethan, grinning. He stretched out with his hands behind his head. "Brady so deserved it. The bastard deserved it."

Dan moved towards Harry. "And... they're going to shut the school. I think that's what Greenway said."

"No!" Harry looked out at the police again. "I can't go home!"

"I thought your dad was away," said Daniel.

"They didn't need him in Poland anymore. He's returned to his barracks. He's coming home."

"I'm sorry, Harry."

"Sorry? We don't all have rich, happy families like you, Dan."

"Doesn't mean anything. I'm the second-best son. My family doesn't care what I do."

"Shut up, Dan!" said Ethan. "We may not have to go back, Harry, not if our parents won't take us. They'll have to keep us here."

"That's right," said Daniel, nodding. "We can tell them to refuse to take us home."

"They'll have to if a killer's on the loose," said Harry as he slipped away from the window.

"On the loose here?" said Daniel.

"Yes. Or..." Ethan stood and moved closer to Daniel. Then he lowered his voice to a near whisper. "It could be... the Grey

Friar."

Daniel swallowed. "The Grey Friar is just a story. Matron uses it to scare the new kids, to keep them in their rooms at night."

"Is it, though, Dan?" said Harry, copying Ethan. His eyes were wide open. "They say he appears in the library and howls like a wolf. Then he walks up to the dormitory at night."

"It's just a story!"

"People have seen him, Dan. You know they have."

Daniel shook his head and refused to be drawn into their game. "You're just... mental, Harry."

"I reckon Brady saw him, and the Grey Friar looked at him. That's when he kills you—when he sees you. Just one look is all it takes, and he curses you. You're as good as dead." Harry burst out laughing. "You're crapping yourself, Dan!"

Daniel was quiet for a moment, and his left eye twitched as he was thinking. He turned to Ethan. "Out of everyone, you hated Brady the most."

"I'm not the only one! I reckon you killed him, Dan—you found out he was screwing your mum."

"Ignore him, Dan," said Harry. "He's just jealous. He wanted to screw your mum first."

"I could get you both in trouble for those bottles you're keeping under your beds," said Dan, his twitch worsening.

Ethan mimicked him. "I don't think so, Dan, do you? Not if you don't want to end up the same way as Brady."

There was a thump on the door. "Time for lunch, and then there's an assembly." It was Matron in full prison officer mode. "Everyone to the dining hall, now!" She repeated the message along the corridor, knocking on all the doors as she went.

"God, an assembly," said Harry. "This is it, then. They're sending us home."

They stood in silence for a moment, and Daniel wondered if

Harry could be right. He didn't want to go home either—it was worse than school. They heard a sudden cacophony of younger boys running around the rooms above theirs.

Daniel looked up. "What the..."

"They'll be coming through the ceiling in a minute," said Ethan.

Daniel moved over to the window, forcing Ethan to move. He put his head outside and looked up to the floor above him, looking left and right, listening to the noise. He could see the white frames of the attic windows above and the dark, leaded ledge.

"Don't panic, Dan. It's just the Year Sevens," said Harry. "They can see the police in the woods from up there."

Harry pulled Daniel back inside while Ethan watched the police cars drive away.

The library was one of Greenway's priorities and a showpiece feature on the school prospectus and website. He often said that nurturing a child started with encouraging them to read, and *reading is where the magic begins.*

It was as large as any small town library and well-stocked. Ample light came through the large arched windows, giving it the appearance of an ethereal temple of learning. Over a century ago, it was a ballroom and the scene of many lavish entertainments for the rich. Now it was a place of silence and reverence for words.

Alice Church was the school's head librarian. She made it her mission to instil a passion for reading in the students, and her enthusiasm was infectious. Greenway especially admired that quality in her.

She was never seen without a cardigan, even in the summer,

and that morning she wore it buttoned up to the neck against the draught that was always present in the library. She had complained about it for years, but she had been told on many occasions nothing could be done. She had always claimed the draught came from the fireplace, even though it had been bricked and boarded up decades ago. Nobody knew there was still an open vent to remove the damp concealed above the chimney breast. This was linked to the void behind, allowing a steady stream of cold air.

The library door opened, and Mackenzie Masterson backed in, carrying a toolbox with a mobile phone stuck to his ear. Having been forced out of the staffroom, Mac had made his way to the library for the next job on his list of equipment to test.

"I'm just saying, we were going to talk about it first before anyone... *acted*. He must be dealt with soon, otherwise—" He looked up and saw Alice was watching him. "Anyway, I have to go."

Once he was off the phone, she confronted him straightaway about the draught.

"Not only is it deathly cold, it makes a horrible racket some days when the wind blows from the north," she said. "It upsets the younger boys when they are in here. Can't you take a look?"

"I'm just an electrician, Miss Church," said Mac. "It's Archie you need to talk to, and Cameron has him busy with other things. You forget the house is a listed building. We can't just make changes when we feel like it. The proper authority has to be sought."

"Really?"

"Yes, really. I'll chat with Archie, but I expect he'll say the same."

"It never used to be so loud. I don't know what's caused it."

"It's the wind blowing over the top of the chimneys, Miss

Church, playing them like beer bottles. Probably all that global warming they're preaching to us about."

"I guess so. Seems a pity they closed off the fireplace, but I suppose it wouldn't do to have a fire in a library.

"Absolutely right, Miss Church. It has to stay that way. I seem to recall that it was dangerous behind there—that's why they did it. Nothing we can do about it now. I've always said we should move a bookcase in front of the fireplace. That would reduce some of the noise. Stop the Grey Friar from getting out, too." Mac grinned.

Miss Church sighed in resignation and pulled her cardigan around her.

"I guess you're right, Mac. Poor Mr Brady wanted to look into it for me. He was going to ask Greenway to get the fireplace opened up to find out what was causing it. He was such a lovely man. He always had time for me and came by often."

Mac rolled his eyes. "That won't be happening now. Anyway, I've got to test your power sockets. It's that time of year again."

"And I have a staff meeting I'm late for."

DCI Dinescu didn't go back to the police station straightaway but stopped off at a garage and bought something for lunch. He parked opposite the West Sussex Record Office and walked to the Bishop's Palace Gardens opposite Chichester College. He entered the gardens through a gate in a wall and found a seat under a giant sequoia tree.

The spring colours were bursting through the flower borders in the bright sunshine. After asking them many questions about the trees and the encircling Roman wall, Dinescu got to know several city gardeners who worked there. The gardens were one of his favourite places to hide. A sanctuary from work, where he appreciated the space to recharge.

Something was bothering Dinescu. He wasn't one for feeling melancholy or indulging in self-pity. His thoughts were preoccupied with Cotisham School's long, dark corridors and the ghostly echoes of young voices. Cotisham School had scratched at an old wound. Something from the past had resurfaced, and he vividly remembered his birth mother's expression again on a sad day in November when she'd left him. Beniamin Dinescu was a victim of Nicolae Ceaușescu's decrees for prosperity, which caused crippling austerity for decades in Romania. It led to the abandonment of thousands of children in overwhelmed orphanages. The irony for Dinescu was that the young boys left behind in Cotisham were there because of their parents' wealth, not their poverty. That had tweaked a nerve and unsettled him.

A robin appeared beside him, eyeing the crusts of Dinescu's sandwich.

"*Vrei niste?* You want some?"

The robin bobbed closer, and Dinescu broke off a piece of crust and flicked it towards the bird. It seized the morsel and darted away, returning a few moments later.

"The universe has been kind to us, little bird. We should be grateful for what we have."

Dinescu looked at the time on his watch. He had a briefing to attend. As he stood, he shuddered as if something dark and inescapable had walked over him. It threw him for a moment, and he wondered if he had got up too fast. The feeling subsided, and he took another look at the walled gardens around him.

His phone rang. It was Summers.

"Go ahead, Emily."

"We're back at the nick now. Several officers from Worthing and Brighton have arrived."

"Yes. I requested them."

"Ah, okay. I can get started on the policy file if you are happy? And we have an operation name: Birchwood."

"You know what needs to be done, Emily. It's all good."

"I know, but... Yes, boss. Are you coming to the briefing?"

"Of course. I'll be in shortly. Have you had lunch?"

"Not yet. Too much to—"

"Make sure you get something to eat. Take a moment to breathe. See you in about twenty minutes."

He ended the call and sighed. What was he going to do with her?

Chapter Six

Dinescu returned to Chichester Police Station, which was a stone's throw from the canal basin and next door to a modern custody block. Chichester had become the base for the West Division's Major Crimes Team, which Dinescu had led for the last two years.

He topped up the fuel in the pool car and parked at the rear in one of the allocated CID spaces. He filled in the car's logbook and gathered his notes into his folder. The missing gun must be the key to this, he thought to himself. Who had access to the gun cabinet? He mulled over his discussion with Doctor Greenway in the dining hall. He wondered why they'd left it so long before Charles Brady was reported missing. Was Brady well-liked, as Greenway said, or was he someone they were relieved to be free of? They couldn't have been that worried at first. Dinescu checked his watch—he'd better get in for the first case briefing.

A sudden screech of wheels and a deep metallic rumble tore through him. His head thumped against the headrest, and his eyes rolled back as he relived that instant of terror once again...

London, 7th July 2005

Beniamin Dinescu held a book close to his face: *The Alchemist by Paulo Coelho*. Its magic had him caught in a trance, and he didn't notice the people rushing past him down the escalator. A rush of air swept through his hair, and he looked up just as he reached the bottom.

It was 8:47, and he was on the eastbound platform, the Circle Line. He was travelling to meet his friend, Jack Balfour, at Tower Hill for breakfast at nine. Jack was thinking of leaving the police. As far as Dinescu could gather, the section Jack had been assigned to wasn't welcoming of new black probationers. Dinescu was trying to encourage him to stay, and he was angry about how they'd treated his friend. He wanted to fix it, but he knew from experience that minorities had little sway, and it would be buried.

Dinescu's stature held him in good stead with his section. They knew he was useful in a fight, and he could hold his own against those who thought the old ways of policing were better. They soon learned that Dinescu wasn't a pushover. He had a past that had made him resilient, courageous, and not easily broken. And he had made it known he didn't want to be in uniform forever. He was interested in plain-clothes work in serious crime.

The platform was crowded with people pushing from behind to get onto the train first. A young girl with large brown eyes looked up at him, and Dinescu smiled at her. Her Asian mother pulled her closer and frowned at him. He didn't blame her. Then a skinny man in a bright blue suit—corporate sales written all over him—pushed beside Dinescu, wafting floral aftershave. Dinescu looked away and checked his Nokia for any messages from Jack. Nothing. He hoped Jack hadn't got cold feet.

It was 8:49 as the draught from the arriving train rushed into the station. The rails clicked and rasped with the weight of the wheels, followed by a flash of red, white, and blue of the carriages. A girl on the other side of him checked her makeup, and her friend gave Dinescu a simpering smile. He raised his eyebrows and moved forward, standing behind a young soldier in a smart uniform. He turned and looked at Dinescu for a moment, blinking his blue eyes in the dusty air.

The doors opened, and they pushed aboard the fourth carriage. The young soldier slumped into the last remaining seat next to where Dinescu stood. His jet-black boots gleamed like a mirror glaze. The doors closed, the motors whirred, and the carriage lurched forward.

The air soon thickened with human scent, and Dinescu pulled out his book again. He grasped the steel rail above the head of the blue-suit man, and then the platform slid away as the train gathered speed. Dinescu looked through into the third carriage. He saw a seated man through the glass, fidgeting with a rucksack on his lap. The man screwed his eyes shut. A flash of hot light. A deafening crack. Screams and splintering glass sliced through them. The carriage rocked. Then there was fire, smoke, and darkness.

Dinescu's eyes snapped open, and he was back in the present, gasping for air. Ted from Facilities was pushing an empty metal wheelie bin along the wall, dragging and scraping it into its usual position. He saw Dinescu and raised a hand in greeting. Dinescu nodded and stared at the wheelie bin. It was over.

He dried his eyes and got out of the car, steadying himself

against the open door. He waited there for his legs to stop trembling enough to walk. No one saw him as he headed unsteadily into the station. Dinescu slipped into his office and closed the door behind him, taking a moment to settle himself and wait for his head and heart to calm down while he counted slowly. It had only lasted seconds, and it was all over. He was okay. He'd told Occupational Health it never happened while driving, but that was too close for comfort.

He needed to do something normal to clear his head. He logged into his computer, silenced his mobile, and tried to read through some of the initial statements taken from the staff at Cotisham School. It took him a while to concentrate on the screen, but it worked, and he began to absorb the details in their statements. It was clear that no one had witnessed anything suspicious or unusual involving Charles Brady. A couple said they may have heard a gunshot, but it wasn't out of place in the countryside surrounding the school. One said they thought they had seen Brady walking towards the woods, and another thought he was walking away, or maybe it was a woman they saw.

Dinescu opened his office blinds and looked out. He was glad to be back working at his desk again. They'd had to move out for a week while it was their area's turn to be redecorated. Now, the place smelled of fresh paint and carpet glue—the whole station had had a facelift. Dirty cream walls were brighter, and charcoal grey carpets replaced the ancient coffee-stained blue tiles.

Through the blinds, he saw everyone getting ready for the briefing, including an extra twenty detectives that he had requested from Worthing and Brighton. There was a knock on his door, and Summers put her head inside the office.

"Ready when you are, boss."

"Just coming."

When he left his office, the banter ceased, heads looked up, and the room went silent. Dinescu took his time to look at all the officers' faces. There were several he didn't know at all. His core team sat at the front. Aside from Emily Summers, there were Sarah Burgess, Gareth Booker, Chester Kirby, and Ross Taylor. They were all experienced, proactive officers and Dinescu's go-to team for the last two years. Summers was sitting a short distance from them, rehearsing the details in her notes.

"Good afternoon, everyone, and thank you all for your prompt attendance. For those who don't know me, I'm DCI Beniamin Dinescu, and I lead the West Division's Major Crimes Team.

"This is the investigation into the murder of Charles Brady, aged forty-eight years, from Chichester, now designated as Operation Birchwood. Charles Brady's putrified body was discovered by the police this morning during a missing person search. Mr Brady appears to have suffered a gunshot wound to the chest from close range."

Dinescu turned to the whiteboard behind him. A blown-up photograph of Charles Brady was pinned beneath the words *Op Birchwood*, underlined in red. The photo looked like the one from the school's prospectus. Also pinned around the board were photographs of the school, including Charles Brady's office and the tower where Brady was found. The concrete platform on the third level of the tower was also shown. The scene was minus Brady's body, but it still showed the smeary, brown stains where the decomposed remains had been removed.

"Charles Brady worked at Cotisham private school, a few miles north of Singleton, just off the road to Midhurst. He was reported missing by the school on Friday, the 21st of April, at 10:20 hours. Brady had not turned up for work all week, but his vehicle was in the car park. His car and flat keys had been left in his office. The deputy headmaster, Andrew Winston, visited

Brady's home on the Friday, and after checking with the neighbours, he called us to report him missing.

"Brady had been the Head of Mathematics at Cotisham for the last six months. According to statements from the other teachers, Brady was well-liked and respected by the staff. They said he didn't take any nonsense from the students but would go the extra mile to help any student who needed it.

"The last reported sighting of Brady was when he walked past the school staffroom at around 15:05 hours on Monday, the 17th of April. He had no other lessons that afternoon, and his usual practice was to retire to his office and perform administrative tasks and mark work." Dinescu looked down at his notes on Brady and had reached the end. "Emily, what more do we know about Charles Brady?" He sat on the edge of a desk as Summers stood and gathered her notes.

"I'm DS Summers, acting deputy SIO." She saw them shuffling in their seats and the looks that passed between the core team. She cleared her throat and read from a notepad. "Charles's mother is Irene Brady. She is his next of kin and lives in a nursing home in West Wittering. Sadly, Irene has Alzheimer's and couldn't understand what had happened to her son. According to the school, Brady was divorced and had no children. We know nothing more about his ex-wife at the moment, but we plan to gather information from his home later." She paused, cleared her throat again, and licked her lips. "As the boss said, statements from the staff tell us that Charles Brady was liked, but he kept himself to himself. He was quiet and introverted, an observation repeated by several staff members. There was some trouble with one of the older students, which we need more details about. Apart from that, nothing was out of the ordinary. That's all we have so far, boss."

Dinescu nodded. "It's still early days, and several lines of enquiry need to be kicked off. The location of the murder weapon, the search of Brady's home, the forensics report, and the postmortem results. We need to know all about Charles Brady. Who his friends were, more information on his ex-wife, his interests, and his history."

Dinescu stood again and pointed to the board. "We don't have a timeline. We know when he was last seen, but nothing else."

"So, as usual, we have our first three questions. Why Charles Brady? Why was he killed in the tower, and why was he murdered when he was murdered? What are our first credible hypotheses? Anyone?"

Dinescu looked around at the surrounding faces.

"One of the students at the school had a grudge?" said Booker. "We've already heard of trouble with one of the older boys."

Dinescu looked at Summers and held out a dry marker to her. She took the pen and wrote down Booker's first hypothesis.

"Good. Any more?"

"An angry ex," said Burgess. "Wife, lover."

"Would they come to the school to kill him?" asked Summers.

"Maybe they would. I was thinking, why was he up in the tower? Perhaps an assignation?"

"Write it down, please, Emily," said Dinescu. "Any more?"

"An accident?" said Chester Kirby. "Some horseplay gone wrong?"

"He didn't come across as someone involved in horseplay," said Summers. "Everyone said he was introverted. Kept himself to himself."

"Why else would he be up the tower?" asked Dinescu. "Apart from an assignation."

"A business meeting or a deal gone wrong?" said Summers. "If it was one of the school's guns that killed him, then we could be looking at the school staff. We need to look in depth at his relationships with those who had access to the guns."

"Yes," said Dinescu. "Write it down. Who was it who saw him last?"

"David Roberts, the Head of Sports," said Gareth Booker. "He met him in the corridor outside the staffroom. Roberts told us he spoke to Brady. Nothing in particular—polite conversation —but Brady ignored him as if he was thinking about something else."

Dinescu pinched his lips with his thumb and forefinger. "Perhaps he was on his way to meet someone. While I'm thinking about it, what was the issue with the student?"

The team looked at each other, and there were a few shrugs.

"Doesn't look like we know, boss," said Summers.

"Okay, let's find out more details about that. A grudge is as good a motive as any to kill someone. Gareth, tell us about the shotguns."

Gareth Booker stood and faced the others. "Okay. The weapon that killed Charles Brady was almost certainly a shotgun. The school owns six of them for shooting clays, and they comply fully with legislation. They are all double-barrelled with a single selective trigger. Upon inspection of the gun cabinet, we discovered one gun was missing. The book they used to sign out the guns wasn't filled in, and no one has claimed responsibility for taking it from the cabinet. Three members of staff have keys to the gun cabinet. Doctor Greenway—although it's his PA who looks after his key— Cameron Hyde, the caretaker, and David Roberts, the Head of Sports. They run a clay pigeon shooting club for the over-sixteens at the school twice a month on Sunday afternoons. They think the missing gun was last used on Sunday, the 16th, and that all the guns were locked away securely by Cameron Hyde. The remaining guns have been seized under the boss's orders as a precautionary measure, and they've been bagged up for forensics."

"Thanks, Gareth," said Dinescu. "So, one shotgun is missing." He took the pen from Summers and wrote it on the whiteboard. "We have a search team going through the school grounds as we speak. I've talked to the ACC on the phone and the police search advisor. An underwater search team has been authorised to check the pond, which will start this afternoon.

"So, we all know what needs doing, and we must act fast to preserve as much evidence as possible. The headmaster is happy for us to attend school when necessary. If you are assigned a task at the school, don't get drawn into conversations with the students that need an appropriate adult present. Uniformed officers will also visit the school to reassure the students who aren't going home." He looked at Summers. "Emily, over to you to wrap up."

DS Summers stood next to Dinescu; she was at least ten inches shorter than him. "Gareth, you can oversee the background checks on all the staff and the older students. I'll assign some of the officers from Worthing and Brighton to help with that. We'll also need to get straight on with house-to-house enquiries in the village, so some of you will be going to Cotisham shortly." Summers took a breath and looked over at Taylor. "We also need to learn more about this so-called trouble with the older student. You can take that, Ross.

"We haven't recovered Brady's mobile phone yet. We've been told he didn't like smartphones, so we may be looking for a simple brick-like phone. That will narrow down the information we can extract from it. Chester, start the financial checks on Brady. If you can find out who his mobile provider is, get the ball rolling on that, too.

"Sarah, you can come with me to look around Brady's flat, and I'll assign some officers to talk to his neighbours."

"I'll come to his flat, too," said Dinescu. "It might help to have another pair of eyes. It also means I won't have to attend a finance meeting at HQ."

"I think we'll be okay if you need to attend your meeting."

"No. I'm coming with you."

"Fair enough." Summers turned away from Dinescu and lifted her voice. "So, before you all disappear, I'm the disclosure officer for this case, and like always, all updates should be entered ASAP. If anyone is unsure of what they should be doing, come and see me now."

Summers's words, *fair enough*, had grated with Dinescu, but he decided to let it slide. He watched the detectives as they picked up their assigned tasks—some left the office, others had gone onto the phone. Then he went to see DS Summers at her desk. A male DC from Brighton was trying to engage her with a charm offensive, but she wasn't having any of it.

"Emily."

"Yes, boss." She looked glad for the interruption. The Brighton DC had got the hint and moved away. Summers looked over her shoulder and rolled her eyes. "Tosser."

Dinescu caught the officer looking back at them.

"I can send him back to Brighton if he's causing you a problem."

"I think he got the message, sir," said Summers. She sighed as she ran her fingers through her hair.

"Emily, I appreciate your hard work, but it's not for you to do everything." He waved his hand in front of her face to get her full attention. "Is everything okay with you?"

"Yes, sir?" She looked puzzled. "I was just trying to save you extra work when—"

"I meant personally. Is everything okay with you?"

"Me?" She blushed. "Just stuff going on at home, sir. Nothing I can't handle. I can relax at the weekend. I'm going to see a show on Saturday with a friend. A musical. I'm looking forward to that."

"Great! You can sing out your heart."

She looked down for a moment. "It's sing your heart out, sir. Other way around. Sorry, I wasn't being rude. I just thought..."

Dinescu looked curious, with a hint of a smile. "You'd think my English would be perfect after thirty-three years."

"It pretty much is, boss. Better than my Romanian, anyway."

"Vă mulțumesc."

Summers smiled. "You're welcome?"

Dinescu went back to his office, leaving the door open. He had to email the chief super, his boss, in Brighton. DS Summers updated the whiteboard with officers' names and their tasks. Burgess was standing behind her, reading the notes she was making. She spoke briefly to Summers and then tapped on Dinescu's door.

"Sorry to bother you, sir. I was saying to the sergeant that I've heard there's a strong connection between the school and the village next door. Are you happy if I ask a few questions at the local pub, the New Moon? It might get us some background intel."

"Did you ask DS Summers?"

"She told me to check it with you."

"Yes, go for it. My old tutor used to tell me to follow my nose. It took me years before I understood what he was talking about. You always follow your nose, don't you? We'll see you at Brady's flat in a couple of hours. Take the search kit with you."

"Thanks, sir."

Chapter Seven

Cameron Hyde's workshop was opposite the school, across the driveway, and near the woodwork huts and the vegetable plots. It was about the size of a large garage, with double doors leading onto the driveway and a single door at the other end. Cameron had installed workbenches, a lathe, and a pillar drill, and it was large enough to store the school's sit-on mower and the wood-chipper. No one entered the workshop without his permission, and he guarded it as if it were his personal castle.

Cameron had called his father after his earlier talk with Archie. Jason Hyde was once the school caretaker and had passed the job on to his son when he left to work for himself. He told Cameron to wait in the workshop for him. He was coming over with a small gift.

Cameron had been watching the police search the woods, nibbling at his fingernails until they were red and raw. A dirty-grey Nissan pickup drove across the driveway and parked next to the workshop, out of sight of the police. Cameron looked through the perspex window as his father, a burly man in his late fifties, brought out a cardboard box from his pickup and entered the workshop, whistling the same indiscernible tune he had whistled since Cameron was a boy. His father was in his usual red lumberjack shirt and blue jeans.

"Alright, Dad?" called out Cameron. "What you got there?"

"Not what you're hoping for," replied Jason.

Cameron's heart sank, and he felt his stomach turn over again.

Jason Hyde dropped the box on the workbench, and Cameron heard the chink of glass bottles. Jason gave a sly smile and opened the box, pulling out a bottle of brown liquid.

"This'll cheer you up, Cam. Home-brewed and ready today. Bottled last September, eight per cent proof."

"I can't drink that here! I'll be out on my ear."

"I won't tell if you don't. Come on, son!"

Jason dug into his pocket and pulled out a Swiss Army knife. He opened two bottles and passed one to Cameron. Jason lifted it.

"Cheers."

Cameron laughed. "Cheers. What are you like?"

"Figured you needed this. Why are you so worried? It'll turn up. Have you checked someone hasn't put it back with the others?"

"No one's been in here, Dad. I can't exactly go and check *now*. I reckon someone's pinched it, and it'll have my finger-prints all over it. With everything that's—you know—going on. They'll think it was me."

"I wouldn't blame you even if you did, but if you've done nothing wrong, then there's nothing to worry about."

Cameron wiped his face with his hand. "I've done nothing wrong."

"I know." Jason examined the liquid in his bottle by holding it to the light. "Think about something else for a while, son. How's that woman of yours? Is she still being testy?"

"Could say that. I don't know what's got into her."

"She needs putting over your knee if you ask me. Can't do that nowadays, they tell me. Never did your mother any harm when she forgot herself. She knew I loved her, though."

"I don't hit women, Dad. I'm not like you."

"Too right you're not." Jason shook his head, sucked on his bottle, and pulled up a stool. "Her and that maths teacher. Was it him who was...?"

"Yes, Brady. He deserved that slap I gave him, and I still don't care what Leah thought. But as far as I'm concerned, that was that. He didn't do it again."

"As I said, I'd have shot him myself after what he did to her."

"Well, someone did, and with the gun that has my bloody fingerprints all over it!"

"They were probably all queuing up for him. He was full of himself, shouting the odds at me, Mac, and Archie. All excited over nothing."

"Shouting the odds over what?" said Cameron.

"Never you mind, son. Brady was just full of shit and had a big mouth."

Cameron looked again under the covers of the chipper machine and sighed. "I just don't get it. This is where I left it."

Jason Hyde sipped his beer. "Archie said a big bald fella's leading the investigation."

"I've just seen Archie. He said the policeman was a foreigner. His name's *Danube* or something."

"A foreigner! Don't they have British policemen anymore? We didn't win Brexit so that bloody foreigners can tell us what to do!" Jason sucked air through his teeth. "I heard they're sending the day students home. Bloody stupid, if you ask me! I'll tell you something—Archie and me will keep out of PC Foreigner's way. Probably end up saying the wrong thing."

"The students are in assembly now. Greenway's telling them. Surprised you didn't meet the angry parents on your way over." Cameron took a long swig from his bottle and put it back on the workbench. "This is good, Dad. Strong though. You sure it's only eight per cent?"

"Thereabouts. You ought to give a bottle or two to Leah. She'll be all yours for the evening."

"Can't get near her, Dad. Won't let me touch her. She's breaking my heart."

"Archie said he's got some poison for you. Maybe that would work on her." Jason gave a wheezy laugh.

"The kitchen will be grateful. They had some enormous rats up there last week. Big as cats, they said."

"Big as cats, my arse! Anyway, those spare bottles are for you. I'm off to find Mac—he's here somewhere. Between you and me, he reckons he's only got six months, poor tosser."

"He's been saying that for the last ten years, Dad."

"He wants to carry on working until he drops. Makes you think when you get to my age, and you lose the mates you've known all your life. Me, Archie, and Mac—the Three Amigos we called ourselves. We were the bee's knees."

"I bet you were." Cameron rubbed the ends of his sore fingertips. "Thanks for coming in. I need to keep looking."

"Stop worrying, boy. It'll turn up."

"Bloody hope so, Dad. I bloody hope so."

Chapter Eight

DC Sarah Burgess drove to the New Moon pub, which was down a narrow lane off the Midhurst road. It wasn't much to look at from the outside—tired and needing a lick of paint and replacement window frames. But it overlooked thousands of picturesque acres of farm and woodland. Burgess could see the top of the folly tower from the pub's front door, which was only a few feet above where Charles Brady had died.

Burgess was glad to be out of the office. Summers had caused a lot of tension since she started, questioning how the team worked and pushing her way of doing things. Burgess knew Summers was insecure and trying to make her mark. Surrey Major Crimes was a larger outfit than here, and they would have had to fight to be noticed amongst the competition. Chichester was very different. A more rural division and a smaller and closer team. Burgess just wished Summers would chill.

She unzipped her leather jacket, ran her fingers through her hair, and pushed open the main door. The New Moon was the only pub in Cotisham and was popular with cyclists and walkers on weekends, but this Monday afternoon, there were only a handful of stalwart customers. Burgess thought it wasn't the best day of the week to talk to the locals.

She stood near the door, and her hand went to the nape of her neck. She looked around at the open fireplace, the brasses, and the agricultural equipment that hung on the walls, and it was much like every other pub she'd been to in these parts. Sarah and her husband enjoyed trips to the countryside and a pub lunch afterwards. When she was training to be a PC, days out together were precious times now stored away as cherished memories.

She walked over to the bar, turning the heads of the men there who had been lost in their thoughts and alone with their pints. She guessed they didn't get many black women walking in by themselves.

A short woman behind the bar did a double-take when she saw Burgess and smiled at her.

"What can I get you, my darling? On your own?"

"Yes. Just a small lime and soda, please. I'm working."

"Sure," said the woman as she got Burgess her drink. "Working, my darling?"

Burgess pulled out her lanyard from her jacket. "I'm a detective constable from Chichester. We're investigating the death of a teacher at the school."

"Gosh, I heard something had happened!" The woman turned around and shouted out into the kitchen behind her. "I was right, John! Something happened at the school. We've got the police here. It was a teacher! Dead!" A man at the bar put down his drink with a thud, picked up his wallet, and walked out.

A grey-haired Geordie came out of the kitchen wearing a chef's cap. "What's happened, Janet?" He looked straight at Burgess. "You police, pet?"

"Yes. I'm trying to find out if anyone's heard of any trouble at the school. Maybe something about one of the teachers there."

"Was it that deputy head fella?" said John.

"No. His name was Charles Brady."

"Charlie's dead!" The woman gasped, slapping her hand to her mouth. "Not Charlie."

"What happened to him?" John pulled a tea towel off his shoulder and dried his hands.

"He was found dead this morning by police officers. I can't go into details. I'm not sure my boss wants it known just yet. I can only say that he was missing for about a week."

The woman leaned towards Burgess with her elbows on the bar. "Charlie was a sweetheart, wasn't he, John?"

"Aye, he was a good man. He was quiet, but once you got to know him, he was friendly. He used to talk about the history of the school, Lord Aversham, and the first Queen Elizabeth. That sort of thing. He told us some very peculiar stories. They hated the Catholics back then, I can tell you."

"He didn't live around here, but he'd come in and talk to the locals," said Janet, "gleaning information from them, I reckon. The whole village has a connection to that school, you see. People either worked there or knew someone who did. We've got ex-pupils living here in the village, too."

"Did Charles ever tell you of anyone wanting to harm him?"

"You mean he was murdered, like?" asked John.

"I didn't say that." Burgess tapped her payment card on a small device and sipped her drink, which was too sweet for her. She would have preferred a Jamaican rum.

"Harm him? No, but..." The woman leaned in even closer. "There was one evening Charlie came in here. He had a nice lady friend with him, and he'd had a couple of our stronger beers—they loosened him up a bit. He said there were evil people at the school. He kept asking the woman *what they had done with her.* Something like that anyway—not word for word. The woman tried to keep him quiet. He then went all maudlin, and the woman said she'd take him home."

"When was this?"

"Two months ago."

"And who was the woman?"

"I don't know. We'd never seen her before. Blonde, attractive, difficult to give an age. Maybe about your age, or could have been older—one of those faces. That's all I can remember about her."

"Huge tits. I remember that," said John, laughing.

Burgess raised an eyebrow.

Janet cackled. "John! Trust you."

Burgess remained straight-faced. "Were they in a relationship, do you think?"

"No," said John. "She was professional-looking. Well dressed and had a notebook. Writing stuff down."

"Do you think she could have been a reporter?"

"Not sure, my darling," said Janet. "Maybe. She was a looker. He's only been in a couple of times since then. Alone both times."

"You didn't hear her name at all?"

"Cathy, Caprice? Something like that."

Burgess took their names and made a note of their comments. She glanced up at the walls and above the bar. They didn't appear to have CCTV.

"Thanks so much. Here's my card," she said. "If anything else comes to mind, call me or leave a message."

"Please send our condolences. John and me thought Charlie was a troubled soul. It was like he was looking for something. Sad to hear he's gone."

"You've been very helpful. Thank you. Oh, and I'd get some

CCTV installed if I were you. You never know when you'll need it."

"CCTV?" said Janet. "Nothing ever happens here to warrant it. Not like we have murderers walking in."

Chapter Nine

Sombre and silent, the boys were ushered away from the assembly hall in year groups. There had been a time of reflection for Mr Brady. Although Greenway was honest and direct, he never used the word *murder*, but they all knew. It had leaked out like a black stain, contaminating the school and conjuring deadly shadows in dark corners and phantoms in the passageways. The Grey Friar was being spoken about, and someone said he'd been seen in the library again, but no one knew by whom.

Leah Turnbull had watched the older students at the back of the hall and had seen the cocky smirk on Ethan Bishop's face as he stood next to Harry Price. An idea had entered her head, but she struggled to reconcile the Ethan she knew as creative, passionate, and talented with Ethan, a cold-blooded murderer.

Greenway's pleas for anyone with information to do the right thing were repeated, aimed at staff and pupils alike. The teachers had remained stony-faced on the end of the rows and had fixed their gaze on Greenway as he spoke. They knew that one of them could have killed Brady and were conscious of the accusing glances from the boys sitting across from them.

Some students were glad to be going home early for the week, while others were subdued and fearful as they looked out for families outside. Leah had encouraged the younger ones, telling them it would be all sorted soon. She stood beside them and ensured they had their coats and bags with them while they waited to be called by Matron. Leah felt there had been a change in the air. The wind had changed direction—it was coming from the north now. Miss Churchill, the librarian, had been telling her about the noises in the library.

Parents of the day students had already gathered outside the school as they waited to hear further news. There were loud, complaining voices waiting for an official statement about Brady's death. They'd heard from their children that he had been murdered, and Greenway was trying to cover it up. Emails were sent, and letters were handed out to those outside the school. There were reassurances their sons were safe, and sending the day students home was a temporary and precautionary measure after advice from the police. For the time being, schoolwork would be continued at home, as it was in the dark days of the pandemic. A hush descended on them as their children appeared at the door.

Leah moved to stand outside the entrance as she watched the boys meet their parents. A mother of a Year Seven blind-sided her.

"Does the school know how inconvenient this is, Miss Turnbull?"

Leah turned and looked startled. "We do. And it's a sad day for us, too."

"I've had to take the afternoon off work. God knows what I'm supposed to do with him for the rest of the week. I can hardly take him to work with me."

"I don't know. Look, excuse me. I have to do something."

Leah never liked confrontation, and she wasn't in the mood.

She walked away, her head down, pulling the sleeves of her thigh-length cardigan over her fingers. The wind had a bite to it now. She followed the path around the side of the school, and as soon as she was out of view, she took her mobile phone from her pocket and typed a message into WhatsApp:

> We need to talk, Cam. What do you know about Charles?

She put her phone away and continued to walk along the side of the house until the laurel hedges hid her. She didn't want these complications in her life right now. She walked to her classroom in the art block and sat alone behind her desk, which was covered with collages her year eight class had dropped there before they left. Leah's phone pinged, and she read the reply:

> What do I know? FFS! Do you even know me at all?

Then her phone rang—he'd called her.

"Why do you have to react every time, Cam? It was a simple question."

"I thought you were accusing me of something," Cameron replied.

"I'm not! I wanted to know if you had heard anything. God, Cam! Can't you just..."

"I'm sorry, okay! You know how it's been. Where are you?"

"The parents are picking up the day students. And I'm busy."

"Come over to the workshop. Let's talk about this."

"You know they'll want to talk to you, Cam. Don't you?"

"What are you talking about?"

"The police, Cam! You can be so dim sometimes. After everything that happened between you and him."

"I know! Okay. I've got another problem here, too."

"What problem?"

"I can't talk about it right now. Come over. I need you, Leah. I don't understand what's happened to us."

"Not now, Cam!" Leah ended the call.

Cameron always made her feel guilty, even when she was in the right. Even when he should have been the one to apologise. She didn't want to return to the cottage tonight, but what else could she do? Where else could she go? Her parents'? But that would mean moving away.

Leah locked her phone and thought about Charles Brady again. The day he apologised to her, she saw how vulnerable he was. Of course, she felt nothing for him, but that wasn't the point. He had misconstrued her kindness for affection, and he said he was mortified. Cameron couldn't see it that way. No, he had to teach Brady a lesson. Idiot!

Leah had to clear up the classroom before she could think of anything else. There was a knock, and the door edged open. Standing in the doorway was a man in his forties, wearing a smart grey suit. He was handsome and tanned, with greying hair and beard stubble. He gave an apologetic smile of perfect teeth and raised his shaped eyebrows.

"Forgive me, but I'm lost," he said to Leah.

She frowned. He wasn't someone she'd seen before in the school.

"Who are you?" She felt she had the right to challenge him, no matter how charming he was.

"Ah, yes." He pulled out a lanyard from under his suit jacket. "I'm Detective Constable Ross Taylor from the Major Crimes Team in Chichester."

Leah was taken aback, and she studied the warrant card on his lanyard. He appeared to be who he said he was. "Who are you looking for?"

"Are you Leah?"

"Yes."

"Can I come in for a moment?" He entered the classroom, and Leah saw he was carrying a black leather folder. "Doctor Greenway told me you might be here."

"Did he? Okay. How can I help?" Leah didn't understand why her heart was pounding. The police officer didn't look like he was about to arrest her for anything.

DC Taylor pulled up a stool and sat in front of Leah. She couldn't help but notice his dark brown eyes. He put his hands on his lap and engaged with Leah. "As part of our investigation into Charles Brady's murder, we need to paint a picture of him." He enjoyed the pun as he looked up at the self-portraits on the walls. "I've been tasked with talking to the teachers at the school who knew him well."

"I didn't know him *very* well," said Leah as she pushed herself back into her chair.

"Okay..." DC Taylor flashed a puzzled expression. "We've been told by two other members of staff that Charles had had a run-in with one particular boy in the school..." Taylor brought out a notepad. "And I was told you may have some insight into what that was about."

Leah's cheeks flushed. "Who said that?"

"I can't tell you, I'm afraid."

"I know nothing about it." She folded her arms across her chest. "You'll have to talk to the deputy head."

"The boy is Ethan Bishop."

"He's eighteen, not a boy."

It was a tart response, and a smile escaped from the corners of Taylor's mouth. "Of course. Can you tell me anything about an incident between him and Charles Brady? What could it have been about?"

"No." Leah shrugged. "Sorry. Talk to the deputy head."

"Thank you, I will." He frowned and looked at his notes. "Looks like I've been misinformed."

Leah raised one eyebrow. "Obviously."

"What can you tell me about Charles? Did you work closely with him?"

"Hardly. He was the Head of Maths, and I'm an art teacher. He was a nice man. We spoke about the history of the school a few times. Nothing major. I think he had an interest in that sort of thing. He gave me a lift home once when my car broke down. He was reserved. A bit of a loner, I think."

"Why do you think the other staff thought you knew him well?"

Leah laughed. She knew who it was but wouldn't drag Charles's name through the mud. "No clue, I'm afraid. They've made a mistake."

DC Taylor held eye contact a little longer. He appeared to be trying to suss her out. "Thank you for your time, Miss Turnbull. Not that painful, was it?"

"No."

"If anything does come to mind..." He reached into his jacket pocket and brought out a card. "These are my contact details. I'm not always working, although my husband would disagree. You can leave a message on the answerphone."

"Great, thanks."

DC Taylor stood and looked around the classroom. "I loved art when I was a kid. I can't draw for toffee now."

"It just takes practice," said Leah. "And a little direction."

"Direction? In my job, we get a lot of misdirection. Thanks for your time." Taylor smiled and left Leah to herself.

Chapter Ten

The lecture theatre was almost empty. The animated chatter of young voices was drifting out into the corridors of the university, and the students were heading towards their seminars. Lisa Dinescu was a senior lecturer in creative writing at Chichester University. She knew if they were noisy after a gruelling ninety-minute lecture, then they were enthusiastic about what they had heard. She had done her job. Thankfully, Virginia Woolf was someone Lisa could teach about with passion.

She gathered her notes and her phone from the lectern. There were the usual hangers-on who had questions for her, but Lisa was impatient to finish after reading the message from Beniamin, which had pinged her phone during her lecture. She'd made a joke of it at the time but was embarrassed that she hadn't silenced her phone. She had caught the first few words when she glanced at her mobile mid-sentence, and it had thrown her completely.

She read the rest of his message as she walked out of the theatre. Beniamin had had another PTSD episode. He wasn't driving—thank God. She bit her lip and stared out onto the campus grounds, wondering what to do.

"Come on, Ben," she said under her breath. "Not now, my love."

Lisa had hoped that these episodes were a thing of the past. Beniamin had come off the meds two years ago, eighteen months after he transferred to Sussex from the Metropolitan Police. Things were going well for them. Lisa had got a job at the university in Chichester, and as she had family nearby, it was like moving back home. Their daughter, Sophia, who had struggled in her old school after problems with bullies, settled quickly into her new school. She was excited to be near her uncle and grandparents again.

Yet Lisa knew Beniamin continued to carry the trauma of an event that changed many people's lives. It had changed Lisa's, too, even though she was over seventy miles away when it happened.

Lisa remembered the awful nightmares he used to have. He would scream and thrash out, and more than once, she had caught a hand in the face, and Beniamin was a strong man. He felt ashamed and guilty afterwards, and Lisa struggled to know what to do. It almost broke them apart.

She searched through the contacts on her phone. She still had Doctor Maguire's number—Doctor Siobhan Maguire. Lisa prayed she was still available and practising. Lisa and Beniamin would have lost each other if it weren't for Siobhan's help.

Lisa sent a message back to Beniamin, not expecting an answer, but he returned with a call straight away.

"Ben, is everything okay? How are you feeling?"

"I'm okay." He was speaking quietly, and she could hear voices and laughter in the background. "It took me by surprise, but it didn't last long. I promised you I would let you know if..."

"Yes, thank you. What do you think triggered it?"

"Just before, there was a loud sound. A wheelie bin, of all things. It just sent me back there. There was nothing I could do in time to stop it. I knew it was coming. I'd been thinking about when I was a kid, and I think one thing led to another under the surface."

"It's okay. It's only been once, right?"

"Yes. The first for a very long time. I just wanted you to know, not to worry you. I'm wondering if there's something about this case I'm working on. It's in a private school—the murder of a teacher. I'm going to be okay, Lisa. It's nothing to worry about."

"Do you think it's worth talking to Doctor Maguire? I know it's been a while, but..."

"Dr Maguire? Look, I don't know. She said it could return now and then. I really don't want to go back on the paroxetine again."

"You may not have to." She could hear the anxiety in his voice.

"It made me feel so sick, and my concentration—"

"Hang on..." Someone passed close by, and Lisa turned towards the wall and lowered her voice. "I said you may not need to, Ben. Please, call her. It would be good for you to—"

"It's *only one* episode, Lisa. I don't want to open those wounds again."

"I know." Lisa sighed. "And I don't want you to go down that horrible road again. What are you doing now?"

"I'm on the way to search someone's flat. I'm okay."

"*Esti sincer cu mine, Ben?*"

Beniamin paused. "I am always honest with you. I love you, Lisa. I'll be fine."

"I love you, too. That's why I'd like you to call Doctor Maguire, even if it's just to catch up. We can afford it."

"Look, I have to go. I just wanted you to know I'm okay."

He ended the call.

Chapter Eleven

Dinescu had parked the car a short distance from Charles Brady's flat. He watched Summers extract the door key from a plastic bag, and they stepped out of the car together.

Sarah Burgess was there to meet them, carrying a box containing the search kit. As they walked towards Brady's flat, she updated them about her visit to the New Moon pub and her conversation with the owners.

"But why would Brady contact a reporter?" asked Summers. "Did they get what paper she was from?"

"She had a notebook, but I'm not sure she was a reporter, Sarge," said Burgess. "The woman was professional-looking, they said."

"We'll bear it in mind," said Dinescu. "I don't suppose they had CCTV?"

"No, boss. I had a quick look."

They found the location they had been looking for. Laburnum House was a block of flats built on the site of the old Royal Military Police barracks in Chichester. The stonework for all the properties was a dull, sandy-grey colour, making all the buildings look much the same. You'd never know they were flats or houses from the outside. Charles Brady's flat was number five. There was another opposite and one next door.

The block wasn't like some of the usual hovels Major Crimes had attended. There was no smell of urine, scratched-up doors, or syringes in the stairwell. It smelled of lemon and was bright, upmarket, and expensive.

The flats were run by a property management company, and Brady had rented his apartment for three years. He had never been in arrears and had never been the subject of complaints. The management company told Burgess over the phone that Brady had kept himself to himself—a model tenant.

DS Summers inserted the key into the lock. She looked at the others to see if they were ready. Gloves were on, and the body-worn video cameras were recording.

"They're not allowed pets," said Burgess before Summers pushed the door open. "So we won't find a dead cat or dog in here."

"That's a relief," said Dinescu.

Brady's flat opened onto a short hallway with a kitchen to the left and a bathroom to the right. Ahead was a living room, and beyond the living room was a bedroom. All the rooms were large, even the bathroom. Everything was clean and cream. Modern appliances were fitted into a kitchen that was large enough for a small dining table and chairs. The lounge was tidy, with a coffee table in the centre covered with piles of books, papers, and two items of particular interest to the police officers.

Burgess photographed the laptop computer and the mobile phone on the table. She then went from room to room. The bedroom had an unmade bed, but aside from that, it was clean. Dirty laundry was in a basket, and a set of weights was gathering dust in the corner.

The three detectives went into the living room, and Burgess

brought out handfuls of evidence bags. She bagged up the phone and laptop and moved into the kitchen.

"We can make a start on all this," Dinescu said to Summers. He was looking at the collection of papers and books on the coffee table.

He and Summers sat at opposite ends of the sofa and looked over everything. He picked up a book that lay open, pages facing down: *Tudor Country Houses and Architecture.* Dinescu could see that Brady was interested in the house where he worked; the page was left open at Cotisham House. Dinescu read the text, which mentioned Lord Aversham's dispute with Queen Elizabeth the First over a planned visit with her retinue. Apparently, it was something Aversham couldn't afford. This was all beyond Dinescu.

"What is the meaning of *retinue*?" he asked Summers.

"It's like an entourage."

Dinescu then slipped into Romanian. "*Un anturaj.*"

"If you say so, boss."

Dinescu read aloud a paragraph below this, describing Nicholas Owen's stay at Cotisham Manor in 1597. "*He wanted to be some distance from London*, it says. *In gratitude for Aversham's help, Owen had overseen the work done to the house.*" Dinescu sighed. "It's all history. I thought Brady was a mathematics teacher."

Summers passed Dinescu a few photographs she'd found. They were black-and-white images of various rooms. He flipped them over to read the comments on the back. They explained the photos had been taken in 1987 and showed work done to improve the dormitories, the removal of the old kitchens, and some building work in the library.

"Fascinating," quipped Dinescu.

Summers agreed. "He was into his research of the place, boss. It's all rather odd, don't you think?"

Dinescu picked up three more photographs, all in colour. "And there are more."

One was dated 1990, according to the note written on the reverse side, and it was taken at the front of the school. The hedges were shorter, and there were huts in the fields that weren't there now. The boys' uniforms were smarter, with white shirts, striped ties, and blue blazers.

"They look like deer caught in headlights," said Summers. "That was over thirty years ago."

Dinescu looked at Summers. "That was the year my foster parents brought me to England." He looked away again, but Summers held her gaze a moment longer.

The next photo was one from the 1980s. There was a question mark after the year. It appeared they had girls and some very young children at the school back then. The look on their faces grated with something inside Dinescu. They were like the children he had left behind in Bacău. He studied the photograph closer. A circle had been drawn around two faces, a boy and a girl, standing side by side.

"That's when it was a mixed school," said Summers. "I wonder why Brady circled those two. I can't quite make them out."

The third photograph was different—dark and macabre. The light came from a camera flash, which bleached the brick walls pink and was perhaps taken from inside a wall cavity. Laid in a row on the floor, placed side by side, were five or more tiny skeletons covered in a cloth that had disintegrated into fragments.

Summers gasped when she saw it. "Shit! That's horrible. Are they babies?"

"It looks like it."

Burgess came in from searching the bathroom and kitchen.

"Nothing of any interest yet," she said. She saw the expression on Summers's face and looked at the photograph. "Ew! That's not nice! Where's that from?"

Dinescu turned over the photograph. *"The Priest Hole, 7th May 1986."*

"Priest hole? Is that in Cotisham?" said Burgess.

"It could well be," said Summers.

"What is a priest hole?" asked Dinescu. "I've never heard of it."

"It's a place where priests could hide from capture," said Summers.

"Who were they hiding from? Their congregation?"

"No, boss." She didn't realise he was joking. "Being a Catholic was illegal in this country, and priests were sentenced to a horrible death. This would have been in the time of Queen Elizabeth the First, mid-1500s to early 1600s, if my history GCSE serves me right. Some of these old country homes were owned by staunch Catholic families, and they had hiding places for visiting priests. It was serious stuff in those days."

Burgess and Dinescu exchanged looks.

Dinescu studied the photograph more closely. "So, these remains were in the priest's hiding place?"

"Looks like it, boss," said Summers.

"It's still just a history exercise for Brady," said Dinescu. "I'm more interested to know why he's circled those two children."

"I'll get on with the bedroom," said Burgess, backing away.

"Thanks, Sarah," said Summers. "I think it would be a good idea to bag up everything, boss, just in case it's important."

"I agree."

Summers took more stills on her police mobile and put each of Brady's photographs in separate evidence bags. They then moved on to some A4 copies of what appeared to be building plans, all with the title *The Lord Aversham Tower*.

"These are plans for the folly," said Dinescu. "Why is Brady studying this in so much detail?"

The diagrams showed a few more ornate features than the actual tower had. It was almost the same, with the central building, the three levels, and a cylindrical support on either side. The platforms were not open to the elements in the original plans, but they were fitted with glass and iron grills. They may have been damaged over the years or never completed. Dinescu saw the stairs were designed to have an iron handrail. He traced a thick, zig-zagged line drawn beneath one of the supporting columns with the words *to the tunnel* beside it.

"What is this line, do you think?" asked Dinescu.

"I don't know. I'm not an architect."

"I'm just asking for a suggestion, Emily."

Summers frowned. "Storage? An escape tunnel?"

They went through all the other notes on the table, and by the time Burgess reappeared from Brady's bedroom, they had one curious note left to examine. It was an A4 piece of lined paper.

Summers looked up at Burgess, who had something in her gloved hand.

"Anything?"

"There are a few out-of-date packets of condoms in his bedside drawer, and I'm wondering if this was the woman with Brady in the pub." Burgess held out a business card with grey, embossed letters.

Candice Lee
Private Detective Services
07700 909009

"I'll try calling the number. It may be worth following up," said Burgess.

"Okay," said Summers. "She may talk to you. It looks a bit tacky not having a landline or email address."

"True. I've also found another number. It's for someone called *Mary*, left on a Post-it note on his bedside table. It's a local landline number. It could also be the blonde woman's number. I'll try that too." Burgess sat on the arm of the sofa next to Summers. "What's that list?" She pointed at the lined paper sheet.

14-05-87 Maisy reported missing
22-06-87 Social services review
24-08-87 Gerald Faulkner-Williams/Aversham College closes
23-10-88 Aversham report published
3-09-90 Cotisham School for Boys Opens

Head - Gerald Faulkner-Williams (died 3/01/99)
Matron - Ruth Lambert (alive),
Nurse - Juliet Butterworth (alive) "A, J, M were black. A. needed <u>compress.</u>"
Nurse - Helen ~~Scott~~ Saunders (?)
Sports - Grant Wilkie (died 2019), Sally Ramsay (died 4/04/09)
<u>*Other Teaching Staff*</u>
~~*Miriam Cohen*~~

Next Actions: Call the police, missing persons.
Hand over evidence.

<u>*Is she there beneath us?*</u>

"Is who there beneath us?" said Burgess.

Dinescu tapped the A4 sheet. "This is definitely an investigation. I think he was looking for someone."

"I think you're right, boss," said Summers. "Maybe it's someone called Maisy. Let's bag all of it."

~

DC Gareth Booker rubbed his eyes. He'd been staring at his screen for too long, working through a list of teachers he had to check on PNC and local databases. He was hoping for something juicy to give DS Summers, but so far, he'd only come up with speeding tickets and complaints about noise.

Booker looked at the time on the computer. There were only a few hours to go. His fiancee, Chloe, had invited her parents over that evening, and Booker didn't want to leave work late. So he hoped the other detectives would find something of interest soon.

This case wasn't straightforward—they had to be missing something obvious. The lack of positive leads was frustrating for everyone. No witnesses and no CCTV. Ross Taylor was digging for someone with a good enough motive to kill Brady, and Booker argued that there wasn't always an apparent motive. But now he was having second thoughts. Brady's death wasn't a random killing.

Booker pulled up the next name on his list to check: Cameron Hyde, date of birth: 05/07/1994. Within a few seconds, Hyde's offences appeared on the screen. He had received a caution for common assault just a few months ago, and the victim was Charles Brady. Booker sat forward—this might be it. He picked up the copy from the printer and looked into Dinescu's office. The boss had already left to search Brady's flat with DS Summers.

Chapter Twelve

It was the end of the evening meal, and the dining hall was emptying. Only the boarders had dinner, so the day students having been sent home didn't affect the evening service. Everything was the same as usual, except for the main topic of conversation: Mr Brady and the Grey Friar. The younger boys hadn't wanted to stay in the dining hall for long that evening, especially as the sun dropped lower and the shadows grew longer.

The kitchen was clattering with dishes and cutlery. Pans were being stacked into the stainless steel industrial dishwashers. Only a handful of boys were left to finish as they scraped and stacked their plates and trays, sliding them onto the trollies.

Ethan Bishop was taking his time with his meal, moving the food around his plate as he watched Leah Turnbull from across the hall. His eyes followed hers, and he imagined staring down into them and the soft curve of her breasts beneath him. She closed her book and gathered her things together. She looked up at the high windows and the fading light, then looked at her watch.

"You on duty tonight, Miss?" Ethan had appeared opposite her, startling her.

"Sadly, not Ethan. I'm off home. I have a cat and a boyfriend to feed."

Ethan could tell she was lying. "How is Munchkin?"

"He's good. Still bringing in dead mice, though." Leah's eyes were wide. She watched Ethan lean over the back of the chair towards her.

She stood and swung her bag over her shoulder. Ethan could see her eyes were a little red as if she'd been crying.

"Everything okay, Leah? It's been a bad day."

"*You* call me Miss Turnbull. Not really, Ethan. I think we're all upset about Charles. Mr Brady."

"Yes. You were good friends."

Leah tilted her head a little. "No, we weren't, but all the staff liked him. Well, most of them."

"I expect Cameron didn't like Mr Brady much."

Leah frowned. "Why do you say that?"

"Brady was always trampling on his wildflowers. Oh, yes, there was something else, too. Brady tried to finger his girlfriend."

Leah's nostrils flared. "Cameron was just *fine* with him!"

Ethan smiled, his eyes fixed on hers. "Well, I expect you're busy, *Miss*, but you're welcome to join me. I can show you my photos for the project."

"I can't, Ethan." She backed away. "Don't forget—it has to be in by the end of next week."

Ethan watched Leah walk out of the dining hall and into the long passage towards the reception. He followed her, and she turned when she heard his footsteps.

"Ethan!"

He stood close to her. They were alone. He felt her breath on his face and the scent of her perfume gathered around him. His hand slipped behind her and rested on her backside, which he pushed towards him.

"Are you sure you don't want to come up, Miss?"

Leah gasped. His face was inches from hers now. He knew she could feel his fingers stroking her.

"No more, Ethan! Please. I don't want this! It's more than my job's worth... You know I like you, but... no more."

She stepped back and pushed Ethan's hand away.

"Okay, *Miss*! Stop fucking teasing me, then. You can't keep treating me like this."

"I'm not teasing you! You have to stop, or I'll report you to Mr Winston. Now, stay away!"

Leah walked off, straightening her skirt, leaving Ethan clenching his hand as he watched her go, still intoxicated by her scent.

Harry's voice came from nowhere. He was standing with Daniel.

"Come on, Ethan!" Harry jogged over to him and lowered his voice. "I've got it. I went into the prop box behind the stage, where you said it was. Loads of costumes and crap in there from Romeo and Juliet. I found the old monk's outfit. This is going to be bloody brilliant! We can scare the crap out of Matron."

Ethan was quiet for a moment until Leah disappeared around the corner. A WhatsApp message pinged his mobile. It was Leah.

> I meant what I said, Ethan. I only want to see
> you in lessons. Otherwise, stay away.

Ethan's eyes prickled with tears. "No. Fuck all of that, and fuck this place! I've had enough of it. I'm going out for a walk."

"It's dark! What's got into you?"

"Nothing. Leave me alone!"

Ethan left Harry and Daniel behind, and his anger burned as he thought of Leah. *I don't want this*, she said. It didn't feel like she didn't want it—not to Ethan.

He ran into the reception hall and crashed out of the main door, heading into the darkness. Leah had gone. He caught sight of a pair of tail lights as they turned out of the driveway. He walked across the pea shingle drive and towards the workshop. Leah's words were punching around in his head. He thought she had feelings for him. She was passionate—she wanted him. He stood still in the cool evening air, staring up at the stars peeking through the clouds and wondering what he could do now. He felt life was playing a cruel trick on him. He wiped his blurry eyes and walked deeper into the darkness. He didn't know where he was going, perhaps to the footpath and the side gate leading to the village. It would be locked, but it was easy enough for him to vault over.

A moving shadow caught his eye. A figure in black was coming out of Cameron's workshop. It stopped and froze when it saw Ethan.

"Cam?" Ethan called out. He couldn't see who it was—just a hooded silhouette. Hot breath rose as a cloud of vapour above them. "Who is it?"

Ethan's heartbeat grew louder in his ears. He saw the hooded figure in a long, baggy robe drifting towards him. Of course, Ethan thought of the Grey Friar—a stupid thought, he knew, but the shape and build was right for it.

Ethan suppressed his impulse to run and tilted his head as he tried to make out who it was. He stepped backwards, and the friar-like man stepped forwards. Ethan walked back a few more steps, and the silhouette followed him again.

"Who is it? Cameron? Mr Roberts?"

The figure kept walking towards him. Then he saw something like a claw hammer in its hand.

Ethan's stomach flipped, and his vision blurred. He turned and ran towards the gate. He could hear footsteps behind him, but Ethan was much faster. He picked up speed and vaulted the gate in one leap. There were trees on either side of the footpath, so he headed into them, leaping over brambles. He ran further and dropped right down behind a fallen oak trunk. It was pitch black where he hid, but there was enough light from the house to see the shadow as it climbed over the gate.

Ethan felt his blood pounding in his head. This was a shit night, he thought. He took deep breaths. He should have run the other way. Was that the Grey Friar? The shadow was too short for Cameron and too wide for Roberts. Did he believe it now? It stopped on the path, waiting and listening, raising the hammer above its head. Ethan wasn't sure how long he had remained there before the shadow moved away. He watched it continue along the path and back over the gate into the shadows of the woods. It didn't return. What was it doing in Cameron's workshop? There was nothing worth nicking in there.

Ethan stepped out from under the cover of the trees and moved back onto the path. It was in complete darkness now. He headed towards the lights of the house, flicking on the torch on his mobile phone. Why hadn't he thought of that earlier? He went back over the gate and ran towards the front door. He took one last look behind him. Was the Grey Friar still there? Ethan reassured himself, thinking how stupid that was. He must have deterred a burglar—as simple as that. He went back into the school and headed towards the common room to join the others.

Lisa slapped her palms onto the surface of the kitchen worktop. She was grateful Sophia was having tea with her grandparents, so she didn't have to listen to them arguing.

"Honestly, Ben! I don't understand you sometimes. You know how dangerous this is for you, and you're ignoring it!" She folded her arms, gripping her sides.

Beniamin stood in front of her. "I'm *not* ignoring it, Lisa. If I were ignoring it, then I wouldn't have told you. It was a one-off."

"Really?"

"Yes."

"I've heard you at night. You've been struggling in your sleep again."

"No, I haven't!"

"You have, Beniamin! Don't hide it from me." Lisa walked away from him and stood on the other side of the kitchen island, her hands on the granite worktop, leaning her weight onto her arms.

"I've had a couple of bad dreams. Everyone has bad dreams."

"Not like you." Lisa bit her lip and looked away. "Not like you."

"I don't need to see Doctor Maguire." Beniamin stepped back and pinched the bridge of his nose. "It will be a waste of time."

"Don't you remember what this did to us? You nearly destroyed us!"

Beniamin jutted his head forward. "Me? Do you think this is something I do by choice?"

"That's not what I meant! You know it isn't. I need you to do this for us. And for Sophia."

"I can't believe you think I'd put us at risk, Lisa. You and Sophia are everything to me."

"Then stop being so bloody pigheaded and speak to Siobhan! Do the right thing by us, Beniamin."

"I always do." Beniamin's voice was quiet, and his eyes were wet. He reached for his car keys and mobile phone. "I always do."

"Where are you going? We haven't finished!"

"I have."

"If that's how you feel, find some pretty young thing to spend the rest of your fucking life with! Wake her up with your nightmares and see how long that lasts!"

Beniamin didn't turn around. He closed the door to the sound of Lisa calling him. He got into his car and sped out of the driveway. Blood was thrumming in his ears, and Lisa's words replayed over and over: *You nearly destroyed us.* He felt bile rise in his throat, and he drove too fast along the Birdham road and headed north. He came to a roundabout and went eastward along the Chichester bypass. Roundabout after roundabout until he was heading north. He could taste Lisa's bitterness in his mouth. He hit the bends too fast and had to brake hard. He couldn't return to therapy. Not again. He stepped harder on the accelerator, taking him further north and up into the hills. He passed Goodwood and took a sharp bend to his left. A short distance further on, Beniamin turned left into a narrow lane. It was dark now, and by the time he had arrived at the Trundle, the car park was closed. Instead, he parked alongside a bank on the slope of the chalky lane.

He stayed in his car for a while, looking at the view over Chichester, the harbour, Portsmouth in the west, and Little-hampton in the east. Although it was dark, lights from the towns and roads lit the sky, and he could make out the Isle of Wight across from Portsmouth.

After a time—he didn't know how long—Beniamin stepped out of the car and pulled his jacket around him. He walked a short distance and sat on a bench. This was where he used to take Lisa when they first started dating. They'd come with a bag of chips and a flask of tea. Lisa would tell him about her plans to move to London, to travel Europe, and to write a novel. He was just happy to listen to her for hours. She was his world. She had helped him through the darkest of nights and loved him through everything. She had a lightness and positivity that Beniamin had never seen before.

He gave a deep sigh. He couldn't believe that they had fallen out over this. They never argued about anything. He dug his hands into his pockets and shuddered, regretting what he had said. Memories of him and Lisa snuggling under a blanket to keep warm flooded back, and the pain in his heart was horrible. If he could click his fingers and make it better, then he would.

Headlights brushed over the treetops as another vehicle came up the lane towards the car park. Beniamin shook his head. He wanted to be alone, but this was a popular spot for youngsters to go after dark for a quick snog and a fumble. The car parked a short distance behind his, and the headlights went off. He didn't hear any doors closing or the car's suspension creaking, so he was glad to be left alone.

His mind drifted in the silence, punctured only by the bleat of a lamb in the fields below. He thought about the case and the old Tudor house. It brought back memories of his childhood. Cotisham School was haunted by something in its dark corridors and halls. He thought about the plans they'd found in Brady's flat, the plans of the tower, and that mysterious reference to a tunnel. There was something in Brady's research that bothered Beniamin. He was obsessed with the house and its history. What had Brady been looking for?

A cool breeze coming down from the top of the Trundle cut through Beniamin. He thought about climbing the footpath up the dome-shaped hill for a moment. Although he would get a better view up there, his sadness had sapped away his energy. He wondered if he had blown it big time with Lisa. Why was he being so stubborn? He knew she was right. He rubbed the chill from his arms and stayed where he was, blending into the darkness of the hillside.

"I come with chips."

Lisa's voice from behind him startled Beniamin. He turned and saw her shadow, wrapped in a blanket and carrying something that smelled very much like chips from a chip shop. He struggled to hold himself together. Lisa sat beside him and covered him with half the blanket. She moved closer to him until their thighs and shoulders touched. The tension in Beniamin's body left him.

Lisa held out an unwrapped bag of steaming vinegary chips. "Do you want one?"

There was the slightest reflection of light from somewhere, enough to see the tracks of her tears on her cheeks. Beniamin took a chip with one hand and stroked away Lisa's tears with the other.

"I'm sorry," she said.

Beniamin nodded. "Me too... Why would I ever want to be with anyone else but you?" They hugged, crushing the chip wrapping, and Beniamin kissed Lisa's forehead.

Lisa took a soggy chip. "I guess I have my own bad memories of that time, too."

"I know. I forget that sometimes. I will call Siobhan and make an appointment. I promise."

"Thank you."

Beniamin and Lisa finished their chips, wiped their fingers on the paper, and pulled the blanket around them. They watched the lights of the giant container ships drifting in the misty Solent, and they sat in silence together, enjoying each other's warmth.

A blue light strobed as it raced along a road somewhere below them, and they followed its journey for a while.

"We're okay, aren't we?" Lisa whispered.

"Of course we are. We have each other. Always."

Chapter Thirteen

Beniamin Dinescu raised his head and saw the bodies blackened by fire, screaming for help. Then came the pall of billowing black smoke that swallowed and suffocated everything around him. Twisted, creaking wreckage blocked the way back. The only escape from this nightmare was back through the tunnel and the smoke. Someone was calling him, tapping his face, and Beniamin awoke when a gentle and shaky finger pressed into his nose. He was home.

"Beep, beep! Got you!"

He flicked open one mad, rolling eye, and the girl responsible screamed with laughter as she did when she was half her age.

"Who dares to wake the Sleepy Bed Monster!" Beniamin sat bolt upright and jerked his head to look at the girl.

"Dad! I'm thirteen, not six. Still makes me laugh, though. Your breakfast is ready... Stinky!"

The girl pushed a paddle forward on her wheelchair, and she whizzed out of the bedroom, almost hitting the door, and escaped back into her room. Beniamin jumped out of bed and ran after her. His daughter squealed, but by the time he had got to her bedroom, the chairlift was already whirring, and Sophia was descending.

"Ah!" shouted Beniamin after her. "Every time! It's not fair."

"Tough!" Sophia replied.

Beniamin paused and shook off his restless night of bad dreams. He could hear Lisa moving around downstairs, laughing with Sophia—probably at him.

He stretched, and his eyes caught a shaft of morning light coming through the bathroom window and onto the landing. He closed his eyes, took a deep breath, and smiled as the sunlight warmed his face.

He put on his favourite blue dressing gown and grabbed his mobile phone. He had an idea, one that would be important to Lisa. He found Siobhan Maguire's website. She had an online appointments page for introductory meetings. After checking his diary and a few taps on his phone screen, he went down the stairs to find Lisa with a grinning Sophia.

"Sleepy Bed Monster?" said Lisa. "Is that the best you can do?"

"I didn't want to scare her." Beniamin ruffled his daughter's hair and kissed her on the cheek. "They told me stories of the evil *Muma Pădurii* when I was in the home in Bacău."

"Muma Pădurii sounds like a friendly fairy," said Sophia.

"Some say she was kind to animals in the forest, but she's really a hideous old hag who steals lost and naughty children. When she finds one, and she *always* finds at least one, she snatches them and drags them away, kicking and screaming. But no one can hear them scream." Beniamin made his eyes bulge, and Lisa laughed. "She takes the children into the forest and eats them with turnips and carrots. We used to be afraid she would come for us."

"I'm not surprised!" said Lisa.

"That's horrible, Dad!" said Sophia.

"So, you prefer my Sleepy Bed Monster?" Beniamin said to Sophia as he jabbed a finger.

"Always."

"Come on, let's get some breakfast," said Lisa. "No more old hags. We're having almond croissants."

Beniamin joined Lisa in the kitchen, hugging her a little harder that morning. She pulled back and smiled, tracing her finger along his bottom lip.

"I'll make the coffee," she said

Beniamin switched on the oven. "How many croissants do you want?"

Lisa didn't hear him. She was reading a news article that had just pinged on her mobile phone.

"Is this what you were doing yesterday? You said you went to a private school." She showed him the headline.

School Mystery Death Puzzles Sussex Detectives

Beniamin frowned and read the short article. "I wonder who leaked this? It doesn't help us."

"No real details, to be fair," said Lisa, "but they're inferring it was suicide. But if it's you investigating, I doubt it was."

"They're right about one thing. It is a puzzle."

"It's a private boarding school. I assume they are all well off."

Beniamin nodded. "The parents have money, yes."

"Did it remind you of your orphanage?"

"I think it must have."

"There's something about the school that rings a bell. I've heard of it before."

"Before today?"

"Yes. Years ago... I don't remember now. If it comes to me, I'll let you know."

Beniamin set the table for breakfast, and they sat together for croissants and coffee.

"All good for school today, Sophia?" he asked.

Sophia nodded. "All good. Double maths to start with, so I'm happy."

"Ah, maths. That's numbers, right?" Beniamin winked.

"No, it's letters at the moment." Sophia gave him a clever smile.

"Of course. How silly of me. I didn't do any maths until I came to England."

Sophia copied her father's voice. "*And I had to learn to speak English...*"

"Cheeky!" Beniamin looked at Lisa. "See how cheeky *your* daughter has become!"

"*My* daughter. She's more like you than me."

Beniamin cleared away the breakfast things, took a shower, and dressed quickly. He wanted to tell Lisa something before he left for work. He kissed Sophia goodbye and waited until she had gone up to her room to get changed. He found Lisa in the study, sorting out a pile of books.

"I have to go," he said. Lisa turned around to face him. "I've made that appointment with Doctor Maguire."

Lisa's face lit up. "Really? That's great! Gosh, that was quick!"

"I booked it on her website, and there was a slot free tomorrow."

"Thank you for taking it seriously. We all need you to be well."

"I know." Beniamin picked up his car keys. "Let me know if you remember anything about that house. Ask your brother, too." He kissed her on the cheek. "Are you okay with Sophia getting changed?"

"Yes, it's fine. You go."

Beniamin sat in his Mercedes in the driveway. He wasn't looking forward to his next task. He was grateful, *always* grateful, for his family. The face of his birth mother came to mind at that moment, and a pang of sadness came over him when he thought of all that she had missed with Lisa and Sophia.

He checked the clock in the car and his face in the rear-view mirror. "*E timpul să mergi la muncă.* It's time to go to work, Beniamin."

Chapter Fourteen

DCI Dinescu left Charles Brady's postmortem and headed for the toilets. He was responsible for attending as SIO, and he didn't want to ask Summers to do it on his behalf—not in the condition Brady was found. He scrubbed his hands and splashed his face and head with cold water—anything to get rid of that smell, which could permeate and linger in clothes all day. It was a gruelling morning, and he was glad he wasn't the one who had to take the photographs. Yet it was hard to unsee those images. So he thought of his family and counted. It was something that worked for him in stressful situations. Counting up or counting down.

He dried his face with a paper towel and looked at the plastic bags on the surface next to him. They were the exhibits he had seized from Brady's body and clothing, including a watch, a wallet containing till receipts, bank cards, and a driving licence. No cash.

On his way back to the car, Dinescu received the news from DS Summers via text that the shotgun hadn't been found in the pond or the woods. He wasn't surprised, but they'd had to look. The hypothesis that the gun taken from the school was used to kill Brady was still likely, but the killer must have taken the gun with them.

He was glad to leave the mortuary and drive back to the station. It was early afternoon, and the briefing was just with his core team in one of the meeting rooms on the first floor.

He sat at the head of the long table and checked his mobile phone. He'd had a WhatsApp message from Sophia: three red hearts and a good luck message. He smiled to himself and replied with a kiss emoji. Sophia knew when her father had something bothering him.

"Whenever you're ready, Emily."

"Thank you, sir," said DS Summers. "Shall we start with the postmortem?"

"Okay. It was... unpleasant, but nothing unexpected." Dinescu pulled out his notes from a folder. "I expressed gratitude for how quickly they returned these results to us. Charles Brady had been shot once from approximately four feet away. This was confirmed by the size of the wound, the penetration depth of the pellets, and the splatter on the brickwork. Brady's insides should have covered the person pulling the trigger if he had been standing in front of him when he was shot. But Forensics are initially saying there was no splatter shadow. So, it looks likely Brady was shot from the steps leading to the platform. The assailant would have been protected from blood splatter to a greater extent, and the distance would be right, too. The gun, however, would have been very messy."

"And the gun would have been easier to conceal from below," added Gareth Booker.

"True. A forensic entomologist was also present at the postmortem and had been measuring the length of maggots and reviewing measurements from photographs taken at the scene. She stated that the time of death was Monday, the 17th of April, in the afternoon between three and six, considering the warm weather."

"Did they find any evidence of a struggle?" asked Summers.

"There were no defence marks or skin under the nails."

"Thanks, sir. So, the search of the pond by underwater search teams late yesterday afternoon was negative. The murder weapon is still unaccounted for. Gareth, where are we with background checks on the staff?"

Gareth stroked his moustache and beard with his forefinger and thumb like he was examining a chess puzzle.

"Between us, we've PNC-checked every member of the teaching staff, including the learning support assistants and reading volunteers. Today we'll look at catering and office staff. There are a few minor traffic convictions and a public order from fifteen years ago. David Roberts, the head of sports, was arrested on suspicion of the sexual assault of a boy at the school. It was dropped when the boy admitted it was a false and malicious allegation."

"How long ago was Roberts arrested?" said Summers.

"Four years ago, Sarge. No further action was taken by Social Services either. Now this is interesting. On New Year's Day this year, Cameron Hyde was arrested for common assault against Charles Brady."

"What are the details?" asked Summers.

"Well, Sarge, Cameron accused Brady of making a pass at his girlfriend, Leah Turnbull, during the school's New Year's bash. They held it at the school a week after they started the new term. Turnbull is an art teacher. Brady apologised for his indiscretion, but Cameron punched him anyway."

"Brady supported the prosecution for the assault on him?"

"Yes, and Cameron accepted a caution, but as he didn't teach or work independently with the students, he was allowed to keep his job."

"What does he do at the school?" said Dinescu.

"He's the caretaker and looks after the grounds, cuts the grass, trims bushes—that sort of stuff. He has a few part-timers in to help. He also helps with the clay pigeon club."

"Let's put his name at the top of our board," said Summers.

"Ross, what do we know about any trouble Brady's had with the pupils?"

Taylor put his hands behind his neck and sat back. "Rumours and more rumours. Brady had a run-in with Ethan Bishop, who's in his last year at Cotisham. Two staff members say it's connected to Brady's unseemly grope of Leah Turnbull at their New Year's party. I had to go to the deputy head, Andrew Winston, to get the full, unadulterated details. Somehow—and no one knows how—photographs were taken of Brady in action."

"By staff?" asked Booker.

"No. That's the strange thing. It was taken by Ethan or one of his roommates—Daniel Curtis or Harry Price. They were somehow able to spy on the party, and photos were taken. Anyway, the details of Brady's attempt at a kiss and a flash of Turnbull's knickers were photographed. Ethan took it upon himself to post prints of the original photograph around the school."

"What an absolute shit," said Booker.

Taylor nodded. "And they got Cameron's punch, too."

Summers was trying to catch up with her notes. "So what did Brady do to Ethan?"

"No one knows for sure. But the day the photos were taken down, Ethan mysteriously walked into a door and broke his nose. Ethan was suspended for four weeks—this was in January."

"Brady hit him?"

"It looks like it, Sarge."

"Ethan Bishop can go underneath Cameron Hyde."

Dinescu rubbed his temples. "Sarah, we need to trace Brady's ex-wife. At the moment, no one is mourning him. Once we've contacted her, there'll be a press release."

"Yes, sir," said Burgess. "I'll also call those phone numbers we found yesterday at Brady's flat."

Summers pointed her pen at Kirby. "Chester, what's come back from the financial checks?"

"Nothing yet, Sarge," said Kirby. "I'm still waiting for a reply."

"Oh, come on, Chester! We needed those by this morning. What have you been doing? Give them a kick. Tell them it's urgent. Otherwise, go down to Brady's bank and sit on someone. Do I have to do everything myself? How about mobile calls?"

Kirby's face darkened like he was about to have an outburst. "His phone service provider promised to get back to me this morning."

"Make sure they do." Summers continued to look down her list of tasks, and the team shuffled in their seats. "Ross, we need to talk to Brady's neighbours. Find out what they knew about him—any gossip."

"That would be an ideal job for one of the civilian investigators," said Taylor.

"I'm asking you to do it, Ross," said Summers, looking down at her notes.

Taylor raised his eyebrows. "Of course, Sarge."

"I assume you've all read the updates from yesterday," said Dinescu. "We're working on the hypothesis that Charles Brady was investigating a historic missing person case with a connection to the school. I will keep following this line of enquiry in case there's a link to Brady's murder."

Summers looked irritated. "Do you think that's a valuable

line of enquiry, boss? What does that have to do with anything? We'd be better following up on Cameron Hyde."

Dinescu's pale face flushed, but he bit his lip. Booker coughed and looked away, tapping his fingers against the table.

"I'll be trying to uncover Brady's social network," said Summers. "I'll task the rest of you to look into the movements of the school staff when we believe Brady was killed. Perhaps someone heard a shot or saw something suspicious. That's a lot of legwork. Sarah, you can help oversee that once you've made your calls."

"Yes, boss... Sorry, yes, Sarge."

Dinescu tilted his head and looked at the pissed-off faces around him, but then there was a knock on the door. One of the Worthing detectives poked his head into the room.

"Sorry to interrupt, sir, Sarge. The headmaster of Cotisham needs to speak to you urgently. He's caught the caretaker, Cameron Hyde, returning the missing shotgun."

Dinescu glanced at Summers, who was about to speak. He raised his hand to stop her. "Chester, call the duty inspector. Let him know Hyde needs arresting—suspicion of murder. You may need some assistance."

"Yes, sir."

"I'll catch up with you all later. Emily, wait here with me."

Chester was the last to leave, and he caught the look from Dinescu. When the door clicked closed, Dinescu leant forward with his elbows on the table.

"Sir?" said Emily, licking her dry lips.

"You came from Surrey Major Crimes, didn't you?"

Emily frowned and looked puzzled. "Yes, sir."

"I've spoken to Detective Superintendent Desai about you."

"Why?"

"To be frank, Emily, I don't think it's working. You are a very, let's say, *eager* detective. There's nothing wrong with that.

You work hard, which is again admirable. But your people skills are terrible."

"What? How can you say that?"

"All I have to do is observe how you speak to the team. You are trying too hard to please me. And by doing so, you are putting down members of your team. That's not how you manage people, Emily."

Emily rose to her feet. "Is this a disciplinary? Because if it is, there should be—"

"Emily, sit down! I'm trying to help you. You need to chill and trust your team to do their jobs. Chester is a good detective. If you had spent time getting to know him, then you'd know that he would have done everything he could to get those financial checks back from the bank. He's as frustrated as you are. Beating him won't make them come back faster."

"How difficult can it be?"

"Ask him. And when he's explained it to you, you can apologise to him. The detectives in this core team are some of the best in the county. They wouldn't be here if they weren't. I have taken the time to get to know them, Emily."

"But—"

"No buts! You have trodden on everyone since the moment you arrived here. You need to decide what you are going to do because the way things are at the moment, I will request you be transferred out of here."

Emily's face was a deep red, and her hands trembled. She nodded.

"Also, it's one thing to correct my English, but quite another to question my decisions in front of the team. I will decide what a valuable line of enquiry is. Not you. Is that clear?"

Emily nodded again.

"I said, is that clear, Emily?"

"Yes, sir."

"Good. I'm happy to hear any doubts you have, but in private. That's how it works here. The last time I looked, the police service was a disciplined service with a rank structure. Do you understand that?"

"Yes, sir. I'm sorry."

"Is this how it worked in Surrey, Emily? Were you fighting to survive?"

"No, sir. I just wanted to do well. To make a good impression. I want this job to work. Everyone knows about this team, and there was a difficult selection process to get onto it. I wanted it so badly. My work is all I have."

"Your work is all you have? I'm sorry to hear that. You have a partner, don't you?"

"Yes, sir."

Dinescu decided not to follow that line of questioning. He could tell something was wrong there.

"Do I request a transfer for you? Or will things improve?"

Emily looked up with wet eyes. "I want this job so badly."

Dinescu smiled. "Then... chill. Trust your team. If anyone doesn't pull their weight, then you'll know—really know. I need you to win them over, not impress them."

"Yes, sir. Thank you."

"Go for a walk for twenty minutes and get some fresh air. I want you to interview Cameron Hyde when he's brought in. I'll be watching on the video feed."

"Yes, sir."

"I'm going to give you another chance. *One* more chance."

"Thank you, sir."

Emily Summers sat alone on a bench overlooking the Chichester Canal, watching the insects flitting around on the meniscus of the water. Her attention turned to a pair of moorhens swimming in and out of the reeds, stirring the muddy water as they searched for food.

Dinescu had stirred muddy waters, churning emotions and memories and raising them to the surface. She remembered the day she last saw her father as he headed for Spain. Emily's mother used to take her down to see the ships leaving port while they stood on the Round Tower in Southsea. She would wave at the people on the giant ferries heading out to sea, and they would wave back. One day, her father went out on one of those ferries and never returned. Of course, she blamed herself. Her father was perfect in every way; it could only have been her fault. Would he have left her if she had worked harder at being a better daughter? She would never know, but she'd never allow the lack of trying to ruin her life again.

Emily called Anthony, but he didn't answer, even though it was his lunch break. She needed someone to talk to, and her mother would be at the library.

Emily knew Dinescu was right. She had been trying too hard. She wanted to hit the ground running in Chichester, but it was very different from Guildford. She even heard herself and cringed when she laid into Chester and Booker on that first day. You can't lead a team like that. Her face flushed with embarrassment, and her eyes were tearful again.

"Come on, Emily!" she shouted. She looked around her, but only the moorhens had heard her. "You can do this."

Maybe if Anthony had been more understanding, she wouldn't be like this, perhaps if he didn't hit the bottle as soon as he got home. Her fingers moved to the bruising on her shoulder, and she shook her head.

"You can do this, Emily. You can start a new life for yourself."

She checked her watch. She had to get back. As she got up from the bench, her phone rang. It was Anthony.

"What is it?" he said. He sounded irritable.

"I just wanted to talk to you."

"What about?"

"It's been difficult, and I—"

"Look, Em. I'm busy. I've had no chance for lunch, and they're queuing all the way down to the X-Ray department for their prescriptions. We can talk later."

"Sure. But we really must—"

He'd hung up.

"Talk."

Chapter Fifteen

Emily Summers arrived in the custody building after her walk by the canal. Cameron Hyde had been brought in, and she was about to interview him.

She went into the toilets, tied back her hair, and checked her face in the mirror. She waited for the custody nurse to finish drying her hands and leave. Her head ached, and her shoulders were stiff. She looked tired but didn't realise how tired she felt until now. It didn't help that she'd only slept a few hours last night. Anthony wanted to argue, but she wouldn't play his games. He had come in late from work after a *disgusting day*—to use his words. New rules at the hospital meant he had even more work and less time. But Summers was tired, too. She was struggling and was having a bloody awful day today. He never wanted to listen. He just wanted to drink.

"Stop whining, Emily," she said to her reflection.

It was all she could do to stop herself from crying. She tucked in her white blouse, brushed off a mark from her grey trousers and took out some makeup from her bag. After a subtle application of lippy, she looked at herself again. Better.

"You can do better than him, Em." She was repeating the

words her mother had said to her not long after she'd met Anthony. She tucked away a stray blonde hair and took a deep breath. She knew her mother was right, but she didn't think she had the energy or the willpower to pack up and move out, to start somewhere new. "Come on, Em. You've got this."

DS Summers picked up the folder next to her and focused on the job at hand. She left the toilets and walked out to the custody bridge, the mottled blue raised platform where the custody sergeant was waiting for her.

"Are you ready for him, Emily?" he said.

"Yes. Bring him down, please. Interview room one."

She heard someone walking up from behind her. When she turned, she saw Chester Kirby waiting for her.

"The boss said I was to do this interview with you," he said.

"The boss did? Okay." Summers knew she'd been set up. "Look, Chester... I'm sorry about earlier. I shouldn't have spoken to you like that. It didn't help either of us."

Kirby stared at her for a few moments. "Okay. Thanks, Sarge. I've got news back from the bank, by the way."

"Great! We can look at it after the interview. Are you all prepped?"

"Yes, Sarge."

"More than I am. Come on."

Summers and Kirby went straight to the interview room and made themselves ready. A few minutes later, Cameron Hyde entered the room with the duty solicitor, and they sat in front of them.

"I'm Mark Pratt," the solicitor said.

"DS Summers."

"Are you sure there's no disclosure for me?"

"Yes, quite sure, Mr Pratt." Summers returned a thin-lipped smile and waited for Hyde and Pratt to settle down. "Do you need any water, Cameron?"

"No, I'm fine, thanks." Summers saw Cameron Hyde was a tall, good-looking man with long, blonde hair. She noticed his large hands, which had seen a lot of manual work.

Summers explained the interview process to him, and Cameron paid close attention to her. When he and Mr Pratt said they were ready, she pressed the record button.

"This interview is being video recorded in an interview room at Chichester Custody." Summers checked her watch. "It's now 14:20 hours on Tuesday, the 25th of April, 2023. I am Detective Sergeant Summers, warrant number NS3432. Also present is..."

"DC Kirby, warrant number NK4110."

Summers looked at Pratt and waited.

"Mark Pratt, duty solicitor."

"Cameron, please state your full name and date of birth."

Cameron hesitated and licked his lips. "Cameron Henry Hyde, the 5th of July, 1994."

"I see you've taken up your legal right for free and independent legal advice with the duty solicitor. Have you consulted with Mr Pratt?"

"Yes."

"Thank you," said Summers, who briefly smiled to reassure him. "Before we start, I need to caution you. It's the same caution you were given when you were arrested. You do not have to say anything, but it may harm your defence if you do not mention, when questioned, something that you later rely on in court. Anything you do say may be used in evidence. Do you understand what that caution means, Cameron?"

Cameron ran his long fingers through his hair. "I do. I've heard it before."

"Good. Cameron, you were arrested today at Cotisham School at 12:10 hours on suspicion of the murder of Charles

Brady. Tell me about the events that led up to that arrest. What happened this morning?"

Cameron looked at his solicitor and then at Summers. "I had the missing shotgun that belonged to the school, and I returned it. Eric saw me and called the police."

"Tell me who Eric is—for the record."

"Eric Greenway, the school headmaster." Cameron rubbed his thumb into his palm.

"Is this the shotgun the police have been searching for?"

"Yes. I think so."

"Why do you think the police were searching for the shotgun?"

"You wanted to know if it killed Charles Brady?"

"And as it was missing, it was a police line of enquiry. Why did you have the shotgun?"

"I borrowed it Saturday morning to shoot rats and rabbits. The boarders wouldn't be returning from their Easter holidays until the next day, so there was less chance of them getting in the way."

"That was Saturday, the 15th of April?"

"Yes."

"Where were these rats and rabbits?"

"The rats were around the back of the kitchens, and the rabbits were digging up the school fields."

"Did you ask permission to borrow the gun?"

"I didn't need it. I had a key to the cabinet."

"But you knew the police were searching for this gun. I assume you had seen the search teams and the police divers. Yet you said nothing. Why?"

"I'd mislaid it." Cameron shifted in his chair. "Look, this is going to sound rubbish. I was going to use it the next day, the Sunday, for the club, so I hid it under the cover for the chipper in the workshop. Then I locked up and left."

"Why didn't you return it to the gun cabinet?"

"I realised I didn't have a key to Greenway's office, which meant I'd have to find Matron and get her to let me in. I couldn't be bothered."

"Am I right in thinking you had the gun in your possession for over a week, including Monday, the 17th of April, until this morning?"

"Sort of."

"Explain, sort of."

"As I said, I borrowed it Saturday morning and shot a few rabbits. It was too difficult to shoot the rats without causing a lot of damage and mess. I asked a mate, and he said poison would be better. Anyway, the older boarders were all back on Sunday, so we decided to run the clay shooting club just to get them settled back in. That was around four o'clock. I went to get the gun out of the workshop..."

"And?"

"I couldn't find it."

"The gun wasn't where you left it?"

Hyde looked away, and his face flushed. "No. I know it sounds stupid, but... I thought I'd lost it. I looked everywhere. I panicked."

"Did someone take it?"

"No. I don't think so."

"A break-in?"

"No. I don't understand it."

"Did you tell anyone the shotgun was missing?"

"No one."

"Did you sign it out in the book when you took it out of the gun cabinet?"

"No."

"Why?"

"I just forgot, okay? And... this morning, I came in to turn the workshop upside down to look for it. Then I found it. It had fallen underneath the chipper somehow. I couldn't have seen it."

"It appeared again?"

"No, it didn't *just* appear. I found it. As I said, it must have fallen underneath the chipper somehow."

"And that's when you thought you'd return the gun to the cupboard instead of handing it to the police?"

"When I heard about Charles, I really panicked. I'd found the gun, and it didn't look good. I knew I had to get it back somehow. So I sneaked into Eric's office first thing, but he caught me."

"Tell me if I've got this right, Cameron. You went to get the shotgun from your workshop on Sunday, the 16th, but it wasn't there. You had mislaid it and didn't tell anyone it was missing. You didn't tell anyone for over a week. You went in early this morning, the day after Charles Brady's body was discovered, to have a good look for the gun again, and this time you found it underneath the chipper machine. You then tried to return the gun to the cabinet with no one knowing because you didn't want to be caught with it. Is that a fair summary? Have I got that right?"

"Yes, but I know how this looks."

"You do. Good. Who took the shotguns from the gun cabinet for the clay shooting club on Sunday the 16th?"

"Me."

"I suppose if someone else had, they would have seen only five in there."

"Yes."

"Who returned them afterwards?"

"Me."

"Why didn't you tell anyone the gun was missing?"

"It was a mistake. I should have, but I wasn't feeling right. I had a rotten toothache, which turned into a migraine, especially after all that shooting. I needed to get the guns away and get home. The toothache went right into my jaw and set off the headache, which got worse and worse. I get terrible migraines, and I just wanted to get home. I couldn't be bothered to go back to the workshop."

"Did you lock the workshop that Sunday?"

"I think I did."

"Can you be certain?"

"Not absolutely. But I usually do. But, as I said... I wasn't well."

"Did you use the shotgun on Monday, the 17th of April, or anytime afterwards?"

"No. I couldn't find it, anyway."

"Did you return to your workshop on that Monday?"

"I may have done."

"Either you did, or you didn't. Which is it?"

"I did."

"Did you see the gun when you returned?"

"No! How many more times do I have to tell you?" Cameron's hands were shaking. "I'd left the gun under the chipper machine cover at the back. But it must have fallen underneath." He coughed. "Can I get some water? My throat's dry."

Summers paused the interview. "I'll give you a minute."

Kirby brought in a cup of water, and Summers gave Cameron a few minutes to calm down and talk further to his solicitor.

Summers and Kirby were waiting outside in the corridor when Dinescu joined them. He had been watching the video feed at his desk. Summers leaned against the wall, arching her back to avoid the alarm strip.

"Either he is our murderer, or he's incredibly stupid," said Summers.

"He mislaid it," said Dinescu with a smirk. "Not a great defence. We still don't have a connection between him and the crime scene, and we don't know if that shotgun was the murder weapon."

"I know. It is possible someone came in and took the gun from the workshop. It's clearly rattled him, though. I'm about to ask him where he was when Brady was murdered. His solicitor looks smug, so I'm guessing he has a reply. He knows it's coming. So, I'd better get back in there, boss."

"Yes. I think it's all a bit too easy with Cameron having the gun, anyway. Would he hide it in his workshop if he'd killed someone with it? Would he try to return it? Go on. I'll talk to you later."

Kirby knocked on the door and stepped back into the interview room. Summers sighed and rubbed her eyes.

"Emily, are you okay?" asked Dinescu. "Not a great day for you."

She faced him again and gave a wry smile, shaking her head. "No, sir."

"Are you okay to continue?"

Emily forced a grin and knew it was overdone, but she would have bawled in front of him if she hadn't. "It's fine. Just tired—nothing else. I'm glad Chester is in there with me. He's quiet, though."

"I call it letting you take the lead," said Dinescu. "Talk to me if you need to. I wasn't trying to break you today."

Emily nodded and then returned to the interview room.

Cameron looked less shaky now and a little more confident. Summers guessed the solicitor had told him there was still insufficient evidence to convict him of anything. She rechecked her watch and restarted the interview.

"Where were you on Monday, the 17th of April, in the afternoon?"

Cameron looked at his solicitor.

Pratt sat forward. "My client is more than happy to answer questions about his whereabouts at the time of the alleged murder, which has taken a long time coming, I might add."

"Fair enough," said Summers, unable to stop herself as she rolled her eyes. "Cameron?"

"I was in hospital having a tooth removed. I can show you the gap if you want to see it?"

"No, thank you. Which hospital?"

"Chichester, St Richard's. My appointment was at 1:45, and then I went home to my dad's after four. I'm sure the hospital can confirm it. My dad will, too."

"Thank you, Cameron. We will check."

Emily frowned and checked her notes. She felt pissed off and didn't know why.

"Cameron, describe your relationship with Charles Brady."

He looked at his solicitor again, who nodded his head. "No comment."

Pratt raised his pen to interject again. "My client has given his verifiable whereabouts at the time of Mr Brady's death. He does not want to answer questions about his relationship with Mr Brady."

"Cameron, is it right you don't want to describe your relationship with Charles Brady?"

"No comment."

"Okay. Can you tell me what happened on the night of Friday, the 6th of January, and the events that led up to your arrest that evening?"

Cameron put his head in his hands and closed his eyes. "No comment."

"That was the night you were arrested for assaulting Charles Brady, and I believe you accepted a caution for common assault."

"No comment."

"In a statement from that evening, witnesses saw you punch Charles Brady after he made a pass at your girlfriend, Leah Turnbull. How was your relationship with Mr Brady after that night?"

"No comment."

"When did you last speak to Mr Brady?"

"No comment."

Pratt sat forward. "Sergeant, at the risk of repeating myself, my client has already given an account of where he was at the time of Mr Brady's death—nowhere near the school. What is the point of continuing with these questions?"

"Very well." Emily flipped over her wrist and checked her watch. "We will consider talking with Doctor Greenway regarding the lax safety of shotguns at the school and your actions. This interview is terminated."

Archie Faulkner was watching Celia type on her computer. When she noticed he was standing there, her brow creased, and she looked him up and down. She had never been very good at hiding her dislike of him, and Archie enjoyed winding her up.

He flashed his bright blue eyes at her.

"Celia, my *sweetheart*," he said with his usual cheeky-boy grin. "Where's Cam? I've got some rat poison for him. Do you want to try some? It's delicious."

Celia's face was stony. "He's not here this afternoon."

"When's he back?"

"I don't know."

Archie rolled his eyes, but instead of leaving, he walked into the office, hands by his hips like a gunslinger.

"Anything else?" said Celia as she looked over the top of her glasses.

"Police are still here, then?"

Celia sighed. "Now and then."

"I see all the kids have gone. The place is deserted."

"The day students have been sent home. Back next week."

"Is that because of the murder? Bloody scary, that. One of your own, too."

"Look, Archie, I'm busy. I don't have time to chat."

"Fair enough, fair Celia. I'll drop the poison into the workshop. I've got a key."

"Fine. You do that."

As he left the office, Archie turned and blew Celia a kiss. She tutted and looked away. He went to his car, removed the box of rat poison, and walked across one of the smaller fields to the gardening unit and workshop. A small group of students were out photographing trees for a project. Leah Turnbull was with them, strolling backwards and forwards, keeping an eye on them. Archie could never resist Leah, even if she was Cameron's girl. He knew she was strong and clever, too. Far too smart for Cameron and young enough to be his daughter.

"Leah," he called out.

She looked up as if she were waking from a dream.

"Hi, Archie."

"God, you look glum, girl. Everything okay?"

He was standing beside her now, and she couldn't look him in the eyes.

"Not great, Archie, if I'm honest."

"Where's Cam? Celia said he wasn't here."

Leah looked around her to make sure the boys were out of earshot. "Arrested. He's been a total dick."

Archie stepped closer so he could lower his voice. "What's he done?"

"I don't know. He kept one of the guns locked in the workshop. He said he forgot to return it. When he saw the police were searching for it, he tried to sneak it back into the gun cupboard. It looked really dodgy, Archie."

"Shit! What a tosser. Is he still there?"

"Yes. I've had enough of him. I can't keep doing this. He's put me through so much."

"It's just not fair, Leah. You don't deserve that." Archie rubbed her shoulder for a second. "It sounds like he just didn't think. He's not a killer, is he?"

"I don't know! Do you think that's what the police are thinking?"

"God knows." Archie shook his head. "I doubt even the plod knows what they're thinking." He looked down at the boxes he was carrying. "I'm going to put this stuff in the workshop. It's going to be okay, Leah. He probably just made a mistake."

"I hope so, Archie. But this is the final straw."

Archie glanced back at the school. "Is that blond kid still coming onto you?"

Leah looked horrified. "How did you know?"

"Come on, Leah. It's obvious. When I was putting up the cable trunking in the computer suite the other day, you were both in there, and he was watching you like a dog in heat."

Leah shook her head and turned away. "I don't ask for it, Archie. I'm sick of it."

Archie wondered if some of that was put on. "Of course you don't, Leah. Lads that age have no self-control. It's a well-known fact. They can't help it. They see a beautiful girl, and the hormones kick in. Don't know what to do with themselves."

A boy was calling for Leah, and she frowned. "Coming!"

"I'm sorry, Leah." Archie looked down at his feet. "If ever you want a chat, you know where I am."

"Thank you. You're so kind."

Archie watched Leah for a moment as she walked away. "You're such a tosser, Cam," he said to himself. "You're going to lose her to a kid."

Archie opened up the workshop and flicked on the lights. It was full of the comforting smell of creosote, grass, and oil. He put the boxes of rat poison on one of the workbenches and looked around at Cameron's domain. He even had a mini fridge with an opened milk container and sausage rolls. Archie checked the date on the packaging and pocketed them. Then he unscrewed the milk container, gobbed in it, and replaced the lid. He switched off the lights, locked the workshop again, and smirked. There would soon be a vacancy for a caretaker at Cotisham School.

Chapter Sixteen

DC Sarah Burgess turned from the front door and looked around her. She was waiting for someone to answer. She remembered patrolling the Swanfield Estate as a brand-new PC. She had been a naïve twenty-two-year-old, venturing out for the first time with her tutor. One of the most valuable lessons she learned from him was always to know the name of the street before you walk down it. That advice saved her life once. She stroked the scar on her left cheek, and the front door opened.

"Mary Brady?"

"You're Sarah?"

Burgess showed her warrant card. "Thanks for agreeing to see me, Mary."

Mary led Burgess through a narrow hallway into a small lounge diner. She offered her a seat on a tired-looking sofa and switched off the TV.

"It's all a bit cryptic. You're a detective, you say?"

"Yes, a detective constable with Major Crimes in Chichester."

"Major crimes? Gosh, that sounds serious. What is it? Have I been caught littering?"

Burgess gave her a polite smile as she opened up her folder and pulled out a notepad.

"I wish it was as simple as that, Mary. You told me on the phone that you were once married to Charles Brady."

"Yes. We were divorced about ten years ago. I have nothing to do with him anymore."

"I regret to say, Mary, that Charles was found dead yesterday at Cotisham School."

Mary's cheeks blanched, and she covered her mouth. "He's dead? Have you told his mother?"

"We have."

"I can't believe it. What happened? It must have been sudden. Was he unwell?"

"I'm sorry to say that Charles was murdered."

"No! That's... Who would want to do that to Charles? He could be a bit irritating sometimes, but never... I just need a moment. I'm sorry."

Mary Brady left the room for five minutes, which gave Burgess time to nose around her front room. There were no photographs of Charles anywhere and no children. She went over to the mantelpiece to look at a birthday card.

To Mary,
Happy birthday
Love and fond memories,
Charles.

There wasn't any bad feeling, thought Burgess. She returned to the sofa just as Mary came back, teary-eyed and holding a tissue to her nose.

"Sorry about that."

"Please, it's understandable," said Burgess.

Mary took a deep breath and looked at her, ready to answer more questions.

"When did you last see Charles?"

"Gosh, it must have been two years ago. A funeral for an old neighbour. Charles and I got along okay. There was no animosity between us." She pointed to the birthday card. "I got that from him two weeks ago. We used to send Christmas cards, too."

"I see. What sort of person was he? After talking to his colleagues, they said he was reserved but friendly, and they all liked him."

"I'm glad to hear that. When I was with him, he was all of that and secretive, too. He didn't always tell me things. He tried to keep his past from me. It had me wondering if he was one of those bigamists. He wasn't, of course. He had a difficult child-hood, which made it hard for all of us."

"How was his childhood difficult?"

Mary squinted as she tried to make out Burgess's features.

"Forgive me for saying, dear, but your hair is beautiful. Does it take a long time to dry?"

The sudden change in conversation threw Burgess off track.

"I use a hairdryer. Not too long."

"I suppose I ought to tell Richard. Not unless you have?"

"Who's Richard?"

"Our son."

Burgess was taken aback. "You had a son together?"

"Yes! Richard."

Burgess made a note. "The school said there was just you."

"Charles had disowned him. Richard and Charles never saw eye-to-eye about anything."

"Is he Richard Brady?"

"Yes."

"What's his date of birth and address?"

"So you're going to tell him. It's the 2nd of January 2000. He was almost a millennium baby. Last I heard, he was in Little-hampton. One minute." She went over to a small bureau and found an address book with a tatty brown cover. She flicked over a few pages and found what she was looking for. "He's in Rich-mond House on South Terrace. Number eleven."

"Have you got a phone number for him?"

"Not anymore. He kept changing his number. He got himself into trouble over money. He had to keep moving about."

Burgess made some notes. "You said they didn't get along?"

"No. But you're going to have to talk to Richard about that. I'm not putting words in his mouth."

"Earlier, you said Charles's childhood was difficult. How was that, Mary?"

Mary played with the tissue in her hands. "His older sister died young. I think it really affected him. She was all he had in the world."

"We didn't know Charles had a sister."

"Yes. They were boarders at that school together."

"Where? Cotisham?"

"Yes, dear. It was the strangest thing when I heard he'd got a job there. Why would anyone do that? Especially after every-thing that happened."

"Was Charles's sister's name Maisy, by any chance?"

"It was! Do you know about her?"

Burgess made more urgent notes in her notepad.

"Tea?" said Mary as she stood up. "I know I'd like one."

Mary returned after ten minutes with a tray of tea and a few biscuits on a plate. On the tray, she had placed a couple of photographs she had dug out from under her stairs. She placed the tray on a low mahogany coffee table beside Burgess.

"Thank you, Mary. What are the photos?"

"I don't know why I still have these. Charles never picked

them up or just forgot I had them. I kept meaning to chuck them or give them back to him."

Mary handed Burgess two photographs, both of a young Charles. He must have been about ten or eleven, and there was an older girl, likely his older sister, Maisy. She was pretty, with bright blue eyes and blonde hair. She was about thirteen or fourteen in the photograph.

"This is Maisy?"

"Yes. It was a school photo they sat for together. Charles said that Maisy used to watch out for him. More like a mother than a sister. The photo was taken a year before she died."

"How did Maisy die?"

"Is it important? Aren't we talking about Charles?"

"Anything could be important."

Mary hesitated for a moment, debating with herself if she should say anything. "Well, you are police. When I say she died, the truth is, nobody knows what happened to her. She disappeared one day. The police searched for her, but Charles said they didn't take it seriously enough."

"Really? Did Charles talk a lot about Maisy?"

"Often too much. It became a bit of an obsession. I'd go as far as to say that we drifted apart because of it."

Burgess sipped her tea and took a chocolate digestive. "Was he still looking for her?"

"That's it precisely, dear. He was *always* looking for her."

Burgess spent a moment writing Mary's comments down and underlining words.

"Did Charles ever talk to you about anyone he'd fallen out with?"

"No. That was the sort of thing he kept to himself. As I said, he was very secretive. I can't believe he's gone! Do you need anyone to identify him?"

"Bless you, Mary, but no. It wouldn't be appropriate under the circumstances."

Mary frowned and raised her head. "But why? I knew him better than anyone."

"Sadly, Charles's body was unrecognisable when he was found. He'd been missing for over a week."

Mary covered her mouth. "Poor Charles!"

"Do you know if he was in a relationship with anyone?"

"You're asking me? He wouldn't talk to me about anything like that. I imagine he could have been. He liked the comforts of the flesh, as my mother used to call it. He needed physical contact. Probably something to do with having such a traumatic past."

"Mary, you've been so helpful. Thank you. Would it be okay if I took these photos?"

Mary nodded. "Was he alone when he died? I guess he couldn't have been if he was murdered."

Burgess put down her cup and slid the photos into her folder. "Thank you." She leaned forward and squeezed Mary's hand, waiting for her to dry her eyes again. "Call me on this number if you remember anything else." She placed a business card on the coffee table.

As she left, Burgess wondered if Charles had turned up something about Maisy. She sat in the car and thought about the blonde woman in the New Moon pub. The landlady couldn't put an age on her. Could that have been Maisy? Had Charles been looking for the living among the dead? Burgess called DS Summers.

"How did the interview with Cameron go, Sarge?"

"He told us he'd lost the shotgun for a week. He'd locked it in his workshop, and it went missing. Do you think that's feasible?"

"I think it's feasible, Sarge. Someone could have taken it."

"How did you get on with Mary Brady?"

"Maisy was Charles Brady's sister."

"Really!"

"They were at Cotisham School together in the 1980s. Maisy had gone missing and was presumed dead. By the looks of things, Charles didn't let it rest and was still looking for her. Maybe he found her."

"Why do you say that?"

"The blonde woman he was with in the New Moon pub—I'm wondering if she could have been Maisy. I may go back there. I have a school photo of Maisy and Charles together, taken a year before Maisy disappeared."

"Good one, Sarah. Let me know how you get on."

Good one? Was that praise from DS Summers? From the look on Dinescu's face after the meeting that morning, they all knew that he would have a word with her. Questioning his judgement like that. Perhaps he'd taken her down a peg or two.

Burgess had a hunch. After following the Midhurst bus for five miles with a windscreen covered in muddy spray, she arrived back outside the New Moon pub twenty minutes later.

The pub looked busier today. She smelled wood smoke as she entered, and something was cooking in the kitchen. Again, she turned heads as she walked to the bar, but this time with more confidence.

"Hello again, my darling," said Janet behind the bar. "Back again. How are things?"

"All..." Burgess was about to say *good*, but investigating a murder was never good. "Moving forward, thank you. Can I show you a photo?"

"A photo? Okay."

Burgess passed the school photograph to Janet, who looked a little bemused.

"I know this girl is young," said Burgess, "and it was taken back in the 1980s. But can you see any resemblance to the woman Charles Brady was with when he came in?"

Janet scrutinised the photo. "I'll just show John. Won't be a mo."

She was gone for a few minutes and then returned. "Well, the girl is blonde and pretty. Is that young Charlie there?"

"Yes. And he's with his sister."

"Sister? I suppose she could have been his sister. Difficult to say. Sorry, my darling."

Burgess's disappointment had shown. "No, it's okay. It was just an idea. People change."

"They do. They didn't act like brother and sister. More like professional and client."

"Client? Do you think she could have been a private detective?"

Janet looked blank for a moment. "I suppose she could have. That would fit."

"Thank you, Janet. You're a star."

Burgess left the pub and considered her conversation with Janet. The blonde woman could have been the private detective, Candice Lee. Yet she couldn't discount the idea that Brady had found Maisy; if he had, wouldn't he have let the police know?

Chapter Seventeen

Emily Summers dropped into the chair in front of Dinescu's desk and massaged her forehead. Her head was thick, and her muscles ached. Not only was she shattered, but she was also late off duty, too. Dinescu looked as calm and collected as ever. She didn't know how he did it. He was always steady and unflappable. Summers wondered if he had a portrait of himself hidden away somewhere in an attic—a portrait of him as an angry, drunken misogynist. Perhaps looking something like Anthony.

"Sarah has an update from her visit to Brady's ex-wife," she said. "I'll let her tell you when she comes in. I've checked Hyde's alibi with the hospital, and it was confirmed."

Dinescu shrugged his shoulders and sat forward, arching his fingers together. His cuffs had slid up, and Summers tried not to stare at the scarring on his forearms.

"Well, that's good," he said. "We know he didn't kill Brady. That's one person we can eliminate from our inquiries. It just raises the question—what happened to the shotgun? Hyde should be released now."

"I'll get onto it."

"Ethan Bishop needs to be questioned. I'd like to know

where he was on the Monday Brady was killed. We know he had a motive to harm him."

"Ross can get onto that, sir."

"Any more news on Brady's finances?"

"Chester's heard from the bank, and... I apologised to him for this morning."

Dinescu thought for a moment and nodded. "He told me."

"Chester's gone through Brady's statements. He had a credit card but seldom used it. His finances were pretty sound. He had about twenty grand in savings. His biggest expenditures were rent, food, and a weekly cash withdrawal for three months, stopping last month. Anywhere between three and four hundred pounds a time. That's a lot of money every month."

"There was no cash found on him," said Dinescu. "We didn't see any signs of gambling or drug abuse in his flat."

"No, sir. We have no idea what he was spending it on. Perhaps it was this so-called private detective?"

"Possibly."

There was a rap on the door, and Sarah Burgess poked her head into the office. "May I interrupt?"

"Sure," said Dinescu. "How did you get on with Mary Brady?"

"That's why I'm here, sir." Burgess took a seat next to Summers. "The long and short of it is that Mary was indeed his ex-wife, and they've been divorced for about ten years. There was no major bad feeling between them, according to Mary. She was quite cut up when I told her about her ex. I think it was genuine. Anyway, sir, that photograph we found of the school—the one with the girl and boy circled—that's Charles and his sister, Maisy. Mary confirmed they went to Cotisham School back in the 1980s. She gave me an old school photograph she had."

"Maisy?"

"Yes, sir." Burgess looked across at Summers. "They were boarders there at the same time. She went missing from the school when she was fourteen but was never found. Mary said Charles was trying to find out what had happened to her. He was obsessed with it. She said it drove them apart."

Dinescu produced the note he'd found at Brady's flat. He tapped a line of text: *14-05-87 Maisy reported missing...*

Dinescu passed the copy over to Summers. "There could be a connection between what Brady was investigating and his death."

Burgess shrugged. "I had wondered if he'd found her, given the description of the blonde woman he was seen with in the New Moon pub. But I've found no evidence to support that."

"It was worth a try, Sarah," said Summers.

Burgess looked at her notes. "Also, Brady had a son. He didn't tell the school because they didn't get along, and he'd disowned him. His name is Richard Brady, date of birth: 2/01/2000, which makes him twenty-three. PNC says he's got previous for possession and robbery. His mother said her son was in some kind of trouble over money."

"He's someone we should look at," said Summers. "Are we overcomplicating it with the whole sister angle?"

"We could be," said Dinescu, "and we don't know enough about any of these Bradys yet. I'll do a bit of digging into Maisy Brady's disappearance. Perhaps we can discover why Charles Brady was still so interested in the school." He tapped another line from the note: *Is she there beneath us?* "It looks to me that he believed his sister could've been buried there."

"I agree, sir. It looks like that. But did he have any evidence to support it? Otherwise, it's nothing more than the beginning of conspiracy theory."

Dinescu nodded. "I feel we need to keep poking around until something moves."

"I was going to check his activity on Facebook," said Summers.

"But we don't have his laptop back yet," said Burgess.

"I know, but I have an idea."

Summers left the office, logged into her computer, and opened Facebook on a web browser. Dinescu and Burgess followed right behind and stood by her desk. Summers searched for the Cotisham School Facebook page and began scrolling down, reading the comments. They were left by complaining parents, moaning about the lack of communication with the teachers.

"We don't know Brady's Facebook account name, boss. It could be something obscure, being that he was a teacher. I was wondering if Brady had ever left a message or liked a comment on the school's page. Because if he did..." Then Summers found what she was looking for—someone called *BraadEC* had liked a post. Then she clicked on the profile photo of a younger Charles Brady holding a guitar. "I can get his Facebook profile." Dinescu leaned over her shoulder, and she could smell a hint of Hugo Boss aftershave.

Brady's list of friends was public. That gave them forty-eight friends for the team to check. Summers copied a link to the page and pasted it into an email. Then she allotted Brady's friends from the list to members of the team to investigate. She clicked the send icon.

"That should help us find some of his friends and acquaintances, anyway."

Dinescu smiled. "That will do for a start. Good one, Emily." He leaned over so she would look into his face. "Now go home. You look exhausted."

"I will, sir. I just need to get Cameron Hyde released."

Summers headed over to Custody. She explained to the custody sergeant that Cameron Hyde's alibi was solid. He couldn't have killed Brady, according to the timings from the entomologist. After a brief conversation with the duty solicitor, she had Cameron Hyde released.

She walked out of the custody building, and the cool evening air hit her. She was flagging now. As she walked back to the office to get her coat, she still couldn't shake the pressure she'd had all day in her head, neck, and shoulders. It was the stress caused by Anthony's mood and her run-in with Dinescu earlier. She couldn't go on like that anymore. Anthony needed an ultimatum—the drink had to go. Summers paused for a moment and checked her personal mobile. Anthony had sent another apology. Maybe it was too late for yet another ultimatum. She'd lost count of how many of those there had been. She deserved better. She felt something tickling her cheeks and then a salty taste in her mouth. She sniffed. What are you doing? For God's sake, Em! Before swiping her warrant card to reenter the station, she stopped, leaning against the wall. It was like she had felt the burden he'd put on her for the first time. It was time for things to change.

Chapter Eighteen

Beniamin arrived home to the spicy aroma of homemade curry. Sophia was in the kitchen with Lisa, singing along to something loud and thrashy. Lisa had come home early from work and cooked dinner, even though it was Beniamin's turn. They would have been hungry, waiting for him to cook something. Lisa preferred recipes, and Chef Beniamin Dinescu's concoctions were made up as he went. He always said they were as unique as fingerprints. Never repeated.

He leaned in and kissed both his girls, and he was grateful when Sophia handed him a cold beer from the fridge.

Sophia picked up a spatula and stirred the curry sauce. "How was your day, Dad?"

"A challenge. We could do with your brains on the team. We have a puzzle to solve."

"I like puzzles. What is it?"

"Sorry, I can't tell you."

Sophia rolled her eyes, and Lisa fluffed up the basmati rice and tipped it into a bowl.

"What time is your brother coming?" asked Beniamin.

"He's already here," said a voice behind him.

It was Kieran. He was leaning against the door frame with a glass of white wine. Beniamin and Kieran hugged, ending with a lot of shoulder-slapping.

"Did I surprise you, Ben?" asked Kieran.

A yellow labrador sat at his feet and looked up, dewy-eyed, at him.

"Ah, Bella!" said Beniamin. "I assume you caught the bus then if Bella's here?"

"No, I drove." Kieran laughed. "You should have seen the carnage!"

Beniamin shook his head and laughed. "I meant you didn't get a lift."

"No, Dad couldn't bring me today. Mum's got a retirement meal to go to."

Lisa took a long sip of wine. "Kieran was reminding me about that school you're investigating."

Kieran took that as a cue. "Yes. The Cotisham Babies. I remember listening to a podcast a while ago. I hope I've remembered it right."

"You two get out of my kitchen and sit at the table," said Lisa. "Sophia and I are dishing up. Your turn tomorrow, Ben Dinescu!"

Beniamin saluted her and led Kieran to a chair in the dining room. Bella, the labrador, lay down beside him.

"What's this about babies?"

Kieran sat forward, and the enthusiasm carried in his voice. "In the mid-1980s, builders found six skeletons of young babies in a priest hole at the school."

"The 7th of May 1986."

"Oh. You know about it?" Kieran looked a little deflated.

"Not much. It's on my list of things to do. Please carry on."

They were interrupted by Lisa and Sophia with her walking

frame. After a few journeys, Lisa put out all the food and served Kieran's dinner.

"Where was I?" asked Kieran.

"The priest hole."

"Yes!" His face lit up again. "Did you know about Ruby Paddock, the baby farmer?" said Kieran.

"A baby farmer?" Sophia laughed. "That's either a very young farmer or a person who grows babies."

"You can tell she's her father's daughter," said Lisa.

"But seriously?" said Beniamin, scooping up the pasanda sauce with a poppadum. "*Baby* farmer?"

Kieran turned his head towards Ben, finishing a mouthful of curry. "In Victorian Britain, baby farmers used to take on babies for payment, usually unwanted and born outside of marriage. The term has a bad reputation because of the stories of mistreatment and murder of children. This may be a bit close to home for you, Ben." Kieran reached out a hand and found Beniamin's shoulder.

"It's okay. Carry on."

"Well, the school you're investigating is connected to Ruby Paddock. She was a nurse there when it was still the Aversham family's country manor. Paddock had a sideline as a baby farmer from about 1900."

"I read a note about a Ruby Paddock in a history book recently."

"She's quite infamous. She was hanged for drowning three babies in a local pond. Young female servants from the rich houses would be sent to her if their masters abused them. But to avoid the costs and hassle of raising the children, she killed the babies instead. There were thought to be more, but they only found three—until that day in May 1986."

"That's so, so horrible," said Sophia.

A deep frown creased Lisa's face. "It doesn't bear thinking about. Makes me shudder."

"So, what about the babies in the priest hole?" asked Beniamin.

"Do you know what a priest hole is?"

"My team has educated me."

"The bones were found when they were checking out a chimney. Radiocarbon dating determined them to be from around the time Paddock was at the school. It's a fascinating but horrible story."

"A chimney?"

"Yes. It's clever. One room had a false chimney. It led to a forgotten priest hole where the remains were found."

Beniamin looked at Sophia. "This Ruby Paddock sounds like *Muma Pădurii*. Don't you think? I told you she was real."

"Stop it, Ben!" Lisa slapped the top of Ben's hand. "You'll give her nightmares."

"Thank you, Kieran. That was very helpful."

Lisa smiled at Beniamin. "He's a clever little brother, don't you think?"

"Don't tell him that. He won't get his head out of the door, and he'll have to live here with us."

"Yay!" shrieked Sophia.

"Well," said Kieran, "a priest hole is a great place to hide a murder victim, don't you think?"

Beniamin froze for a moment. Kieran had hit on something. A priest hole. Maybe it was too far-fetched, but it was a hypothesis worth exploring. There may have been a link. "Which chimney was it where they found the priest hole?"

Kieran shrugged. "I don't remember. I'm not even sure they mentioned it in the podcast."

Dinescu squeezed Kieran's shoulder. "Thank you. Now I have a cold case I need to examine."

Chapter Nineteen

By the time Emily Summers arrived home, Anthony had fallen asleep on the sofa with the TV on. He was hugging a glass in one hand against his chest, and an empty bottle of red wine was next to him.

It looked like a bomb had gone off in the front room. Emily thought Anthony must have had another tantrum, probably something to do with her.

On a side table was a photograph in a silver frame. Emily stared at it for a few moments. She remembered when it was taken—their first holiday together, touring the Loire Valley in the summer of 2019. The best holiday she'd ever had. What happened? Covid, lockdowns, and work pressures for both of them exposed the cracks. Those pressures tortured Anthony, and the only relief he found was the drink. It started with a small glass of red in the evening, just to take the edge off. Then it became two glasses and then a bottle. Then came the slamming of doors, the punching of walls, the grabbing, the pinching, and, two nights ago, the hand around her throat.

He was good-looking back then. He had warm eyes and was

funny and caring. Now he was cold and empty, with nothing left to give. He hated himself more than anyone else.

Emily switched off the TV and collapsed into the armchair opposite him, still in her jacket. She studied his drunken face—the man she once loved. The man she had even thought she would marry one day—the person with whom she could start a family. And her mother's words returned to haunt her once again. She knew she could do better than Anthony. He had never filled that love-shaped hole left by her father.

She put her elbows on her knees and dropped her head into her hands. She could have woken him, but she didn't know what mood he'd be in. Angry, no doubt. He was always angry about something, and she felt it was always directed at her.

She wondered what she had done to deserve it, but she stopped herself. She wouldn't wallow in self-pity. That wasn't her. Anthony needed help, but Emily had to admit to herself that she wasn't the one who could give it.

She pulled her mobile phone from her jacket pocket and brought up her mother's phone number. She stared at it until the screen went dark again. If she did this, then it would be final. There would be no turning back. She was always good at making a decision and sticking with it. She got up and stood in the hall.

"Hi, Mum, it's me."

"Hello, love. Is everything okay? You sound a bit... different."

Emily swallowed hard. She couldn't break down on the phone. "I was wondering if I could stay with you for a while?"

"Emily? Is everything okay?"

"No. Mum. Can I move back into my old room? Until I find somewhere else."

Her mother processed what Emily had asked. "Of course, my love. I'll change the bedding now. When will I see you?"

"In about an hour, I think."

After Emily finished the call, she felt different inside. Her mind had been made up. With Anthony still asleep and drooling on the seat cushion, she went upstairs and began packing her things into a suitcase. Everything precious to her was packed first, followed by her clothes and shoes from the back of the wardrobe. She found a couple of large bags and another suitcase, then went to the second bedroom. She packed her certificates and passport and unhooked her old college photos and framed degree. She placed the bags and a packed suitcase by the front door and moved into the kitchen, trying not to make a sound. Her tea towels from a friend, her hot chocolate, and her lemon and ginger tea bags were there. She remembered the cheese the friend had brought back for her on holiday was still in the fridge. She had filled another suitcase and two large bags by the time she was done. Then she loaded everything into her car with only the sound of rustling bags to give her away.

When she returned, she had everything important to her in her car. She looked around the house, and everything else was his. His house. His decor. His TV and sound system. His books. He had just slotted her into his world, where and when he wanted her. The realisation that there was nothing shared between them made her shudder.

With her keys in her hand, she paused, wondering if she had forgotten anything. Then, when she had reassured herself, Emily shook Anthony's shoulders and stood over him.

"Anthony, wake up."

Anthony frowned, licked his lips, and then wiped his cheek.

His eyes were tight and squinting as he sat up to look at her.

"Emily," he said in a thick voice, "what is it? I was asleep." He licked his lips and held his head as if it were about to fall off.

"Anthony, I'm going. I've had enough of this." She waved at

the bottle of wine, the glass, and at him. "All of this. I've had enough of you. I don't love you anymore. I'm going."

Anthony jolted forward and rubbed his eyes.

"Why? What are you talking about? What's wrong with you, woman?"

Emily shook her head. There was no point in replying. She placed her house keys beside him on the sofa and walked out the front door. She could hear him calling after her as she left, crashing around as he tried to follow her. But she didn't turn around. And every step away from him she took, the better she felt.

She got into the car, locked the doors, and started the engine. Anthony stumbled out of the front door, falling into the side of her car.

"Emily! Don't you dare go anywhere." He tried to open the door, slapping his palms against her window. "Emily! Where the fuck are you going?"

Emily flipped him the bird. "Screw you, Anthony!" She selected first gear and drove, watching him in her rearview mirror as he fell off the kerb, landing headfirst in the gutter.

Chapter Twenty

The rain was heavy enough for the roads to flood on Wednesday morning. Everyone struggled to get to work on time except DS Summers. Dinescu saw she was already at her desk when he arrived twenty minutes early, but she didn't see him. She was focused on something on her screen. A holiday request, as far as Dinescu could make out. She didn't see him pass her or respond when he said good morning.

Dinescu put down his bag and hung up his dripping coat over the radiator in his office. After logging in to his computer and reading an email from Forensics, he looked out at Summers again through the blinds. She was still sitting there, staring at the screen.

Dinescu made them both coffee, placing Summers's drink on his desk.

"Emily?" It took a few moments for her to hear him.

"Sir?"

He called her into his office with a motion of his head and saw the pained expression on her face as she heaved herself out of her chair. "Come and sit down, Emily. I've made you a coffee. And shut the door, please."

Summers was grateful for the coffee and cupped her hands around the mug. Dinescu studied her, making Summers blush and look down at her cup.

"I walked past your car as I came in this morning," he said. "It's full of your stuff. You're either sleeping in your car now, or you've had to move out of your home."

"Yes, sir."

"I assume it's the latter?"

Summers nodded.

"Tell me to keep my nose out, but have you split up with your partner?"

"Anthony. Yes, boss. They don't call you a detective for nothing." She laughed. It was tired, delirious laughter.

"I ought to try it as a day job." He smiled and pulled down on the cuffs of his shirt. "Where are you living now?"

"My mother's." Summers sighed, and her lip quivered a little.

"Do you want to talk about it? It could help."

Summers averted her eyes. "I'd had enough of his drinking, his temper, and the constant blame for his wasted life. He manipulated everything to make it my fault. Now, his abuse is getting physical. That's where it all ends. I don't love him anymore."

"Then you have made the best decision for you. Have you slept?"

"I got a few hours. But I'm okay. Honestly, boss. I know I've done the right thing and made up my mind."

"Good. Do you need to take some time off? You can take it as compassionate leave."

"God, no! My mother will fill me with tea, cake, and sympathy all day. She's lovely—don't get me wrong, but I need to work."

Dinescu looked over Summers's shoulder and saw the office

filling with wet detectives. He refocused on Summers. "You need to be fit for work if you are here. I'm still wondering if this job in Chichester is right for you."

"But I need to be here, sir!" Her eyes widen. "I've taken onboard your comments from yesterday, and I want to make amends if it's not too late."

"Whether it's too late or not is up to you."

Summers looked up to the top corner of his office, biting on her bottom lip, her eyes wet.

Dinescu smiled. "Once everyone's in, we'll have a briefing."

"Yes, boss. Just what I was going to suggest." Summers forced a smile and stood. "Thanks for the coffee and chat. Just what I needed."

"And Lisa and I will have you over for dinner."

"For dinner?" Summers had a look of disbelief on her face. "You don't need to—"

"It would be good for us to get to know each other if you're staying. It's not compulsory, but it could help, don't you think?"

Summers couldn't speak but nodded with a smile.

As soon as she left his office, Dinescu watched her switch back into detective sergeant mode, lifting her chin and smiling at the incoming questions and comments. He wondered why any man would treat her like her partner did. Maybe her response to Anthony's misogyny was why she was zealous at work, and it was the male staff she had issues with. Whatever it was, Dinescu believed Emily was intelligent and headstrong, but she was also vulnerable and caring. She reminded him very much of Lisa.

Within a few minutes, Summers had gathered the core and wider teams together, where they waited for Dinescu to make his appearance. And again, everyone went silent when he stepped out of his office. He was going to lead the briefing.

"Good morning. This is the Operation Birchwood briefing.

Thank you all for your hard work and the extra hours you've put in. Considering the few leads and progress, it feels like we have come to a hiatus in the investigation. But this is quite normal. Cameron Hyde was interviewed yesterday, and the missing shotgun was recovered. We have been able to eliminate him from our inquiries. However, it does raise a question about what happened to the gun after he *borrowed* it to kill rabbits on the school field." Dinescu turned to the whiteboard and wrote his next statement in red. "The gun went missing for eight days. Hyde told us he could not account for the gun's location from Sunday the 16th until it mysteriously appeared again yesterday."

"Sounds like complete bollocks, sir," said Booker.

"I know, but we have no evidence to discount his explanation."

"But he was the last person to have his hands on the murder weapon."

"That shotgun wasn't the murder weapon, Gareth. I received an email from Forensics this morning saying there are no traces of blood on the shotgun. They said with Brady only a few feet away from the weapon, they would have expected to find some of his bodily fluids on the gun, even if it were just a few droplets. If the gun had been wiped down, they would still have found material in some crevices. But there were also fingerprints from several people found all over the gun, which was expected, considering students and staff used it. This proves the gun hadn't been wiped down. It's not the murder weapon."

Booker shrugged, defeated. "Okay, boss."

"There was something of interest. They found blue and grey fibres—wool and polypropylene—on the butt of the shotgun. Most likely carpet fibres. Your guess is as good as mine. Keep a lookout for it when you are out and about."

"And Hyde's alibi is solid, sir?"

"Sadly, Gareth, as much as it would make our job easier, Cameron Hyde was at the hospital recovering from general anaesthesia when Brady was murdered. He was also seen on hospital CCTV when he left."

Chester Kirby pointed to the whiteboard. "So, are we saying someone took the shotgun from the workshop and then put it back? Why?"

Dinescu scratched his head and looked at Kirby. "Maybe to implicate Cameron. What do you think?"

"If it wasn't the murder weapon, then maybe."

"Who has access to the workshop," said Burgess, "apart from Cameron Hyde?"

"That is what we need to know," said Dinescu. "And since you asked, that is your job to find out or to delegate."

"Yes, sir." Burgess looked amused.

"There are more forensic results we need to discuss now." Bottoms shuffled on seats, and pens were held at the ready. "We were working on the theory that the killer was standing on the steps when they shot Charles Brady. You'll remember me talking about the splatter shadow. SOCO recovered some blue fibres caught on the brickwork. It's possible the attacker leaned against the wall, giving them an approximate height of five foot eight to five foot ten inches. The fibres are the same material and colour as the school uniform fleeces."

"A student?" said Burgess. "Couldn't the fibres have been left there previously?"

"It is possible—something to bear in mind."

"How tall is Ethan Bishop?" asked Kirby.

"I'd say he fits that range," said Ross Taylor.

"And he's got motive," said Kirby. "Especially if he did have a confrontation with Brady. Posting those photos of him around the school was asking for trouble."

"It's still very tenuous," said Summers. "But we could get him in for a voluntary interview."

"I was going to suggest that, Sarge," said Taylor. "From the questions I've asked staff, Bishop is becoming harder to deal with. He's recently become very moody and disruptive. I'll organise an interview."

"Okay, let's make that a priority." Dinescu rubbed Cameron Hyde's name off the whiteboard, leaving Ethan Bishop at the top of the list. "DNA transfer onto Brady is inconclusive. At least six other DNA profiles were found on him, possibly transferred from the backs of chairs and contact with other staff."

"Those fleeces, boss," said Kirby. "I've seen members of staff wearing them, too. I think they pinch them because it gets so cold in the school."

"That's helpful, Chester. Now then, Sarah, update us all on your phone calls."

"Yes, boss. I called Candice Lee, the name on the business card we found in Brady's flat. After several calls, she got back to me. She told me Brady was one of her clients. She wouldn't say in detail what he had hired her for, just that he wanted her to look into the school's history. She suggested that he was writing a book."

"History?" said Summers. "You wouldn't hire a private detective to find out history."

"She kept it pretty vague," said Burgess. "And she became defensive when I pressed her. I tried to set up a meeting with her, but she put the phone down. After some digging, I found out Candice Lee now works for an insurance company in Bognor Regis. The private detective business didn't work out for her."

"Is she a suspect?" asked Dinescu, looking around at everyone. "What do you think?"

"Worth following up," said Kirby.

"I'd like us to visit her," said Summers. "And maybe more will come up from the search of his computer."

"Thank you, Sarah," said Dinescu. I think you should pay her a visit. You were going to oversee the checks into staff movements around the time of the murder."

Burgess nodded. "Yes, boss. Officers spoke to every member of the teaching staff, including the learning support assistants. All teaching staff and students were in their allocated lessons. The only time they went outside was during the afternoon break. One of the science teachers had taken his students in the school minibus to a local copse for a lesson, but that was it."

"Did anyone report hearing anything during that last break period?"

"Grounds staff were using petrol hedge trimmers, and a sit-on lawnmower was out on the school fields."

"A lot of noise, then."

"Yes, boss. Ideal for covering the sound of a gunshot. During that break, one LSA thought she saw a pupil walking towards the woods at about 15:10 hours. She wasn't certain who it was. It could have even been staff in a school fleece—all very vague. A lot was going on at the time, and she may have been confused. She only saw them walking away."

"As vague as that sounds, it could have been Brady," said Summers. "Has the LSA given her statement?"

"Yes, Sarge. No one remembered anything different about the lessons, just the usual visits to the toilet. Ethan Bishop had been a pain in a geography lesson. He'd arrived twenty minutes late."

"Twenty minutes?" said Dinescu. "So, that's from 15:15 to 15:35. Something to put to him, Ross. Is that all, Sarah?"

"That's it, sir."

"Ross, what did you get from Brady's neighbours?"

Ross Taylor still used a police pocket notebook for his notes.

He drew it out with a flourish. "The young woman opposite said she had nothing to do with him and rarely heard him. The couple living next door said he was polite enough. He knocked on their door during the Covid lockdowns to see if they wanted anything from the shops. Apart from that, they rarely heard him."

"So, nothing then," said Dinescu. "Last but not least, Chester. You have an update for us."

"Yes, boss. Brady had a basic mobile phone that he seldom used. The numbers he texted were mainly the headmaster and the school office. There were a couple of calls to Leah Turnbull at the beginning of the year, but we can guess what those were about. Then there were calls to the number given for Candice Lee."

"Any calls around the time of his murder?"

"Sorry, boss. None made, none received."

"Nothing of any help there, either." Dinescu put his hands on his hips and sighed.

"So you have all been allocated a list of friends DS Summers found on Facebook. I'd like those checked ASAP, please, especially if any of them live locally. We need those digital forensic results back for his laptop, but I guess we have to be patient."

"Hopefully by Friday, boss," said Summers.

"Okay. If I can just have the core team for the rest of the briefing."

The officers around the periphery headed off to look at their tasks while the others moved up to sit closer to the whiteboard.

"Thank you." Dinescu waited until he had their attention. "Time and again, we see Charles Brady was obsessed with searching for his sister, Maisy Brady. She went missing in May 1987 and was presumed dead. I am becoming more convinced there is a link to Charles Brady's death. From what we've seen so far, I think Brady believed his sister's body was buried somewhere in the school. Last night, someone gave me an idea, and now I want us to look at the Maisy Brady case and how it could be connected with Charles Brady's murder. I have contacted the cold case unit in Haywards Heath and spoken about my concerns. They are sending one of their investigators to us, Detective Inspector Jonathan Clegg, to outline the case. I have an idea where she could be, but I want to hear from DI Clegg first. Keep this line of enquiry restricted to the core team. I don't want it to leak out to the community. In the meantime, we'll interview Ethan Bishop and find out who has access to the workshop."

Summers had one more thing. "And we must follow up on Brady's son, Richard, known as Ricky. Chester, can you do that, too? He's over in Littlehampton. We need to establish what their relationship was like and if he needs an alibi."

"Yes, Sarge," said Kirby.

Dinescu looked around the team. "Okay. That's it for now."

As the core team returned to their tasks, Dinescu grabbed his coat and cap. Summers stopped him as he passed her desk.

"Just so you know, Sarah and Ross will interview Ethan Bishop after school finishes, and I'll get back to you on that later."

"Okay. I must go out for a while, and my phone will be off. I don't want any interruptions." Dinescu raised a hand as he left.

Chapter Twenty-One

Dinescu walked into the city despite the rain. He had a good raincoat and a waterproof cap and didn't mind getting wet. He'd spent many years of his early life only ever watching the rain from inside a building, wondering what it felt like. He imagined then it would hurt, but as he got older, he figured out that people all over the world must have been rained on and lived. It seemed funny when he thought of it now, but his experience of the world as a child was limited to four walls.

He had to wait at the train barriers for a few minutes while two trains went by, and then he headed north onto South Street. He reached the Market Cross in the centre of the city, which was clogged up with street traders and buskers. Then he turned onto West Street, towards the cathedral, and Dinescu saw that the tip of the cathedral spire had disappeared under a blanket of low cloud. Opposite the Bell Tower was a pub that was once a church. It had changed its name so many times that Dinescu couldn't remember what it was called. Just past the old church, after a small memorial garden, were the offices of Doctor Siobhan Maguire, a private therapist Dinescu had been under several years ago.

Dinescu stooped as he went through the front door and entered a pleasant reception area to the sound of ethereal meditation music. He removed his dripping cap and became aware he had made the carpet wet.

Behind a desk was a young man typing on a computer keyboard. He wasn't there when Dinescu visited all those years ago—he looked as if he was young enough to still be at school.

"How can I help?" he said, looking up at Dinescu as he towered over him.

"Hello. I'm Beniamin Dinescu. I have an appointment with Siobhan Maguire."

"Ah, yes. I'll let her know."

"Sorry about the carpet."

"Don't worry," said the receptionist. "It's been wet all week."

A woman in her mid-forties with long auburn hair came out of a passage behind the desk. Doctor Maguire was from Belfast and was an expert in post-traumatic stress disorder. Dinescu thought that she had changed very little changed since the last time he saw her.

"Beniamin, it's so good to see you again!" Doctor Maguire was one of the few people who could pronounce his first name correctly.

She shook his hand with a broad smile and led him into her room. Dinescu removed his wet raincoat and hung it on the hook provided. He sat on a sofa opposite her and looked around at the soft, calming pastel colours.

"You've redecorated," he said.

Maguire laughed. "Yes. The magnolia has been forever banished. I have a business partner now, too, with his own office."

"That's very good."

"Can I get you a drink or perhaps a towel?"

Dinescu chuckled. "No, I'm fine. Thank you for seeing me at short notice."

"Thank the web booking system. It's very efficient. You know Lisa called me as well? I just wanted to get that out in the open."

"Yes. Thank you. She was worried."

Maguire shifted her position and tucked her hair behind her ears. "Are you worried?"

"No. Well... A little. I didn't think I'd have another episode."

"Are you okay with talking about it now?"

"I'm happy to talk if you are." Dinescu took a couple of deep breaths, and Doctor Maguire focused on him. "I've been having dreams, but I've been able to distance myself from them."

"The same dreams as before?"

"Yes."

"Tell me about the episode that you called Lisa about."

Dinescu licked his lips. "I heard a sound while I was sitting in my car. It was from outside. Someone was moving a metal wheelie bin. It was loud, and the wheels were squealing. It transported me back to the fire, the smoke, and the burned bodies."

"The walking wounded, or were they the people from your nightmares?"

"A mixture of both. Some of it was from my memory, and some from my dreams. I know they're not real. But I saw them."

"Are you under any stress at the moment?"

"No more than usual. I feel fine in myself."

"You're a chief inspector now. That must mean you carry a lot of extra responsibility."

"Yes. I'm enjoying my job. I have an excellent team around me."

"That's good to hear. You must be proud of yourself."

Dinescu smiled.

"Going back to the PTSD episode, were you walking in the tunnel during the flashback?"

"Yes, towards the station. I know the way back. I always know the way back."

"So, it's the same as it was before?"

Dinescu nodded.

"I'm so glad you want to talk about this, Beniamin. That avoidance is no longer there. That's a healthy response. Have you travelled the London Underground in recent years?"

"Not since we did that exposure therapy together. I've been avoiding it."

"Okay. Maybe it's time for you to try it again. Just slowly. I think exposure to the situation would be the way forward."

"Really? That scares me if I'm honest. But I don't want those meds again."

"Then you won't have them, and we won't do the EMDR therapy either."

"What's that?"

"Eye movement desensitisation and reprocessing."

"Ah, yes," said Dinescu. "I remember that." He laughed but shook his head. "That was *not* a nice thing to do."

"Effective."

"Yes, but... not again."

"I'd like you to consider exposure therapy. It's a gradual process, and nothing more than you can bear in one go. We will push the envelope a little at a time."

Dr Maguire went through a set of questions with Dinescu, but the thought of returning to those underground stations was playing on his mind. She suggested a series of trips to London with her and Lisa if someone could look after Sophia. "Perhaps you could work towards it being just you and Lisa, followed by a stay at a hotel as a reward."

"Lisa would like that," said Dinescu.

"And the shopping!"

"You're meant to be curing me of PTSD, not giving me more."

Maguire laughed for a moment but then sat forward. "Beniamin, you've had more than your fair share of crap happen to you, but I see a man who wants to conquer his demons. They are just ghosts. That's all." Maguire sat back and smiled. "And I'm looking forward to helping you bury them for good."

"Thank you, Siobhan. I will speak to Lisa. I may even tell her about the shopping."

Dinescu remembered little more of the consultation but walked back onto West Street with an appointment card and a head full of challenges. He looked up. It had stopped raining, and the tip of the cathedral spire had reappeared. Maybe that was a good sign, he thought to himself.

Chapter Twenty-Two

It was usually a twenty-five-minute drive from Chichester Police Station to Littlehampton, but that morning, Chester Kirby was delayed in a queue of traffic on the Littlehampton road. A police car screamed past him, soon followed by the complete works of emergency vehicles. It irked him that his journey was delayed. He had too much to do to be sitting in a car. But what disturbed him the most was the memory that was trying to surface.

Kirby first joined the police as a PCSO thirteen years ago. He remembered what it was like to be stuck on your own, directing angry motorists. After a few years, he rejoined as a PC, hoping to become a traffic officer after a couple of years. That changed after the first fatality he went to—two cars and a lorry. A family of three, including a child. No matter how hard he tried, he was unable to separate that incident from his everyday life. He was off work for three months after that and couldn't step out of the station for a year. But four years ago, when he was thirty-two, he became a detective constable and had never looked back.

He knew he had to pass the scene, so he steeled himself, focusing on the road ahead. But he glimpsed something. A car on its side, people laughing, a woman shaken but unharmed. All was good—no injuries. He loosened his grip on the steering wheel and exhaled.

He was now driving down Beach Road and heading towards the Littlehampton seafront. Kirby had been brought up in Littlehampton and now lived in Arundel, four miles away. He met his wife, Jenny, in a pub nearby, on the side of the River Arun. He loved the river, which flowed out of Littlehampton, and he loved the beach there.

At the end of Beach Road, he turned left, with the green and East Beach on his right. He passed where an old hotel used to be on the green and stopped fifty yards further on. Richmond House was beside him. It was a brick terrace house converted into flats. There were overflowing rubbish bins outside the front, and the rusty remains of a wheelless bicycle were shackled to the black iron railings.

Kirby updated Control with his location and rang the doorbell for number eleven. It was frustrating that he had no phone number for Ricky Brady, so it would be hit-and-miss whether he would be there. After about thirty seconds, he heard footsteps by the front door. Then a man in his early twenties opened the door a few inches. From what Kirby could see of him, he was wiry, with unkempt blond hair, blue eyes, and a spotty face. He didn't say anything but waited for Kirby to speak. Kirby pulled out a black leather holder and opened it to reveal his warrant card.

"I'm Detective Constable Kirby, Sussex Police. I'm looking for Ricky. Is that you?"

"Yeah. What do you want?"

"Can I come in, Ricky? It's about something private."

Ricky looked Kirby up and down. He stared at Kirby's polished tan brogues and his smart suit.

"No. No one else is in, anyway." He tried to keep himself out of view as if he were about to shut the door in Kirby's face at any moment.

"Fair enough. Have you spoken to your mum recently, Ricky?"

"No. Is she okay?" The door opened a little more. Kirby could see Ricky was in a grubby blue T-shirt and jeans.

"She's okay, I believe. I wondered if she'd called you about your dad, Charles."

"What about him? What's he done?"

"I'm sorry to say, Ricky, your father is dead." Kirby studied Ricky's expression. There wasn't even a flicker. "Did you hear me, Ricky?"

"Yeah. Dad's dead. Good."

"Okay. I take it you didn't get on with him."

"No." The gap in the door grew thinner.

"Can you remember when you last saw him?"

"Not really."

"Did he talk about anyone wanting to hurt him at all?"

Ricky paused for a few seconds, staring at something on the floor. It was a black beetle scurrying over the concrete step.

"Did someone hurt him?"

"Sorry, didn't I say? He was murdered."

There was a flicker now, but not much more. Kirby saw Ricky's Adam's apple rise and fall in his scrawny neck.

"Murdered? Who by?"

"We don't know yet. We are making inquiries."

"It wasn't me."

"Okay."

"Do you think I killed him? Is that why you're here?"

"I would have arrested you by now if I suspected that, Ricky. I'm just trying to find out a bit more about what happened. You being his son and everything..."

The door opened wider, and Ricky rubbed his eyes. Kirby could see his bony wrists. "We didn't get on. I had problems, and he wouldn't help. He said I had to help myself. I got beaten up, and it was his fault."

"Any idea when you saw him last? Was it weeks, months?"

"Months. He could afford to help me. Instead, he kept going on about how useless I was."

"Do you have any idea who would want to hurt him?"

"I caught him with that woman, you see. That's where his money went. On her."

"Are you sure we can't sit and talk? I'm interested in what you have to say, Ricky. It's difficult to talk to you through a crack in the door. We could go down to the beach if it's easier or if there's crap in your flat you don't want me to see."

"Wait there."

Kirby had walked with Ricky Brady down to the promenade and onto the pier. The tide was in, and Kirby was enjoying the walk, listening to the crash of the waves and the rattle of the pebbles being drawn over each other. Ricky gathered his thoughts and answered in short sentences, and Kirby gave him as much time as he needed to tell his story. By the time they were walking along the wooden planks of the pier, Ricky had perked up a little.

"The men that beat you up never came back again?"

"No," replied Ricky, looking out onto the sea from the end of the pier. "Not them. But there were others after me. They took my phone, laptop, and all my cash."

"And you never reported them?"

"Shit! I'm not that crazy. No, I moved from Worthing and came here."

"So, you went to your dad to borrow more money to pay the rest of your debt?"

"He wouldn't do it. He said he'd given me enough."

"What happened?"

"I was fucking desperate. I went to his flat in Chichester. I stood outside his front door for ages, thinking about what to say to him. But I heard him arguing with someone. The window was open. I knocked on the door, and he was right pissed off when he saw me. I told him I'd be dead if I didn't pay them back. There was this woman with him. I was well shocked."

"When was this?" Kirby got out a notebook from his jacket.

"Last Saturday in March."

"You'd gambled away your benefit money by then?"

Ricky looked at Kirby and frowned. "You don't know what it's like. I can't help it. I'd won something. It's better than smack, and I had to try again. If I could win enough to pay back the McCoys, then..."

"But you never really win, do you, Ricky?"

"No. I've stood where we're standing now more times than I can remember. It wouldn't take much just to climb up and drop into the river. Fast flowing. It would take me in a minute."

"Not a good way to go."

"No. I'm still here talking to you, aren't I?"

"You are. The woman who was with your dad—can you describe her?"

"A bit shorter than you. She was young, had long blonde hair, and a silver nose stud. Not skinny, but not fat either. Way out of my dad's league."

"How old?"

"Can't say. Lots of make-up. Twenty, thirty, forty? He'd

obviously paid for her. If he could afford to pay for it, then he could afford to help me. His own son."

Kirby stared at the other side of the river and over at West Beach. People were running and laughing along the path, carrying bodyboards.

"Would you recognise her if you saw her again?"

"Probably."

"Did you get her name?"

Ricky shook his head. "No."

"What were they arguing about?"

"God knows. I think he was going on again about his sister, Maisy. All the bloody time at home, it was. *Maisy, Maisy, Maisy.* She was telling him to leave it—to let it go. Dad was like a stuck record."

"How good was your view of her?"

"She was standing right in front of me. She opened the door, and she was scared. I think she was expecting someone else. But she saw me, and Dad was behind her. Something was going on. And someone was waiting outside in a van, watching. When he saw me leaving Dad's, he looked the other way."

"Any details of him and the van?"

"I didn't hang around. I had to thumb a lift back."

"Did you ever go back to your dad's again?"

"No. That was the last I saw of him."

"Thanks, Ricky. Have you got a phone number in case I need to call you again or you need me for anything?"

"I have. But I don't give it to anyone."

"You need help, fella. Serious help."

"I'm getting help. The old Sally Army in Bognor has picked me up. Early days, but... they've been solid so far."

"That's really good." Kirby handed Ricky his contact card. "Take this anyway. At least you can call me if you need anything or remember anything else."

"Lend us twenty?" Ricky laughed.

Kirby smiled. "Apart from that." He looked Ricky up and down. "Buy some food, Ricky. There's nothing of you."

"A tenner, then?"

Kirby sighed and reached into his pocket. "For food. Nothing else."

Chapter Twenty-Three

Sarah Burgess turned right at the roundabout and passed Hotham Park, heading towards the Bognor Regis town centre. She had a love-hate relationship with Bognor, more often than not related to the weather. It wasn't a place she enjoyed in the rain.

She went over another roundabout and saw the ugly white building she wanted on the left: *Price-Petersons Insurance*. After negotiating a temperamental barrier, she parked in a visitor's space. Burgess didn't know what Price-Petersons insured. She only knew she paid too much for hers.

She walked into the reception and was greeted by a woman with a black bob, who squinted over the top of her glasses to make out who Burgess was. She didn't recognise the lanyard she was wearing.

"I'm Detective Constable Burgess from Chichester CID. I understand that Miss Candice Lee works here."

"Who? Lee? Let me check for you." The woman scrolled down a list on a computer terminal in front of her. "Yes, she does. I think she's new. Do you have an appointment?"

"No, but I need to speak with her on a police matter."

"Take a seat, and I'll call her down."

Burgess sat in a hot leather chair against the large glass window. She swept her beaded hair back over her shoulders and saw from the corner of her eye that the receptionist was watching her. Burgess smiled out of politeness and turned to watch the traffic heading down the high street.

She heard heels coming down a stairwell to the right of her. A tall blonde woman in a tight lilac skirt and jacket appeared. She was slender, had high cheekbones, and a soft but serious expression. She looked sharp and professional in her suit, and her curvaceous profile reminded Burgess of the description given by John at the New Moon.

The woman spoke to the receptionist, who pointed over to Burgess.

"You've come to my workplace?" said Candice Lee, now looking irritated.

"Miss Lee, I'm DC Burgess from Chichester Major Crimes. Can I have a few moments in private, please?"

Lee sighed. "Follow me."

She strutted off in her heels towards a side room beside reception. She didn't look like she could ever have been a private detective.

"This is about Charles?"

They sat opposite each other on low-backed chairs designed for short people. Lee sat on the chair, pulling down the sides of her skirt.

"Yes, Miss Lee," said Burgess with a smile. "I spoke to you on the telephone. I remember you being defensive and evasive, and I wanted to find out why."

"I don't know anything about why he's dead. I don't have to answer your questions. I'm an ex-cop myself."

"That's interesting, Miss Lee. Where did you work?"

"Nothing to do with you."

"Gosh. Sounds like you didn't enjoy it. If you are an ex-police officer, as you say, then you will know we have several lines of enquiry we must investigate."

"Why me?"

"We found a business card in Charles Brady's flat. You've already told me you were helping him uncover some of the history of the school. Why was he researching the school's history?"

Lee looked at her manicured nails. "He was writing a book or something."

"We've discovered that Charles had a sister who went to Cotisham school. Did Charles ask you to research or find his sister?"

"I can't say."

"Why?"

"Is that all you want because I need to go back to work?"

"You may have information we need, and you aren't being forthcoming. I'm going to ask you to come to the police station with me to answer my questions under caution."

"Arrest me? You've got no grounds."

"Voluntary interview."

Lee shook her head. "I know what that means. Look, I didn't want anything to do with Charles anymore."

Candice Lee became breathless, and the colour dropped from her rouged cheeks.

"What's wrong, Candice?"

"Don't tell anyone I spoke to you, okay? I'm not going to put this down in a statement. So don't get your pocket notebook out."

Burgess frowned. "Go on."

"Charles believed his sister, Maisy, was buried somewhere on the school grounds. He thought there was a cover-up, and he'd come back to the school to work so he could find out. He was obsessed with it."

"That's as much as we know."

"I found some old newspaper articles. They found the remains of the babies a year before Maisy disappeared, and they bricked up the fake fireplace to stop the kids at the school from getting to the hiding place. I suggested to Charles that maybe there's a connection to Maisy somehow. I tried to put in a data protection request for details of the teachers at the school in 1987. It was soon after that I started getting messages."

"Threatening messages?"

"At first. I've chucked them since. They said the Grey Friar would come for me if I didn't stop helping Charles. It was some stupid ghost that was meant to haunt the school. I met Charles at a pub and told him about it."

"The New Moon?"

"Yes. He became distraught and angry. I had to calm him down."

"Did you stop working for him after that?"

"Not then. I hadn't had a response about the list of teachers, so I went to the school about two months ago to ask them why. It was dark when I got there, and I was waiting in reception for ages. Someone called me from behind a door that led into a long corridor. I stupidly went through, and then he grabbed me. He was wearing a hood and put his hand over my mouth. I tried to kick and punch him, but he was bloody strong. He dragged me down the corridor and into something like a cupboard. I couldn't see anything. He pushed me against the wall..."

Candice Lee's hands were shaking, and Burgess held them. "It's okay, Candice. Take your time. I've got all day."

"I was sure he was going to try and rape me. He lifted my skirt and everything. But he didn't. He just hissed in my ear. I could feel the hair and bristles on his face. He stank of sweat. He may have had a moustache, but I can't be certain."

"Did he say anything to you?"

"He said he was..." Candice took a breath. "He said he was going to kill me right there, right then. He said he'd warned me to stay away from Brady. Then he had a knife in his hands. He pushed it against my face."

"Did he hurt you?"

"Apart from the gripping, no. I begged him to let me go. I told him I wouldn't speak to Charles again."

Candice pulled her hands away and wiped her eyes.

"Are you sure you don't want to report this formally?"

"No! He said he knew where I lived and was coming to get me. He said he'd count to ten to give me a head start, and then he pushed me out of the cupboard. I just ran and ran. I didn't look back. I got in my car and drove."

"Can you give me any further description of this man? You're sure he wasn't an older student?"

"His voice was too old for a student. He was so strong. I didn't hang about to get a better look at him."

"Did you let Charles know what had happened?"

"No. I blocked him on my phone and got out of my flat as soon as I could. I moved over to Littlehampton to get away from Chichester. This is the closest I ever go there now."

"What do you think it was that touched a nerve with this man?"

"I don't know. Look, that's as much as I'm going to say about it. I'm putting all that behind me and moving on."

"I'm so sorry, Candice. I really am."

"I know you are. Thanks. I was in Hampshire Constabulary for eight years. I was bullied because I didn't fit in."

"Why didn't you fit in?"

"When I joined up, my name was James Lee."

Burgess smiled in surprise. "I wouldn't have guessed. Is it okay to say that?"

"Yes, that's fine." Candice Lee smiled, and her face softened. "Thank you."

Burgess signed out at reception and headed for the doors. She called DS Summers on her way back to the car and updated her.

"Shit, that's horrible! Do you think she could be persuaded to make a statement?" asked Summers.

"Not at the moment, Sarge. Not until we have this creep locked up. She's scared for her life. What she said backs up the boss's hunch—Brady's death is connected with the search for his sister."

"Good work, Sarah. This man is very dangerous. His scare tactics worked for Candice Lee, but they didn't stop Charles Brady. We don't know if he received any similar threats at all."

"No, Sarge."

"So it has to be someone at the school, but who the hell is it?" Burgess heard Summers sigh. "Okay. I'll update the boss with what you've told me. Can you go with Ross to pick up Ethan Bishop, just in case he needs babysitting."

Burgess laughed. "Who, Ross?"

"No, Bishop. He sounds like a moody teenager."

"On my way, Sarge."

Chapter Twenty-Four

Ethan Bishop watched a single droplet of rain trace its way down the window. As it continued its path, it gathered in others and grew in size, falling with greater momentum. The police car crawled through the roadworks, the wind buffeting it from the north, and the wipers were at full speed.

Sitting beside him was a black woman with long hair. Every few minutes, she would glance at him, sometimes with a smile, other times watching what he was doing with his hands. No one spoke. The only sound was the weather and the tyres on the wet road.

The detective driving was called DC Ross Taylor. He was straight with him. He said he wasn't under arrest, but it felt like he was. Matron was going to come with him, but Ethan didn't want her. He was eighteen, and DC Taylor told her Ethan didn't need an appropriate adult.

After another thirty tedious minutes, they arrived at Chichester Police Station. The black detective let Ethan out of the car and led him into an interview room. Then she left them, and it was just him and DC Taylor.

"It's not like the TV," said Ethan. "Don't I have to talk to the sergeant and get my photo taken?"

"They only do that if you've been arrested," said Taylor. "You're not under arrest, Ethan. This is voluntary."

He was given a drink of water, and many things were said about solicitors and being free to go—some of it went above his head. He didn't want a solicitor and wondered if he could make something up. He could just tell them he murdered Brady. It would get him out of Cotisham, and he wouldn't have to go home. He could be someone. He'd be famous for a while, and after a few years, he'd be released, and his family would never want to talk to him again.

Ethan sipped the ice-cold water and agreed to something. He wasn't listening. A tone jolted him, and he was asked to give his name.

"Ethan Bishop."

"And your date of birth?" said Taylor.

"21st of September, 2004. It was a Tuesday."

"Really? Are you certain you don't want a solicitor for free legal advice, Ethan? They don't work for the police."

"No. I don't need one."

DC Taylor took a sip of his water. "We need to know more information about how you got on with Mr Brady. People have told me you both had a falling out about something. What can you tell me about that?"

"Why?" Ethan knew that it sounded like he was being awkward. "What have people been saying?"

"You had an argument after you put up those photographs around the school of him and Miss Turnbull."

"Oh, that. He was being a prick and wanted to cover it up. He literally abused her and then just said sorry, like he didn't mean it. As I said, he was a complete prick."

"So, you put photographs up around the school as revenge? Payback for assaulting Leah Turnbull?"

"Sure, I did. Leah wouldn't have done anything about it. She's too nice about everything."

"When did you put the photographs up, Ethan?"

"I don't know. Soon after their crappy party. The Sunday after."

"That was the 8th of January."

"If you say so. Cameron gave him a slap for it, but it took him ages to think about it. People were staring at him, wondering why he did nothing. Cameron punched him and ended up getting nicked for it. Nice bloke, but he's an idiot."

"You weren't there at the party. How did you take the photos?"

"We were there, sort of. I was with Dan and Harry in the passage that runs along the top of the hall—the place is full of them. You get to it from the main stairs and can spy on people in the hall from there. Those Tudors were well weird. Dan took the photos. Harry and I watched. We wanted to see who got pissed first."

"What did Charles Brady do when he found out it was you who stuck the photos of him around the school?"

"He waited for me after dinner and smacked me in the face. He went crazy. Spat on me and everything. He bust my nose. I had to go to A&E, but all the teachers kept quiet about it. They said nothing against him. They blamed me. Said I'd walked into a door. They protected him, and I got suspended."

"How did that make you feel about Brady?"

"I hated him."

"How long have you felt that way about him?"

"Ever since."

"Enough to kill him?"

"I may have wished him dead a few times, yes."

"Mr Brady was killed on Monday, the 17th of April, sometime between three and six in the afternoon. Staff told us you were twenty minutes late for the last period that day. Why were you late?"

Ethan knew exactly what he was doing then. He could feel his face growing hot, but there was nothing he could say.

"I can't remember."

"Ethan, this is important. Do you understand why it's important?"

"Of course I do. I'm not stupid. You reckon I shot Brady. But I didn't. That's all I can say. I wasn't anywhere near the tower."

"So, where were you? Take your time. Your last lesson was geography. Who's your geography teacher?"

"Mrs Williams."

"Do you remember being late?"

"Yes."

"So, you must remember why."

"I can't say. You wouldn't understand."

Something inside wanted to tell him. He wanted to tell someone—was *desperate* to tell someone. Then perhaps Leah would be okay again. All the pressure of keeping it quiet must have been getting to her.

Taylor rubbed his eyes. "Ethan. Don't forget, you can ask for a solicitor anytime."

"I know." He looked up above Taylor's head and saw a video camera with a red light on.

"Are you videoing this?"

"Yes. I told you at the beginning."

"Did you? I didn't hear."

"I'm going to come back to why you were late in a minute. It will give you a chance to think about it."

"Whatever."

"The school has a clay pigeon shooting club, and your name is on the list. Are you any good?"

"Me and Dan are the best shots. I'm better than him, though."

"How many went shooting at the last club meeting? That was a week last Sunday."

"There were only four of us. Me, Dan, Cam, and Archie."

"Cam. Is that Cameron Hyde?"

"Yep."

"Who's Archie?"

"Archie. He's Cam's mate. He does odd jobs around the school. He's a builder."

"Do you have a key to Mr Hyde's workshop?"

"God, no! He doesn't let us go anywhere near it."

"Have you ever been in Mr Hyde's workshop without him knowing?"

"No. Why would I do that? I'm not interested in his stupid workshop."

"Did you remove a shotgun from the workshop at any point after the shoot on Sunday?"

"No! The guns are in the office. In the cabinet."

Taylor paused as he read his notes. "I want to talk about the folly—the tower. You know it well, I assume."

"We all do." Ethan took another sip of water. The questions were going from one thing to another, and he was finding it hard to keep up with them.

"When was the last time you went up the tower?"

"We're not allowed up the tower. Is that some kind of trick question?"

"No trick questions, Ethan. So, you are saying you've never been up the tower?"

"No, I'm not. I'm just saying we're not allowed. But that

doesn't stop most of us. The last time I went up there was after Christmas. We have a smoke and a few drinks in there."

"Have you ever climbed to the top?"

"Of course I have. Lots of people have."

"Did you go up the tower on Monday, the 17th of April, in the afternoon? Is that why you were late for your geography lesson?"

"No."

"So, where were you?"

"I can't tell you."

"Why not?"

"These fucking questions! Because I can't. I'd drop someone in it."

Ethan's head was swimming. He felt the sweat on his back and his top lip. Another sip of water and looked into Taylor's eyes. They were intense and serious. He wasn't being Mr Friendly Cop at the moment.

"We need to know where you were, Ethan. You've already admitted you hated Mr Brady and you wished him dead. If you can tell us where you were, and if someone can give you an alibi, then all the better."

"You can't tell Greenway. Okay?"

"I'm interested in your whereabouts, Ethan. That's all."

"I was with Leah. Miss Turnbull."

"In her classroom?"

"No. Her house. In her bedroom. We were having sex."

Summers and Taylor returned a petulant Ethan Bishop to Cotisham School. He wasn't happy when Taylor told him they would have to check his alibi with Leah Turnbull. He wouldn't talk to them until they had parked the car outside the school.

"So you're going to walk me back in, are you? Make me look a right twat."

"I'm sure you don't need me to hold your hand," said Taylor. "Come on, Ethan. You know we have to confirm what you said."

"She's going to think I've grassed on her."

"No, she won't," said Summers, turning around. "How old were you when you started your relationship?"

"Eighteen," said Ethan. "I've already told your buddy here. Nothing happened before that."

"You know this could cost Leah her job."

"It's got fuck all to do with Greenway!"

Summers shook her head. "You're a student, Ethan!"

Ethan tried to open the car door. "Are you going to let me out or not?"

Summers and Taylor got out of the car and opened his door. They watched him walk away, hunched up in a strop, back through the main entrance.

"I'd never want to be a teenager again," said Taylor. "All those hormones rushing around everywhere."

"Sleeping with a teacher is seriously out-of-control hormones," said Summers.

They began walking towards the school. Summers glanced sideways at Taylor and was impressed by his dapper appearance. He'd never had a hair out of place or a creased shirt since she'd known him.

"You're always so smart, Ross. I look like I've slept in my blouse."

Taylor laughed. "I try my best."

Summers stopped by the front door and searched for a way to say something to him.

"Sarge?" He was puzzled.

"Ross, I've come into the team like a bull in a china shop. It wasn't a good start. It's very different here, and..."

"You wanted to make a good impression?"

"Precisely. I tried to get the best out of people but failed dismally. I'm trying to do better."

"Can we just step out of our job roles for a minute?"

"Sure."

"Chester said you apologised. That was good—impressive, even. It's okay." Taylor looked at his feet. "The boss spoke to us all privately. He said to cut you some slack and let you get your feet under the table. He meant it to be kind and asked us not to complain about you. We're all okay with that. It's hard to come into an established team from the outside. I couldn't do what you do. My opinion is you should cut yourself some slack, too. Yeah, it wasn't a great start, but hey, you haven't seen me when I'm in a bad mood yet." He looked up and smiled.

"Thanks, Ross."

"Back to work then, Sarge."

"Yep." Summers looked awkward for a moment. "Okay. Do you think Ethan's fling with Turnbull was real? Not just some fantasy?"

Taylor shrugged. "Difficult to say for certain until we've spoken to Turnbull."

"And you've considered she could have groomed him when he was younger?"

"Yes, Sarge. According to Ethan, he approached her first."

"Okay. Let's see if she'll confirm his alibi."

Taylor squirmed. "This is going to be embarrassing for her. She's likely to deny it if she thinks she'll get into trouble. She wasn't forthcoming with information about Charles Brady making a pass at her."

Summers pushed the heavy door. "She'll need to verify it. Otherwise, Ethan's still in the frame."

They walked into the school, and after a talk with a friendly receptionist called Janice—back from maternity leave, she

175

explained unsolicited—Leah Turnbull was located. When she arrived in Reception to meet with them, her eyes were wide, and she was biting her bottom lip. Summers reckoned she'd heard Ethan had been interviewed. There was restrained panic in her eyes.

"Thanks for coming out to speak with us, Miss Turnbull," said Summers.

"Is there something wrong?"

Summers looked at Taylor. "Ross, could you update Doctor Greenway for me? Miss Turnbull and I are going to have a chat for a few minutes."

"Yes, Sarge."

"Come and sit in my car, Leah."

Summers led the way to the car park. The wind had turned into a squall, and both women wrapped their coats around them and hurried to the CID car.

Leah became withdrawn and sat next to Summers, who had turned in her seat to face her.

"Leah, we spoke to Ethan Bishop about his whereabouts on Monday, the 17th of April, from around three o'clock to just after 3:30. We believe that's when Charles Brady was murdered."

Leah nodded as she stared out the window into the distance. Her eyes were tearing up.

"He gave us his alibi for that time. Are you able to confirm what he told us?"

Leah looked down at her knees and shuddered. A tear rolled down her cheek, and she wiped it away. Leah nodded again.

"So, you were together at your home during that time? I need to ask, Leah."

"Yes."

"Okay. This isn't a formal interview. I'm not recording our conversation."

176

She looked at Summers. "I was stupid, DS Summers, but he's over eighteen. I wasn't in a good place, and I suppose I was flattered. It wasn't illegal, was it?"

"As you say, he's over eighteen. You'd be under investigation if he were younger."

"Are you going to let the school know?"

"No. It's not my place to. He's an adult. I'm debating if it's a safeguarding concern, and I imagine your school will have a policy against it. Your statement said you had gone home early that day. Did you drive Ethan back to the school?"

"Yes. We were late getting him back, but I made him walk from the gates."

"What time was that?"

"About 3:30."

"Did Charles Brady find out about your relationship with Ethan?"

"No."

Leah looked out of the side window, and her face was flushed.

"Okay," said Summers. "Tell me what happened after the incident at the party in January."

"Me and Charles had become unexpected friends after that. He'd misunderstood something I'd said. I think he was just lonely. Anyway, we got to know each other a bit. He told me about his past connection with the school. It wasn't much more than that. Cameron and I had a big falling out about it. He decided to go all macho, defending my honour like he owned me or something." Leah cleared her throat and wiped her eyes with a ragged tissue.

Summers could see the similarity between Cameron and Anthony. She looked outside. The wind had died down again, and the sunlight was coming through the clouds.

"Why don't we get a bit of fresh air?"

Summers and Leah Turnbull walked around the side of the school and looked out onto the tree-capped hills on the horizon.

"I will be handing in my notice when school finishes today."

"It's probably for the best, honestly," said Summers.

"I don't know what to do now. So much of who I am is tied in with Cam and this place. It's really hard."

"You can start again, Leah. It is hard, but you can. I'm speaking from experience."

"I have to get back." Leah turned to Summers. "I'm not a predator, DS Summers. But I know I've left myself wide open."

Summers nodded. "Thanks, Leah."

Daniel was in the bedroom after lunch. He was finishing a project he had to hand in for history. He saw the police car pull up in the driveway and drop Ethan Bishop outside the school. Ethan was hunched over when he got out of the car. He looked up and saw Daniel watching him.

Harry came in. "Ethan back yet?"

"Just," said Daniel. "He doesn't look great."

"Maybe they tortured him into a confession," said Harry.

"Ethan didn't kill Brady. He's only interested in one thing."

"And that *thing* is?" Harry looked out the window and caught Ethan's blonde head disappearing beneath them.

"Leah Turnbull," said Daniel in a matter-of-fact way.

"Miss Turnbull? Him and most of the school."

"Most? Not you?"

Harry flinched a little. "Who did kill Brady, then?"

"I saw someone with him on the day he died. I'm going to ask someone about it."

"A right proper detective, aren't you."

"I wish. Perhaps I could be a private detective."

"Photograph unfaithful partners in the act?"

"Maybe."

Ethan walked in and dropped himself onto his bed.

"How did it go, mate?" said Harry.

"It was shit," said Ethan. "I think I've dropped someone in it, but I didn't have a choice. I can't stay here anymore. It's just so fucked up."

"Just a few more months, and then we're out of here."

"I don't think I'll make it till then. I've screwed up big time, and I think there's someone after me."

"Who?" said Daniel.

"I don't know. Has to be one of the staff. Maybe Cam."

"Why would Cam be after you?"

Ethan rolled his eyes. "I don't want to talk about it, Dan."

"They can't do anything," said Daniel. "You're over eighteen."

"You just keep out of it, weasel!"

"Ethan, he was being, you know, nice."

"You sticking up for him, Harry?"

"No. Just making the obvious point."

"I'm going to my next lesson," said Daniel. "Glad you're okay, Ethan."

Daniel grabbed a couple of books and a pencil case and left. The school seemed darker than ever today. He felt there were eyes on him as he descended the main staircase, walked through the main hall, and passed the library. He saw Archie Faulkner leaning against the library door, and he stepped out to block Daniel's path.

"Archie," said Daniel. "You okay?"

"Fine, Dan. Fine. Me, Jason, and Mac are heading to the New Moon in the village tomorrow for lunch. Fancy coming along? We'd love to hear any more interesting tidbits you might have."

"Me?"

"Yes, you."

"That would be great. Thanks, Archie! I'd like that."

"Pick you up at lunch tomorrow. We can't be long, but there'll be enough time for a quick one."

"Thanks. See you then."

Archie stepped out of Daniel's way, and Daniel continued his journey to his lesson. He wondered what Archie and the others wanted to know. It had to be connected to everything that was going on in the school. He did have secrets but wasn't ready to share them with anyone yet, not even the police.

Chapter Twenty-Five

Dinescu led Detective Inspector Clegg into the meeting room, where the core team was waiting. Coming in behind them were Summers and Taylor, who had just returned from the school.

DI Clegg was a stout man, a seasoned detective with drooping eyelids and thinning hair. He was accustomed to training crime teams across Sussex and Surrey and was a renowned expert in *mis*sing persons. He was also a police search team advisor, and he had advised on a string of high-profile missing person cases over the years, the vast majority of which led to either the person being found or the perpetrator's arrest.

"Good afternoon," said Clegg. He had a strong Yorkshire accent, deep and throaty. "I'm DI Clegg from the Cold Case Unit, and I'm here to brief you on Maisy Brady. Her date of birth was the 6th of August, 1973, which made her 14 years old when she went missing in May 1987. DCI Dinescu has asked me to brief you on the information we have and to answer any questions. Would you believe this is the sixth review of Maisy's disappearance? The last two were in 2010 and 2020, both of which I worked on. Those reviews led to appeals to the public for further information, including computer-generated mock-ups of what Maisy would look like today. Sadly, no new information came forward—until now." Clegg pulled out some photocopied notes from a folder and handed them out.

"Maisy was at Aversham School with her brother, Charles Brady. They both joined the school in 1986 as full-time boarders. According to school records, Maisy was bright, athletic, and keen to impress. She was popular with other children. Her mother lived in Haywards Heath and later moved down to the coast. She was the CEO of a finance company and a widow.

Maisy was last seen on the 14th of May 1987. She had attended all the morning lessons and had gone to the first lunch sitting. She was seen talking to a group of older boys in the dining hall but left alone. The last time she was seen was in the library. The school librarian at the time was Miriam Cohen. In her statement, Cohen said Maisy looked anxious but didn't want any help. She had the impression that Maisy was waiting for someone. Mrs Cohen said she was about to lock up the library. She was distracted by something for about five minutes, and by the time she returned to her desk, Maisy had gone. That was the last time anyone saw Maisy—we think. That afternoon's weather was much like today—rainy, fourteen degrees Celsius, and windy.

"At about four o'clock in the afternoon, the matron, Ruth Lambert, raised the alarm to the then headmaster, Gerald Faulkner-Williams. He may not have taken the concern seriously. It was later found that Faulkner-Williams didn't take many things seriously—which I'll get onto shortly. It wasn't until the next morning when Mrs Lambert called the police."

Burgess looked up from the sheet in front of her. "Did Faulkner-Williams explain why they left it until the following morning?"

"He told a later inquiry that he thought she would turn up in the evening and that there was nothing to worry about."

"Bloody dodgy, then," said Booker.

Clegg raised his bushy eyebrows. "The detectives investigating Maisy's disappearance thought the same thing but couldn't find anything incriminating. Faulkner-Williams claimed to have been away at a conference in Brighton the day she disappeared, but he later stated that was, in fact, an error.

"After another week of local searches, a nationwide search was called, and it went to the papers and the TV. So, at this point, I'll bring in the other reason Cotisham was famous—perhaps infamous would be a better description."

"For those who don't know, work was done in the library the previous October to improve the heating. It was suggested that the fireplace be boarded up to reduce the draught. There was an inspection by builders, and they found an entrance to a priest hole just above a ledge, right at the back of the fireplace. The ledge was easy to climb onto and was completely obscured. Ingenious, whoever thought of it."

"Nicholas Owen, in 1597," said Dinescu. "A famous priest hole builder, according to Wikipedia."

"Well, there you go. Something I didn't know, sir."

Dinescu smiled. "Anytime."

"The builders went over the ledge and examined the priest hole. There they found—and you've already seen the photographs—the remains of the babies. Their deaths were later attributed to the baby farmer, Ruby Paddock, who was hanged in 1911 for murdering other babies. So, the school already had some bad press."

"Did Maisy go into the priest hole?" asked Booker.

"The fireplace had been bricked over the previous January," said Clegg. "I don't think they'd have gotten away with it today, being a listed building and all. Anyway, no one could have got in there after that. My understanding is that it's remained that way ever since.

"After the search went nationwide, we had reports of Maisy being seen in Brighton and Newcastle. Nothing substantiated. Her mother's house and garden were turned upside down, but she was away in New York when Maisy disappeared.

"Statements were taken from the pupils. One girl thought she saw Maisy running out of the door, heading towards the old tower. She said Maisy was wearing a red coat, but Maisy didn't have a red coat. The girl who had seen Maisy was one of the juniors—nine years old. Her statement wasn't taken seriously.

"So, it's been a perplexing mystery for many years. Amateur sleuths had gone after Faulkner-Williams. Crazy theories about him killing Maisy and hiding her body in the boot of his car. It was about that time that the stories of the Grey Friar began circulating. They said he had been released from the priest hole to avenge the babies. Scary, eh." Clegg feigned horror and smirked.

"What happened to the school?" said Summers.

"Yes, I was getting onto that. The then-Social Services ordered a review of the school after reports of bullying and abuse by staff came out of the investigation into Maisy's disappearance. That's why they wondered if she had run away.

"Evidence was found that the children were beaten for poor work or bad behaviour. There was talk of a culture of bullying from the headmaster down. A school nurse who tried to raise her concerns, Juliet Butterworth, was fired. To cut a long story short, the headmaster was told to resign, and the school was forced to close as Aversham College."

Summers spoke again. "So, was there a link found between the bullying and Maisy's disappearance? Why wouldn't she have just run away?"

"No direct link was found, according to the report," said Clegg. "It was possible she could have run away, but she had packed nothing in her room. All her clothes and bags were there, and she had arranged to meet her brother after school. And it was well known that she loved her younger brother and would often look out for him. No one believed she would have left him on his own."

"Later, forensic tests were done on her clothing in her room. Nothing was found on those. The babies' bones were later carbon-dated to the early 1900s. But there was no link between them and Maisy's disappearance. And that's it."

Clegg took more questions from the team until they started going around in circles.

"Thank you for coming to speak with us, Jonathan," said Dinescu. "I believe that Charles Brady was searching for his sister's body in the school and that this is somehow linked to his death. Now we have a reluctant witness saying she was threatened for helping Brady in his search."

"Well, it is possible, sir," said Clegg. "I can only comment on Maisy's disappearance."

"Who was the young girl who thought she saw Maisy in a red coat?" asked Summers. "Maybe we could find her and talk to her. She'll be in her mid-forties now."

Clegg pulled out a note from one of his files. "Her name was Celia Lambert, the matron's daughter."

"Celia!" said Burgess. "This case is getting more and more weird."

Clegg looked confused.

"She's the headteacher's PA," Dinescu said to Clegg. "We need to go to the school and take the tower plans with us. Maybe it will spark a memory in Celia."

"Okay, boss," said Summers. "Nothing ventured..."

Chapter Twenty-Six

Summers drove Dinescu and Burgess back to Cotisham. Summers and Burgess were mulling over their meeting with DI Clegg, but Dinescu's mind was preoccupied with the thought of travelling to London once more. He remembered the sounds and smells of the underground, which had been his usual method of travel in London. He had known it like the back of his hand. He could read a book, get on and off the right trains, and change lines without looking up.

After he joined the Met, he couldn't imagine working anywhere else, let alone in a rural county in the south of England. He loved the city's noise, the traffic rumbling, and the diversity of culture. He had a group of Romanian friends he would meet with, and his foster parents insisted he never lost his cultural heritage as he grew up. Although Dinescu didn't know until he was eighteen, they had planned to find his family in Bârlad. In later years, they found his mother, after whom Sophia was named, and Beniamin had spent three months with her before she died.

His Romanian friends helped him retain his culture and language. Dinescu wished, above all else, that he could go back to London to meet with them again, walk the streets where his foster parents once lived in Harrow, and visit their graves.

"Boss?" It was Summers who brought him back to the present.

"I'm sorry. I was far away."

"Sarah was just saying we've unexpectedly taken on a cold case alongside Brady's murder."

Dinescu nodded. "These things are rarely straightforward. Not bad in three days' work, though."

Summers was frowning to herself. "If Celia Lambert was the little girl who saw Maisy disappearing, did she tell Charles Brady? Could she identify who Maisy was with?"

Summers turned into the school driveway.

"We will talk to her," said Dinescu. "That was excellent work with Turnbull, by the way, Emily."

"Thanks, boss."

After parking, they were met by Greenway in Reception. Dinescu and the other detectives followed the headmaster into the library.

"These repeated interruptions are upsetting everyone," Greenway said to Dinescu, "including the parents."

"Of course, Doctor Greenway," said Dinescu. His stolid temperament wasn't bothered by Greenway's growing impatience. "And we are grateful that you are as motivated to find Mr Brady's killer as we are."

Greenway harrumphed.

A small class of year eights was choosing books in the library that afternoon. On a central island of tables, the librarian was helping a boy design a poster about his favourite book. The other boys at the table looked up open-mouthed at the three detectives and the apparent giant Dinescu, who smiled at them.

"Miss Church," said Greenway. "Would you mind if we took a corner of your table for a few minutes?"

Alice Church moved her bags and papers closer to make more space. She looked worried as if the detectives were about to ransack her library and burn it down.

"That's fine, Doctor Greenway. Help yourself. The students are about to leave, anyway."

DS Summers thanked her and brought out a pile of papers that she had in a folder. They were copies of the plans Brady had in his flat. She laid them down on the table, and they all gathered around, with Dinescu in the centre.

The class left, the boys craning their necks to have one last look at DS Summers.

"I have the list from our archives you requested, Chief Inspector," said Greenway. "I stopped Celia from throwing them away last week. She was having a clearout."

"Very fortunate," said Dinescu, glancing at Summers.

As the last boy left, Celia Lambert walked in. She looked surprised to see the police officers.

"Oh," she said, frozen on the spot. "Did you need me, Eric?"

"Yes, please, Celia. The chief inspector tells me this is important. Come and look with us."

Dinescu started with the plans of the folly.

"I'm not sure where Mr Brady found these plans, perhaps in the County Record Office. You'll see three different aspects of the tower. We believe he was obsessed with finding his sister, Maisy, who came here with Charles when it was Aversham College in the 1980s."

"Charles came here?" said Greenway. "He never said. That's another one. They're like old pennies."

"Another one?" said Summers.

"Yes." Greenway looked at a printed sheet in his hand. "According to the list of pupils asked for, there's David Roberts, Jason—that's Cameron's father—and Mac. I see Charles and his sister on the list now."

"We didn't know that," said Dinescu. He glanced over at Celia Lambert, who had turned pink. "Eric, you've missed someone. Celia, you were a pupil here too."

"Yes. Only for a few years." Lambert didn't look up but studied the plan of the tower. "My mother was the matron for a while."

"Soon after Maisy disappeared, you gave a statement to the police about a girl in a red coat. You thought it was Maisy Brady."

"Gosh! I can only just remember it. I was only nine. My mother and my aunts used to say I had a vivid imagination as a child."

"Do you think you imagined it?" said Summers.

"Perhaps, DS Summers. I enjoyed all the attention."

"Be that as it may," said Dinescu, "it was a statement you made to the police with your mother present. I have a hunch."

"A hunch?" said Greenway, shrugging his slender shoulders.

"I believe if we find out what happened to Maisy, then we will find out what happened to Charles, and vice versa. I suggest he had a good idea of where Maisy was buried. Brady showed a very keen interest in the folly." Dinescu pointed to the diagram and the words *to the tunnel*.

"A tunnel?" said Greenway. "What tunnel? Celia, do you know anything about a tunnel?"

Celia Lambert didn't answer. Her jaw was locked closed, and she entwined her fingers together.

Burgess stooped a little. "Are you okay, Celia?"

"Do you honestly think Charles's death is connected to Maisy, Chief Inspector?" said Lambert.

"Yes, I do." Dinescu's voice was gentle. "Is your mother still alive, Celia?"

Celia looked straight at Dinescu. "Can we talk somewhere?"

"Yes. I'd like that."

Burgess stayed with Greenway and looked through the lists he had provided from the archives.

Meanwhile, Dinescu and Summers did up their coats and walked outside with Celia Lambert. They followed the path around the school and along the back fields that made up the vast majority of the estate. Lambert walked between the detectives with her gaze on the path before her.

"My mother's name is Ruth Lambert. We were only really at the school because of her work. Our home—mine and my sister's—was her apartment next to the dormitories."

"Your sister?" said Dinescu.

"Olivia, the matron."

"We were unaware you were sisters."

"We're very different. They'd only let one of us attend the school—Liv was just a little too young at the time. She's a year younger than me but was always our mother's favourite." Celia shrugged. "They were different times back then. The teachers wouldn't get away with it now. You'd arrest them. The sports master was terrifying. I think he was murdered years later in Portsmouth. My mother had it tough, but she did what she could. The headmaster was a total bastard to her. Nevertheless, I later learnt she was infatuated with him. I'd go as far as to say he was cruel. But after Maisy disappeared, everything changed. He was kind to her and gave her days off and time with us. I often wondered why."

"And she said nothing to you?" asked Summers.

"She did, but not until last year. And she inadvertently told Charles, too. My mother is in a nursing home in West Wittering. She's been there for years. She has vascular dementia."

"Is she in the same home as Charles Brady's mother?"

Lambert nodded. "A total coincidence."

"Last November, it was my weekend to visit her at the nursing home. She was pretty delirious. We didn't know it then, but she was on the cusp of a UTI. That always sends her like that. She kept saying…" Lambert put her hand to her mouth. "Sorry, excuse me…"

"Take your time, Celia," said Dinescu.

"She kept saying *Maisy's dead.* Repeating over and over. Then she said, *I saw her, I saw her.* I didn't know what she was talking about. Then she repeated so that everyone could hear— *Maisy's dead. She's in the hole.* I looked up, and Charles was there. The new head of maths was standing over us. His face was as white as a sheet. Of course, I knew nothing about it. He kept demanding answers from me, but I couldn't help him. But he recognised my mother. He tried talking to her, but she wouldn't answer. He was asked to leave in the end."

"Did she say anything else to you about Maisy?" asked Summers.

"Just that she was dead in the hole. She said he told her to check—to make sure. I haven't heard her say it since, but the staff at the nursing home have."

"Do you think she was talking about the priest hole? The fireplace was bricked up before Maisy went missing."

"Look, I don't know. I'm sorry for what I said earlier. I didn't want to say anything in front of Eric, but I'm certain I saw Maisy walking towards the tower." Dinescu and Summers stopped walking and faced Celia. "The tunnel is still there, and it runs beneath us. There's a cover that blocks off the steps, but it's hidden now. I can show you. Maisy may be under there."

"Why haven't you told anyone?"

"Because I think my mother killed her."

Chapter Twenty-Seven

Thursday morning was dry, bright, and a little on the cool side for spring. Emily Summers and Doctor Greenway met the team from Kent Police in the Cotisham School car park. They were a specialist search team, experts in searching tunnels and confined spaces. They'd just returned from Dover, searching the vast underground wartime maze of tunnels for a high-profile missing person case. This case wouldn't be so taxing for them. With the help of a structural engineer, they would first assess the safety of the tunnel that stretched from the tower to the school.

Summers led them to the tower, and they met Dinescu behind a new line of police crime scene tape. They had borrowed a couple of special constables as scene guards.

"You okay, sir?" Summers asked Dinescu. He was withdrawn and taciturn that morning. She wondered if he was having second thoughts. "I'm sure this is the right thing to do."

Dinescu returned an appreciative smile. "Thank you, Emily. I'm okay." But she could see he wasn't.

DI Clegg joined them from nowhere and almost collided with two SOCOs waiting in their white scene suits. Clegg was also convinced by Dinescu's reasoning that Maisy's body was hidden beneath them or within the priest hole. He stood with Summers, his hands buried deep in his jacket pockets.

Summers checked her mobile and cursed under her breath. She had to stop that habit. She had blocked Anthony's number after the dozen or more calls from him. He'd even knocked on the door of her mother's house. She pressed and held the off button on her phone and slipped it back into her pocket.

The small team of five search officers had driven up as close as they could with their van and equipment. They set up a table, and Dinescu brought out the plans for the tower. He unrolled them and clipped down the edges onto the table. He spent some time going over the search strategy with PS Jupp, who ran the team.

Summers knew Dinescu was going out on a limb with this, but she trusted his judgement. After the plan had been agreed, the search team moved equipment into the folly's right-hand column. The morning light had slipped through the open arch-way. Before them was a thick, tangled carpet of brambles and nettles. The petrol strimmer was started, filling the air with oily fumes. It made a racket as it began decimating the undergrowth, which they forked away into a pile. Within ten minutes, a shout went up. They had found something.

Dinescu and Summers went into the column and saw for themselves. Beneath the mush of vegetation, there was an iron grate. Despite its age, the ironwork was still intact, made from a lattice of bars. Being underneath the cover of the brick column had protected it to a certain extent from the elements. Two officers wedged crowbars against a stone lip and levered the grate until it lifted away.

"That was easier than expected," said PS Jupp. "We could have lifted it with our bare hands."

Below them was a large, rectangular hole in the ground. Descending into darkness were a set of steep stone steps.

Dinescu and Summers stepped back to let the engineer and the officers make their preparations. Ropes, lights, hard hats, and fluorescent jackets were passed around the search team, and then the engineer made the first tentative journey down the steps.

Summers turned and saw Dinescu standing behind her. His face was pale, and his eyes were fixed on the men and women as they began to make their way into the underground tunnel.

"Part of me wishes they don't find anything," she said.

Dinescu didn't answer, and when she turned again, he was gone. He had walked a short distance away and was pacing the ground. He had a phone in his hands, but it was for show. He wasn't using it. With everyone's attention on the hole before them, Summers slipped away to join him.

"Forgive me for being nosy, but you're not right, boss. Can I do anything?" Dinescu's mind was somewhere else. He was muttering to himself, and he was sweating. "Sir?"

He jerked his head around and looked at her wide-eyed. Then his focus returned. Emily felt her heart beating in her chest.

"Emily. It's you." His shoulders dropped, and he stared at her.

"Yes, sir. What's wrong?"

"I don't like tunnels."

"Tunnels?" She felt stupid just repeating what he'd said, but she was trying to process it. "Do you get claustrophobia, sir?"

"Yes. Sort of. Something happened a while ago, and I had to walk through a dark tunnel. I know it sounds stupid, but—"

"Not at all, boss!" She could see sweat droplets forming on his head. "I can go on my own, or we'll do it together. I don't mind."

Dinescu nodded with a gentle smile.

Someone was calling him from the folly. Dinescu and

Summers returned to find an officer ascending back to the surface.

"It's pretty sound down there," said PS Jupp. "Damp, but it's well built. The tunnel is in a dead straight line and goes beneath the house. We've gone in about thirty metres. The engineer says it looks safe to continue but will stay with us. It's only wide enough for single file, though." He looked up at Dinescu. "I think you'd find it a little low, sir, but it's passable."

"Thank you," said Dinescu.

Summers pressed her arm against his so he knew she was there.

PS Jupp entered the tunnel again after he had reattached a clip to a rope. Another officer was still down there, relaying communications along the tunnel to the surface.

"I didn't even know it was there," said Greenway. He had so far been silent, pressing up against the crime scene tape. "If she's down there, I'm not sure how we'll recover from this."

Celia Lambert appeared beside him. "They are sins of the past. I'm so sorry, Eric. I knew nothing about it until my mother..."

Eric didn't answer her but put his hand on her shoulder.

They didn't know how long the team had been in the tunnel, but they all reappeared and climbed back into the sunlight, their eyes squinting.

Dinescu stepped forward, frowning. "Was there nothing there?"

"Well, sir," said Jupp. "I'm a little confused. We walked the length of the tunnel. Nothing. Just black mould, a few dead rats, and lots of damp. The wind really pushes along down there. At the end of the tunnel are steps going up into the house. They take you to a blackened brick ledge. Below the ledge is a brick wall—that must be the fireplace. Just above the ledge is some kind of rough repair, about three-foot square. They're newer bricks and mortar, not hundreds of years old like the others surrounding it. A real bodge job, done in a hurry. We could poke something through if you want to have a look."

Jupp brought out a camera and showed Dinescu the images of the ledge and the newer brickwork.

"You're right. That lower brickwork is the library fireplace," said Dinescu. "Could we just knock a hole in that from the library and climb through from the other end?"

"We could, sir, but it would need some proper support with the right type of bracket. It could take out the entire fireplace and chimney breast. We also have to bear in mind the school is a listed building. If a body is behind that other wall, it's possible we would bring that area down and destroy the scene. It would be much safer to put in support brackets first and break out of the tunnel into the library rather than the other way around. It depends if you want to preserve a potential crime scene or not. It's a shame these photos don't show it too well."

"Take me down there and show me," said Dinescu.

"Do you want to look for yourself, sir?"

"Yes. Show me."

"And me," said Summers.

Dinescu had made Summers take a selfie of them both in hard hats and crime scene suits.

"Sophia will like this," he said. Thinking of his family was one of his coping strategies.

An officer went with Greenway back to the house to clear the library, with Celia Lambert following behind.

PS Jupp, carrying something like a pickaxe over his shoulder, took the first few steps. "You okay there, sir?" he said. "Be careful going down. The steps are slippery."

Another two officers squeezed past carrying two long brackets they'd taken from the van.

Dinescu felt a heavy weight on his chest and took some deep breaths. He was aware of Summers right behind him. Beneath him were the steps that led to his fear. He teetered on the edge, his feet fixed to the ground, unwilling to move.

Dinescu wondered what it was within him that was making him do this. He thought of Siobhan Maguire and her planned trips to the London Underground. But she had in mind a far more gentle therapy than this. He was walking into his worst nightmare. He could even smell the acrid smoke again and hear the screams and sobbing around him. Back then, he had a job to do. He had latched onto one young man and made him his focus. He was going to bring him to safety. That was his only purpose that morning. And he had a job to do right now, but he struggled to find a focus to start the journey.

Then Summers insisted she would go down first and pushed her way in front of him. After a few steps, she stopped and turned. She offered her hand to him.

"Come on, boss. I can't have you slipping and damaging yourself. I'm not taking this case on by myself." She smiled at him, but he knew what she was doing.

Dinescu took Summers's hand, which became his focus as they descended the steps, their feet guided by torchlight.

"The walls and floor are slimy, sir," said Jupp.

The officers had placed LED lights along the tunnel floor, which now looked more like a runway.

"Okay to continue, boss?" said Summers.

Dinescu hadn't moved since he'd reached the tunnel floor. He took a few steps forward, and his helmet scraped along the roof, forcing him to bend his neck.

The overall smell was of pungent mould and dampness. In front of him, he saw the back of Emily's hat and her slim curves as they moved in front of her. It brought him back to when Kieran first introduced him to Lisa. She was up a ladder, fixing some guttering. He remembered his embarrassment when she caught him admiring her curves.

"Not too bad, is it," said Summers.

Jupp thought she was talking to him. "Not at all. Nothing like some spaces we have to crawl into. Barely enough space to breathe. I've only been stuck twice, though."

Dinescu slowed down, putting distance between himself and the conversation in front of him. Each step forward was another step further from the entrance. The light was now only coming from the LED trail. He tried to focus on it, but the lights appeared to bounce with his heartbeat, which was now pounding in his ears. The sound of the screeching brakes was growing louder. Summers's voice faded, and she walked on ahead. Dinescu turned. Why was he doing this? He could see the light from the entrance. Shadows were moving in the tunnel. Something was coming towards him. The blackened shapes of burned bodies followed them, and behind them was billowing smoke. The way back was blocked. He had to run. He had to get out of there. This had been his nightmare for the last eighteen years. His knees buckled, and he couldn't find the air to breathe.

"Come on, sir. We're almost there. Just another twenty yards and up the steps."

Was it Lisa? Why was she here?

They had come to some rough steps with a low ceiling, and Dinescu had to bend over to climb them. He looked up, and he felt the sweat dripping into his eyes. "Lisa?"

"It's Emily, sir. We're nearly there. Look."

Dinescu looked at where she was pointing. There were three officers there with head torches, examining the brickwork. Dinescu took Summers's hand and steadied himself as he stood back up.

"*Suntem acolo?* Are we there?"

Summers pulled Dinescu towards her, and he gathered his strength again. When he reached the wall, he could now see the brickwork himself. It looked starkly different from the older brickwork. The mortar work was messy as if it had been done in haste. They were on a ledge, and Dinescu could see the curve of a fireplace below.

"What do you want to do, sir?" asked Jupp, unaware of Dinescu's panic attack.

"That's the priest hole behind that wall. We need to open it again. Can you break out into the library without disturbing it?"

"I think we can, sir. Breaking out wasn't the problem. Give us a moment to secure the brackets."

Dinescu and Summers stood back while two brackets, looking like hangman's gallows, were brought in and secured. When he was ready, Jupp aimed his pickaxe at the brickwork below the ledge, and after a few hefty knocks, sunlight and a plume of dust poured in from below them. They saw hands pulling out the fallen bricks. Then PS Jupp dropped down, and he looked up at them with a smile.

"Good news. The library's open."

Dinescu and Summers had removed their crime scene suits, now smeared with the black slime from the tunnel. Burgess and Kirby had joined them in the library as they watched the legs and feet of a SOCO. The chink-chink sound of steel on brick was all they could hear.

"She wasn't in the tunnel, then?" said Kirby.

"Obviously not, Chester," replied Summers with a smile.

"Digital forensics are in, Sarge."

"Thank God for that. Tell me."

"I can't. The email was sent to you and the boss. They called in to ask if you'd seen them."

"Okay. Thanks, Chester."

"And I've been to see Brady's son, Ricky. I've updated the database. There's a mysterious blonde woman involved."

"It's not her," said Summers. "Sarah's paid her a visit."

"Have I missed something, Sarge?"

Dinescu went and stood by one of the library windows. He pulled out his mobile and sent a message.

Kirby turned to look at Dinescu. "Is the boss okay? He looks a bit... peaky."

"Peaky," Summers laughed. "Yes, he's okay. It was a bit of a squash for him in there."

"I can imagine."

There was the sound of something dropping, and then everything went quiet.

"Oh, shit!" It was one of the search officers.

"What is it?" shouted Summers into the fireplace.

The SOCO ducked down, and her face looked pale. "We've found her. She's here."

Chapter Twenty-Eight

The New Moon wasn't that busy, and the men found a dark corner to sit in. Jason Hyde held three pints, pushed together in two hands, with only a slight spillage onto the floor.

"Yours is on the bar, Dan," said Hyde.

Daniel Curtis, who had already shown his proof of age, went off to collect his pint while Hyde, Faulkner, and Masterson took the first sips of theirs. The men were straight-faced. Not a hint of the usual banter between them. Their dark eyes watched Daniel get his drink.

Daniel returned, and the men exchanged a look between them.

"Dan, how's it going, mate?" said Archie. "Thought you'd appreciate a break from that place."

"Thanks for inviting me, chaps," he said, looking pleased to be included. "I've never been in here before. Is this your local?"

"It is," said Archie. He licked his lips.

"All that stuff going on at the school must be upsetting everyone," said Mac. "The young lads, especially. Must be good to get away from it all for a bit."

"Thanks, Mac. But we're okay," said Daniel. "It makes it interesting. Ethan's not too happy about something."

Archie glanced at Jason, who appeared to take it as a signal to begin.

"So, then, young Daniel," said Jason. "Got any more scintillating secrets for us?"

"Ah. I've seen and heard lots of things."

"Secreting yourself in dark places, no doubt."

Daniel smiled. "There are loads of them."

Jason put down his glass with a thud. "Come on then! Spill the beans."

"Well, that big, bald detective discovered a tunnel running under the tower. He's got the plans that Mr Brady had."

"Has he, now?" said Jason, looking at the others. "Clever detective."

Archie frowned, shaking his head.

"Yep." Daniel was enjoying being in the know. "It led him to the girl in the chimney. Bloody awful. Someone said she was Brady's sister."

"Brady's sister? Is that what the police were doing today?"

"Yep. They think it was, too. That's why the library's closed. Looks like Brady was right." Daniel sipped his lager, looking at their faces.

Mac leaned forward. "So, who do you think killed Brady, Dan?"

"God knows!" He tapped the side of his nose. "But I have a couple of suspects."

Mac was a few inches from his face. "Who?"

"Can't tell anyone yet. I'll go to the police first."

Mac sat back and laughed. "Yeah, right."

Archie glanced at Mac and took over. "Mac told us you saw a woman going into Brady's office the day he was killed."

Daniel blinked and frowned. His confusion had brought on his twitch. "How did you know about that?"

"He overheard Mr Roberts telling *everyone* in the staffroom. Roberts said you'd told him."

"That was meant to be a secret."

"Roberts is a teacher, Dan!" said Archie. His voice was lower, darker, and cutting. "He won't keep a secret like that." Archie was drumming his fingers hard against the table. "Who did you see in Brady's office? Did you get a good look at her?"

Daniel slumped back. He was panicked by Archie's demeanour. He didn't look like a mate anymore. Daniel swallowed. "I can't say. I was watching from inside the cavity. They didn't know I was there."

"One of your many spy holes?" said Jason.

"Yes. It was a blonde woman. I know who she was, but —"

Archie cut in again. "Did you tell Roberts who she was?"

"No."

"Maybe they knew you were watching," said Mac.

"No. They couldn't see me, and I was really quiet. She said she had a message from—"

"Shut it, Dan!" hissed Archie, looking around him. "We're not interested, you dumb arse."

Daniel looked at the intense faces surrounding him. "Did I do something wrong?" Archie's face was purple, and he glared at him. "What?" Daniel's eyes widened. "What has she got to do with you?"

"Shut the fuck up, Dan!" Archie turned his face towards the bar and shook his head. "Why did you tell everyone for?"

"But I only told Roberts. Why is it important?"

"And he blabbed to everyone else. You're an idiot. Just like that fuckwit of a friend of yours, Ethan. You've crossed the line, Dan."

"I didn't know he'd tell everyone." Daniel's head twitched. "You don't know her. So, why are you guys so bothered?"

"Let me tell you something, and I want you to listen *very* carefully. Are you listening?"

"Yes, Archie." Daniel's voice trembled.

"You didn't see *any* woman with Brady. If anyone asks you about it, you tell them Roberts was lying. He made it up. Got it!"

"But what if the police ask me?"

Archie sat forward and gripped Daniel's shoulder until it hurt. "If you tell anyone, and I mean *anyone*, then the school will become an extremely dangerous place for you. Accidents happen, Dan, any time of day or night. You saw no one. Do you hear? No one! You know nothing about it. Do we understand each other, boy?"

Daniel had tears in his eyes. He looked in desperation towards the bar, but no one was looking his way.

"You just need to tell us you're going to do *exactly* as you're told," said Mac. "Roberts made it up. You never saw no one."

"I didn't see anyone," Daniel's voice cracked.

"Say that again, dumb arse," said Archie, spitting in Daniel's face. "I didn't hear you."

"I didn't see anyone!"

"Good lad," said Archie, and he let Daniel go. "Just remember. We *will* know if you tell anyone. You don't want that Grey Friar knocking on your door at night, do you?"

"And if he does come knocking, young Daniel," said Mac, leaning forward into Daniel's face, "you'll be dead by the morning. Remember that."

Chapter Twenty-Nine

The Major Crimes office was busy again. Detective Chief Superintendent Faraday was with them, along with DI Clegg. Faraday and Clegg were with Dinescu in his office, and the door was closed.

"There's going to be a press release," said Faraday, who looked too young to be Dinescu's manager. "It's going to hit the news this evening. Inevitably, people will point the finger at the previous SIO in Maisy's case, and there will be questions. The main one will be, why the fuck didn't they look back up the chimney? That's where the babies were." Faraday gave an accusing look at Clegg, but it didn't faze him.

"Don't look at me, sir." He laughed. "I were just a young'un when Maisy Brady disappeared."

Dinescu didn't understand most of that, but he got the sentiment. He struggled a little with Yorkshire accents.

"That was a long time ago, sir," Dinescu said to Faraday. "DI Clegg's help has been invaluable. Finding Maisy has brought to an end thirty-six years of speculation as to her whereabouts."

"You said she was mummified?" said Faraday.

"Yes, sir. Maisy Brady was found in the priest hole. Her hands had been bound, and she was gagged. There's been no formal identification, but she'd been wearing a white blouse and a grey school skirt with her name sewn into them. She was gagged with her underwear. It's highly likely she was sexually assaulted. The priest hole was then bricked over, and she was effectively entombed."

"What kind of monster...?"

"One I'm going to catch, sir."

"Glad to hear it, Ben. You're the SIO, and the buck stops with you."

Faraday stood to leave, and Dinescu stood with him. Faraday gave vague reassurances that the budget was now available for more resources if needed. The press interest in the case had seen to that. As soon as Faraday's foot was out of the door, Summers entered.

"Sir, we have the digital forensics to review—Brady's computer."

Clegg took that as his cue to leave. "She keeps you on your feet, sir."

"We are lucky to have her, Jonathan."

After DI Clegg left the office, Dinescu pulled the core team together in front of the whiteboard. He had brought in a box of something for them, which he placed in the middle of Summers's desk.

"Doughnuts with sprinkles!" said Taylor. "Thanks, boss."

The team dived into the box, and it didn't take long for them all to be taken.

"Thank you for all your efforts with this," said Dinescu. "We're on the right track now, but we have a little further to go."

Summers swallowed the last mouthful of her pink doughnut

and wiped her sticky fingers on the antiseptic wipes Taylor had found in the office.

"Go ahead, Emily," said Dinescu.

"So, we have got the results back from Brady's laptop, and everyone's come back after delving deeper into his Facebook friends. I'll start with that first, boss. We had forty-eight friends on his list. The vast majority were teachers he'd met at various conferences, a few Thai women in bikinis, and a couple of cousins in Perth, Australia. That left us with six contacts. All of them are involved with the school in some way. We have Mackenzie Masterson, Archie Faulkner, Jason Hyde, Celia Lambert, Olivia Grainger, and her daughter, Susan. She helps her mother at the school from time to time. We know about Celia and Olivia. Archie does occasional work in the school for Cameron, and Jason is Cameron's father. I'm unsure what the connection is with Mackenzie Masterson."

"Masterson does the electrics at the school," said Taylor.

"Thanks, Ross," said Summers. "So, there is a connection there, too. Everyone, except Celia and Susan Grainger, lives in Cotisham village. I spoke to the deputy headmaster this afternoon. He let slip that Olivia Grainger and Archie Faulkner have been living together for years, but Grainger keeps that hush-hush from the students."

"I didn't know Grainger and Faulkner were partners," said Burgess. "You'd never know."

Summers pulled out a printed copy of the email she had received earlier in the day. "Computer forensics hasn't turned up anything of interest in Brady's Internet search history. Only what we know already. He's also searched for his sister, presumably trying to find her online."

"It's all disappointing," said Dinescu. "I was hoping for another lead."

"But I think we do have another lead, boss," said Summers, smiling.

"We have his emails. He did most of his communicating via email rather than messaging apps. Here's an email he wrote to Celia." Summers passed around a sheet of paper.

Monday, 17 April 2023 08:48

Celia,

I know why you won't speak to me. Your mother, Olivia, and Archie know something. There's Mac and Jason, too. Do you want Maisy's blood on your hands? I can't believe you won't help me. Well, I'll give you until Friday, then I'm going to the police. They'll be interested in the library, don't you think?

CB.

"It was sent the day he was murdered," said Dinescu. "Celia said nothing about this. Why do you think he is including Olivia and Archie?" Dinescu looked again over the list of pupils who were at Cotisham in 1987. "Archie Faulkner wasn't even at the school. There's a Simon Faulkner-Williams on the list, but no Archie Faulkner. And Olivia was only seven."

"It does sound like Brady had gathered together his suspects," said Burgess. "David Roberts isn't on his list. He was at the school."

"He didn't start there until later," said Dinescu. "Once the trouble had blown over."

"Wasn't Faulkner-Williams the name of the headmaster?" asked Summers.

"Yes," said Burgess. "Gerald Faulkner-Williams."

"This email *is* a new lead for us," said Dinescu. "There's a motive there, even if it's a vague one."

"A pretty good lead, too," said Burgess.

Summers got up and made a list of names on the whiteboard: Mac Masterson, Jason Hyde, Archie Faulkner.

Dinescu studied the list. "We need someone to talk to Jason Hyde and another to talk to Mackenzie Masterson. Perhaps at the same time, so one doesn't call the other. We need to know what they knew about Maisy. Then we need someone to talk to Archie Faulkner. What does he know about Maisy? Was he in contact with anyone at the school back then? Why is he on Brady's list?"

"Okay, boss," said Summers. "Chester, if you go after Mackenzie Masterson, Ross, you do Jason Hyde. I'll talk to Archie Faulkner."

"Yes, Sarge," said Taylor and Kirby together.

"Chester, the boss, and I have read about your meeting with Ricky Brady. I'm not sure what the significance of his account is yet. Sarah, look at the description of Ricky Brady's blonde woman. See if it matches Candice Lee. It might not be relevant, but it's worth a check."

"Yes, Sarge."

Summers look at her watch and sighed. "It will have to be tomorrow. Today's been a busy day. We'll have fresh minds in the morning."

Dinescu caught up with Summers as she was putting on her coat. "I know this is late notice, Emily, but I've spoken to Lisa, and we were wondering if you were doing anything for dinner tonight?"

"Dinner?" Emily looked a little stunned.

"Yes. Unless you already have plans?"

"I have no plans at all. My mother's out, and I was going to order a pizza."

"Well, if you'd like to?"

"Thanks, boss. That will be brilliant! What time?"

"Now?"

Chapter Thirty

Lisa was excited when Beniamin messaged her that Emily had accepted their offer for dinner. When he called her at work about how Emily had helped him in the tunnel, Lisa had burst into tears on the phone. Beniamin had chosen to face his worst nightmare, and Lisa couldn't feel anything other than relief that Beniamin was not alone down there. That was what he was like. He'd always stand up to fear and challenge any threat to him or his family. Emily had helped him, and she couldn't have known. He had only told a few people about his past.

When she first met Beniamin, he wouldn't talk about what he had faced that morning in London. Over the years, Lisa had pieced together Beniamin's account of that day, divulged to her in small, disjointed scenes, one paragraph at a time. She had encouraged him to write his thoughts, emotions, and memories into a private journal to help him express to himself the horror he saw and felt. She had never read his journal, and he trusted she wouldn't. She knew it had helped him come to terms with his post-traumatic episodes when they came. But now she was wondering what the journey into the tunnel at Cotisham would have done to him.

The doorbell rang when Lisa was in her bedroom. Sophia called out from the hallway that she was on her way. Lisa checked her face in the mirror and heard Sophia using her frame. She had got up some speed to get to the door and welcome her much-beloved uncle, Kieran, with Bella. Lisa heard the joy in Sophia's voice as she let Kieran in and even helped him hang up his coat.

"Hi, little brother!" shouted Lisa from the landing. "Just coming."

Kieran made his way in with Bella, who was wagging her tail with excitement.

"Are we getting a takeaway? I don't smell food."

"Ben's cooking tonight," said Lisa as she met Kieran. "He's promised not to poison us. He's bringing a girl with him."

Kieran laughed. "Is this some kind of new, kinky arrangement between you?"

"No, Kieran. We're not into threesomes."

Lisa went to the kitchen, poured her brother a small glass of white wine, and handed it to him.

"Is she single?"

"I don't know. Ask her yourself."

Kieran's face lit up. "How do I look?"

"As handsome as ever."

"Do you think she'll go for a good-looking blind guy?"

"She won't be able to keep her hands off you."

"I'm looking forward to it. Maybe she'd give me and Bella a lift home. I hope she likes dogs."

"What's a threesome?" asked Sophia when she entered the kitchen.

Kieran laughed. "It's when three—"

"No, thank you, Kieran!" said Lisa, putting her hand over his mouth.

Lisa saw the flash of car headlights—two cars.

"They're here," said Lisa. She ran her fingers through her red hair and looked again at her reflection in the oven door. "How do I look, Sophia?"

"Stunning, Mum—always stunning."

Lisa went to the door to welcome them. Emily was greeted like a long-lost friend and looked slightly embarrassed by her reception.

"Gosh, you're so pretty!" said Sophia. "Follow me. Come and meet my Uncle Kieran and Bella."

Emily blushed and turned to Beniamin. Something in that look struck Lisa, and it made her stomach turn.

"Would you like a drink of anything?" said Lisa. "Wine, fruit juice?"

"I have to drive. Juice would be great."

Lisa watched Emily as she walked into the living room. She had let her long, blonde hair loose and wore slim-fitting trousers and a white blouse. Lisa could hear introductions and laughter. She thought there was something strange about seeing Emily in her home—someone Beniamin had spoken about several times. She was indeed pretty, and Beniamin had to work with her every day. There must have been something on Lisa's face that her husband saw. The tilt of the head and the way Lisa raised her hand to her neck. Beniamin wrapped himself around her like a huge cloak, like unbreakable armour, and squeezed her so tightly the air left her lungs.

"Every day, I look at you," he said quietly as she placed her head on his shoulder, "and I know why I lived through what I did. It was for you. You are my everything, Lisa." And, as if he had read her mind, "My love and desire are only ever for you."

He kissed her hair. She couldn't help but take in his scent—it was only his. No one else's.

"Come on, you soppy date," she said, smacking his bottom. "You're cooking, remember?"

Lisa joined Emily, Sophia, and Kieran in the living room. Emily had already enthralled Kieran, and he was enjoying her attention as she listened to him talk about his work for a veterans' charity after he was discharged from the army. Beniamin kept the door open so he could heckle Kieran from the kitchen. Lisa closed it again, telling him to get on with the cooking, but that wasn't the only reason.

"Ben spoke to me and said that you went into that tunnel today."

"Yes," said Emily. "It wasn't very pleasant, but we found what we were looking for—sadly."

"Thank you for what you did for him today."

Emily looked at her half-empty glass of juice. "I don't like spiders. Can't bear them. We all have different phobias."

"I doubt he's told you the story behind his phobia. He wouldn't mind me telling you, but he wouldn't say it himself."

"No. I wasn't aware there was one."

"The 7th of July, 2005."

"The London bombings? Was he caught up in that?"

"The crazy thing is, we wouldn't all be here if he wasn't."

Emily frowned and looked at Kieran. His head was face down, and he was stroking his dog.

"Was he on duty?" asked Emily.

"No. He was on his way to meet another PC for breakfast. Jack, I think his name was. Ben hadn't been in the job for long. He had a full head of hair then, too!"

"Really!"

Lisa laughed. "It's hard to imagine Ben with hair. His friend Jack was considering leaving the Met, and Ben wanted to convince him otherwise. He'd just caught the train from Liverpool Street station. Kieran and Ben tell this better than me."

"Ah, yes," said Kieran. "Well, I wasn't always as handsome as I am now, either."

"Not possible," said Emily.

"Ben, she's flirting with me!" he called out.

Beniamin came in with a tea towel over his shoulder.

"Is she?" he said. "It's all in your mind, Kieran."

"We were about to recount the story, Ben," said Lisa.

He nodded in resignation. "Where have you got to?"

"The train leaving Liverpool Street," said Emily.

"Yes..." Beniamin sat on the arm of Lisa's chair and put his hand on her shoulder. "I was going to see my friend, Jack. He was a probationer, nine months behind me. I took that train at that time, and the rest is history. We were barely a hundred yards from Liverpool Street station, and the bomb went off in the carriage next to ours."

"No!" Emily put her hands over her mouth. "You and your friend?"

"No, just me and..."

"Me," said Kieran.

Lisa could see the penny drop on Emily's face.

"We were hit by broken glass. Everything was on fire—blood and body parts everywhere. When I came around, my hair, chest, and arms were on fire. I somehow managed to put it out. I had visions of being burned to death—rather like our meal tonight. Kieran was lying between two seats, glass embedded all over his face—blood everywhere. It was everything I could do to stop him from rubbing his eyes."

"He nearly smothered me to death instead," Kieran interjected. "He was shouting at me, holding my arms down. I was swearing at him."

"The blast deafened me," said Beniamin. "The fire was spreading, so I had to pick him up and drag him out. Fortunately, he wasn't the fat lump he is now."

"Hey, you can talk!"

"But Kieran was saving me, too. He was my focus. If I could

save him, then I would save myself, too. The next few minutes were a blur. I pulled him out of the carriage and saw things I wish I hadn't. Then we got back to the station."

"And then," said Kieran, "he's made me pay for it ever since by marrying my sister!"

"Is that how you met Lisa?" said Emily.

"Yes. And she saved me, too."

The room went silent, and Lisa noticed Emily's eyes tearing. Sophia moved closer to her and held her hand, and Emily squeezed back.

Lisa picked up her glass. "Ben used to come and visit Kieran afterwards to see how he was doing. That's how we met. I owed him Kieran's life. As did Mum and Dad."

"But then we all realised," said Kieran, "he wasn't interested in how I was at all. It was all for show. He just wanted a piece of my sister."

"Uncle Kieran!" laughed Sophia.

"After meeting Lisa," said Beniamin, "all my hair fell out. So, it was her fault."

Lisa slapped his shoulder.

"What's that awful smell?" said Sophia as she screwed up her nose.

"Dinner," said Beniamin. "Takeaway, anyone?"

"Is she okay in the back?" said Kieran, turning towards his dog on the back seat of Emily's car.

"Sure. She'll probably find some old treats—left-over McDonalds."

Kieran laughed. "It doesn't smell that bad in here if that's any consolation."

Kieran buckled his seatbelt, and Bella pushed her head through the gap in the seats.

"Thanks for taking me home."

"No worries. It's only an hour out of my way."

"What!"

"Joking!" Emily laughed. "Five minutes, max."

"Phew. You had me worried. It's been great to meet you tonight. Just to let you know, I won't be inviting you in for coffee."

It then struck Emily that she hadn't laughed so much for a very long time. She'd had a permanent grin since the time the curry arrived.

Emily turned right and onto the road from Bracksham towards Chichester. "Where's your office, Kieran?"

"Around the corner from my home. There are three of us who work there. I'm fortunate, and it's fulfilling work. Do you think you could be anything other than a detective?"

"Oh, I don't know. When I was young, I liked the idea of running a guest house by the sea."

"When you were young? That's the sort of thing older people aspire to. I don't even know how old you are."

"What do you think?"

"Forty, forty-five?"

"Bloody cheek!"

Kieran laughed. "I'll ask Bella." He pretended to have a secret conversation with his dog.

"Bella says you're thirty-two, and she thinks your birthday is in May."

Emily shook her head. "Did my boss tell you? He must have."

"No, it was Bella. She said you have a lovely voice, are kind and... love cheese."

"I can't believe he told you I like cheese!"

"That's all I know. Apart from that, you're incredibly ugly and have blotchy red skin. Am I close?"

"I could make you walk."

"You wouldn't make a poor blind man and his dog walk home on their own."

"Wouldn't I?"

"What do you think of Ben?"

"I can't call him that." She tried to imagine it. "It just doesn't feel right. He's two ranks above me. I like working for him. You know where you stand. He's always pretty even-tempered, and he puts his team first."

"You mean he's a great manager."

"Yes, exactly."

"He said a lot of good things about you, too."

Emily smiled. "I really love the way he is with Lisa."

"They're soulmates—that's why."

After one wrong turn, Emily found Kieran's house on the corner of a park and some allotments. She helped him out of the car, and Bella found her way to him.

"Thanks so much, Kieran. I can't tell you how much you've cheered me up." She leaned forward without thinking and kissed him on the cheek.

"You'll have to marry me now, Emily," said Kieran. "I don't usually kiss on the first date."

"I didn't realise we were on a date."

"Ah, well, it was a secret date that only you didn't know about. The next one you will know about."

"The next one?"

"Yes. The one this Saturday, at 7:30, KFC. Don't tell me you were too drunk to remember?"

"Oh, yes! I remember. Of course, how could I forget? I'm picking you up, aren't I?"

"So you do remember! You almost fainted when I offered to drive. If KFC is full, then I'll book somewhere else."

"And I'll cancel my evening of music at the theatre. My friend won't mind."

"Ah, whoops! Sorry. Didn't think you may have had plans."

Emily laughed. "Looks like they've changed." Another peck on the cheek. "See you Saturday."

Chapter Thirty-One

It was after nine in the evening when Greenway arrived back at the school. He was in jeans and wore a baggy denim jacket over a T-shirt. He looked out of place, and his clothes made him even more scrawny than usual. His face was dark as he entered his office. Andrew Winston and Olivia Grainger were waiting for him.

"What's this all about, Andrew?" he snapped. "I was ready for bed when you called."

"It was only 8:30, Eric! Ethan Bishop is missing."

"Can't you handle it? Why do you need me here?"

"He's missing! Why shouldn't I call you? It's in our safeguarding policy, for God's sake!"

"You know what Ethan's like. He just wants to cause trouble. He knows how hard things are at the moment."

"Eric. He was upset. We have a duty of—"

"He's been nothing but bad news to this school, Andrew. Him, Harry, and that Daniel—creeping around everywhere. Leah's handed her notice in, and there's a rumour bloody Ethan had a hand in that, too. I refuse to believe it."

"Eric, this is not the time. For now, we must focus on finding him. If anything should happen to him, then it would fall on your head. And ours."

Eric dropped into his chair and scowled. "I've had enough of all of this. That bloody Brady. If it wasn't for him—"

"Dying?" said Winston. He shook his head. "I find your reaction outrageous, if I'm honest, Eric. Totally outrageous. Well, I'm going to do something, even if you're not. I'm calling the police."

"No, you're not. He's probably up the tower or something. Go and look up there."

"I've looked! Of course, I've looked for him. No. I'm calling the police."

"Andrew, have you any idea how close we are to ruin? Have you? Our reserves have halved since Covid. This series of unfortunate incidents has done nothing to help us. I've spoken to six parents. Six, Andrew! Threatening to withdraw their boys."

"Maybe it would be better for them if they did!" Winston's anger had boiled over now, and he was shaking.

"I'm not stopping you if you want to leave!"

"Eric, Andrew!" said Grainger. "Both of you, just calm down. The toerag is hiding somewhere. You're both going to say something you'll regret in the morning. Let the lad sweat it out. He'll be in for breakfast first thing."

Andrew Winston went to the door. "I will follow our policies and procedures, even if you don't. I'm calling the police."

Winston left the office, slamming the door behind him.

The room was silent, with Greenway holding his head in his hands. "Bloody Brady caused all of this," he muttered. "We were on our way up again."

His phone rang, and Grainger saw Celia's name on the screen before he cancelled the call.

"Maybe all this is Brady's fault," said Grainger, "but it will all come out in the wash. The police will work out that

Cameron killed him in a jealous rage, and it will all be over. Archie can take over Cameron's job at the drop of a hat. You'll find a new head of maths, and the troublesome boys will have gone for good in the summer. You need to keep your cool, Eric."

"That bloody Romanian detective. Now that he's found Maisy Brady, what else will he be looking for?"

"That was something that happened a long time ago, Eric. They won't find anything that leads them to the school as it is now."

"It's just more bad news to tell the parents."

"If you play it right, then it will be a subject of interest to the parents. They know it's got nothing to do with you! That was before Cotisham was a boy's school."

Eric's lips broke into a thin smile. "You're right, Olivia. Thank you. We need to stay calm. And then we can replace Winston, too."

"Exactly."

∽

Beniamin sat on the edge of the bed, smiling to himself, as Lisa removed her makeup. She babbled on about how lovely Emily was. He loved it when Lisa was excited by something. He would listen to her for hours as she spoke about her love for Virginia Woolf, A. S. Byatt, and Oscar Wilde. Most of it he struggled with, but he understood her passion.

Lisa climbed into bed and leaned her head on his shoulder.

"I'm sorry for my wobble earlier. She's just so pretty and... young."

"But you are stunning and all mine."

Lisa kissed him on the cheek, pulled up the covers and turned out her light. Just as Beniamin was about to do the same, his work mobile rang.

Lisa groaned. "Don't they know what time it is?"

"Sorry, my love. I have to take this. They wouldn't call unless it was important."

Lisa buried her head under her pillow.

"DCI Dinescu."

"Many apologies, sir, for waking you. But the duty inspector said you should be made aware."

"It's okay. I wasn't asleep." Dinescu checked his watch. It was 11:30.

"This is Sergeant Baker, Chichester Response. A lad from Cotisham School has gone missing this evening—Ethan Bishop. He was interviewed by your team just over twenty-four hours ago."

"When was he last seen?"

"Around 16:00 hours, by another student leaving his room in the dormitory. He said Bishop was angry and scared, saying that someone was trying to kill him—something about a friar. Makes no sense to me. He didn't leave a note or anything. I just wanted to make you aware. He's not a named suspect at all?"

"No, but he's known to our investigation. Who saw him leaving?"

"A roommate called Daniel Curtis. The deputy head called the police."

"Not the matron?"

"No, sir."

"There's nothing I can add at the moment. I'm sure the inspector has it in hand. You have the helicopter looking for him?"

"Yes, NPAS has been called out. Hopefully, he hasn't gone far."

"Does the inspector need me to come in?"

"No, sir, it was just to update you in case you felt you wanted to."

"Okay. I've got a postmortem to attend first thing, so any urgent updates to DS Summers, please. Did Daniel get a direction of travel for Ethan?"

"He saw him walk out of the main drive."

At the end of the call, Dinescu turned off his light and cuddled into Lisa. He thought of the Grey Friar. Those stories, like evil *Muma Pădurii*, were about controlling others through fear. Had someone threatened Ethan? Was someone trying to control him?

First thing on Friday morning, Summers and Burgess drove out to Leah Turnbull's home, a cottage in the village of Singleton. Dinescu, who had gone to Maisy Brady's postmortem, asked for updates when they had them.

Summers had caught Burgess glancing at her several times during the drive. Summers had a fixed grin as she thought about the previous evening. Kieran's sense of humour had floored her. He was fun to be with. Summers wondered why she had put up with being so miserable over the last few years. And Kieran was bloody cheeky, too—she liked that. He'd even asked her on a date without her even knowing it. She was wondering how Kieran, being blind, would work when Burgess spoke to her.

"We're here, Sarge."

They had come to a cottage down a narrow, winding road. Burgess found a lay-by to park the car in, and they walked fifty yards to Leah's home.

The cottage was made from brick and flint, with a low red roof. The small, square windows were overgrown with stunning lilac wisteria. The detectives admired the colour while they waited for Leah to open the door.

Summers had seen Leah Turnbull through the gap in her

bedroom curtains. She was hesitating as if deciding what to do. When she came down, she was wrapped in a long silk dressing gown and coughing at the door. Leah suggested that she could have Covid and wouldn't let them inside.

"Ethan's not here. Why would he be?"

"He's missing, Leah," said Burgess, "and he was in a bad state. Are you on your own?"

"Yes. Just me and my cat." On cue, a large ginger tom appeared, wrapping itself around Leah's legs.

Burgess smiled. "We're going to need to check, Leah. You two were in a relationship. Maybe you still are?"

"I don't have to let you in."

Summers felt in her gut that Ethan was there. As Burgess continued with her soft diplomacy, Summers had a brief conversation with Dinescu over the phone.

Summers stepped forward. "Leah, let me be straight with you. I think you're lying to us. Ethan is here. He's a high-risk missing person. We have to locate him and check on his welfare. I don't care what you've both been doing. He's over eighteen, and you're not breaking the law. What your boss would say is something altogether different. We've already had that conversation. Ethan told a friend that he thought someone was trying to kill him. We have to talk to him."

Leah stared at them for a moment and then swore under her breath. "Come in."

She led Summers and Burgess into a small front room with low ceilings and uneven walls. A few moments later, they heard slow footsteps coming down the stairs. Ethan Bishop appeared, wearing a T-shirt, jeans, and no socks.

"Ethan," said Burgess. "We meet again."

Ethan nodded and looked at Leah.

"We need to check on your welfare," said Summers. "Last

night, you walked out of the school after saying someone was trying to kill you."

"Bloody Dan grassed me up."

"No! I'd say he was looking out for you. He was worried, and the school called the police. Who's trying to kill you? I assume it isn't the Grey Friar."

"What? No." He sounded like that petulant teenager again. What did Leah see in him? Summers didn't like teenagers on the best of days.

"We don't have all day. Get on with it."

"Someone with a hood. I saw him Monday night—he was coming out of Cameron's workshop. He chased after me when he realised I'd seen him. It was dark, but I saw he had a hoodie. Then last night, I was walking to my room up the stairs, and this bloke in a hood came out of the darkness and grabbed me. He held me over the bannister rail. I thought he was going to push me off. He was in the shadows. Honest to God, I thought it was the friar for a moment. I know that sounds stupid, but he looked like him. He said something to me. He told me not to tell anyone I'd seen him on Monday, or... he'd kill me."

"So, you came straight here?"

"No, he didn't," said Leah. "He was walking to Midhurst in the dark. He called me to talk things through with me. So, I picked him up."

"Do you think Cameron would do that to you, Ethan?"

He shrugged.

"I think it's unlikely," said Leah. "He would have just thumped him. That's his go-to response nowadays."

"It didn't sound like Cam. It was strange, like someone was trying to hide their voice. But he had the same top as him. I think he was trying to make me think it was him. He was shorter and bigger than Cam."

"You should have called the police. We've had helicopters and all sorts searching for you. Cost us thousands."

"Sorry, but I didn't ask you to."

"We'll have to tell the school that we've found you. As you're an adult, I don't have to tell them where, but I think it would be better for you both if we took you back now, Ethan. It would look better for Leah."

Ethan shook his head. "No. But thanks. My parents are coming to get me. They're taking me home with them. I won't be back."

"Your parents!" said Summers.

"Yes. They're getting my stuff from the school and meeting me at the police station. They want to make a complaint about me being interviewed. A waste of time if you ask me. So Leah was going to take me, but..."

"Okay. We'll give you a lift."

Ethan got into the police car without saying goodbye to Leah. He couldn't look at her as they drove away. Summers glanced back and saw his bright blue eyes and the tears running down his cheeks. Leah had said nothing more but went inside and closed the door.

Burgess and Summers dropped off Ethan at the police station, where his parents met him. They looked relieved to see him.

"That complaint won't go anywhere," said Summers as they watched Ethan and his parents from a distance. "I'll update the Response inspector and complete the misper report. Then we can grab a coffee and go back to the school. We need to talk to Celia and Olivia."

Chapter Thirty-Two

After a quick phone update from Summers, Dinescu made his way to the mortuary, where Dufour had already started on Maisy Brady's postmortem. The photographer had already begun recording the evidence.

Dinescu watched them in their protective suits as they examined the remains of Maisy's body. A lab technician passed him a coverall in a cellophane bag.

"Good morning, Chief Inspector. So, the mummified body is of a young woman," said Doctor Dufour, "early teens and post-pubescent. Long bones aren't fully ossified, including the femur, tibia, fibula, et cetera. She was gagged with her own underpants, and her hands were bound by her bra. Brutal. I assume you already know about the name tags on her clothes?"

"Yes," answered Dinescu, staring at the caramel-skinned corpse lying shrivelled on the table. She was about the same age as Sophia. He shuddered.

There was a camera flash as the photographer snapped a close-up of her skull. When she backed away, Dufour put his face close to the head. "Her skull was fractured, having been hit three times with a blunt object, causing bone fragments to lacerate her brain, leading to catastrophic haemorrhaging. Within the priest hole, we recovered half of a sixteenth-century brick with matted hair stuck to it. The collar of the blouse is covered in blood, all pointing to the kind of trauma we're talking about."

"So, it's likely a sexual motive?"

"Almost definitely, Chief Inspector." Dufour stood up straight, and his shoulders slumped forward. "We've found staining on her skirt, most likely semen. Under her fingernails are remnants of dirt, skin, and dried blood, probably the attacker's. And we found this little gem..."

Dufour walked over to a stainless steel trolley and brought Dinescu a tube containing a small yellowish-grey peg.

"A tooth?"

"Yes. It's not the girls. Most likely her attacker's. Looks like she tried to defend herself. One way or another, we'll get the DNA profile of a shitbag. Sorry—unprofessional of me."

"No, it's okay. What about confirming her identification?"

"DNA testing of her teeth and bones will hopefully confirm that. As long as it hasn't degraded too far—fingers crossed. We can use the familial match through what's left of her brother, and I understand her mother is still alive?"

"That's right, but she doesn't have mental capacity."

"This girl's been waiting a long time to see the light of day. I understand that her brother kept looking for her."

"He did. She wasn't forgotten by him, at least."

"Whoever sealed in her body did us a favour. It helped preserve the evidence. We owe it to Maisy to do everything we can to get her justice."

"How strong do you think her assailant was?" asked Dinescu.

"Good question. He bound her tightly, with her arms and legs flailing about. You know how difficult it is to arrest someone who doesn't want to be. She was in the dark and panicking, no doubt. I'd say the person who smashed her skull was strong, and I would wager he had help, too, unless he subdued her first. There are signs she was dragged, but I don't know how far."

Dinescu stood back and watched Maisy as she was covered once more and returned to a cold, dark place. He looked at Dufour as he removed his protective clothes and washed himself. His eyes gave away his thoughts as he considered Maisy's murder.

"Do you have children, Chief Inspector?" he said as he dried his hands.

"Yes, a teenage girl."

Dufour looked up. "Me too. We know, don't we. Still, we have to move on. I'll write up the report and email it to you and DS Summers."

Dinescu nodded. "I appreciate it."

When he left the mortuary and could see daylight again, Dinescu unlocked his personal mobile and opened the last message on WhatsApp from Sophia. It was a photograph of a bowl of chocolate ice cream. *Jealous?* she wrote. He typed in a message and then deleted it. She'd think it was too mushy. Instead, he sent her a heart and a shining sun.

"God, how many times have we done this journey!" said Summers.

Burgess was driving again. "So, are we speaking to Celia Lambert first, Sarge?"

"That's the plan, Sarah. Then it's Olivia Grainger."

"Greenway's complaining that he's getting calls from worried parents, threatening to pull their children out of the school."

"I'm not surprised." Summers turned as they drove past a thick bush of white-flowering hawthorn. "I love spring. Don't you?"

"Is everything okay, Sarge? You seem *different* today?"

"Do I? Yes, I'm great. All good. You?"

"Not as good as you, Sarge."

As they neared the entrance to the school, they saw a row of parked cars and vans—the media had descended. The iron gates at the entrance had two heavy PCs guarding them, looking stern with their arms folded. Summers knew the press had been told of this new find. Burgess tooted the horn to get the huddle of photographers out of the way. She showed her warrant card to the officers, and they swung open the gates, barking orders as a few reporters tried to squeeze through behind them.

Summers took a short call from Dinescu. He relayed to her the postmortem results, and she updated him about Ethan. She made a few brief notes as they spoke and ended the call.

"She was raped and had her skull smashed in," she told Burgess. "Then left in the dark for thirty-six years. Maisy would have been fifty now."

Burgess groaned. "Poor girl."

She parked in the car park, and they went inside the school, passing a team of SOCOs still working on the fireplace.

They found Celia Lambert with Greenway in his office. She was puffy-eyed and not in her usual office clothes. Greenway looked even more grey than ever. He offered them a seat in front of his desk.

"This is almost too much, DS Summers," he said. "I'm trying to distance us from this latest horror, but the parents and the press just see the two deaths. The fact that one of them is historic and before we were Cotisham School escapes them. Now, Daniel Curtis has asked to return home, too. Never thought I'd see the day. Do you know how much longer those people in white suits will be here?"

"I don't think you understand, Doctor Greenway," said Summers. "The two deaths are linked. They are brother and sister, and Brady believed Maisy was buried at the school. Things won't return to normal until we get to the bottom of it."

Greenway shook his head and glared at Celia.

"I knew nothing about this!" said Celia. "It wasn't until Mother started rambling that I had any idea. She told me it was all in a letter she had written to me and Olivia."

"A letter?" Summers glanced at Burgess. "This is news to us. What did this letter say?"

"I never got the chance to read it. Liv took it from her."

"Where's the letter now?"

"You'll have to ask Olivia."

"We can't interview your mother," said Summers, "but is there anyone else who would know? Did she confide in anyone?"

"Just Liv, but Liv wouldn't talk to me about Mother. We don't get on. She visits Mother every other week so that we don't clash. She's closer to her than I am."

"You were a pupil at this school when Maisy was here. What do you remember of her?"

"I've answered this already! Maisy was very pretty. She looked older than fourteen and often attracted the wrong sort of attention from the older boys—even from some of the teachers, Mother said."

"You were only nine, Celia. It would have been very astute for such a young person to know that. Is that something you remember, or was that from your mother or the older pupils?"

"Both, I imagine."

"Which teachers gave her the wrong sort of attention?"

"Grant Wilkie, the sports master. Horrible man. He didn't

teach the girls directly but would often come in and... *watch*. He's dead now."

"Do you know of any specific incidents?"

"Nothing specific, but it was constant. I don't think Maisy understood what was going on. Mother said she was a bimbo. An airhead. I do remember she was lovely and never unkind to anyone, but her looks got her what she wanted. She was gullible."

"But she was only fourteen," said Burgess with a frown. "Of course she was gullible."

"Yes, I know that very well."

"Do you remember Charles when he was at the school?"

"Only vaguely. Maisy loved him—always looking out for him."

"Who were the older boys that showed an interest?"

"They were the usual older boys—three of them always hung out together. Mac, Archie, and Jason. Idiots." Celia rolled her eyes. "*The Three Amigos*, they used to call themselves."

"Archie? We understand he's the builder who does work here sometimes—Olivia's partner. And is Mac short for Mackenzie?"

"Yes. They all stayed local after they finished school. Mac is our electrician. The most boring man on the planet, in my opinion."

"But I didn't think Archie was at the school then? We didn't find him on the records."

"He didn't call himself Archie Faulkner then," said Celia. "Not after all the trouble with his father. He was Simon Faulkner-Williams. Archie is his middle name—Archibald."

"He was the headmaster's son?"

"Yes. He's a right prick, too. Still is. Excuse my French. He thought he could get away with anything and was a very good-looking lad then. He still thinks he's the bee's knees."

"And he's still your sister's partner?"

"He is. That's why we don't speak."

Summers stood, signalling they had finished. "Thanks for coming in, Celia."

She noticed Celia touch Greenway's shoulder as she put on her jacket. He nodded in reply. She left the detectives with Greenway.

"It has been the worst week," said Greenway. "We have two deaths, and the boarders are virtually under house arrest. Then a student goes missing, parents are threatening to withdraw their children, and I've lost two members of staff, not including bloody Brady."

"Which staff?"

"Leah Turnbull has resigned. She won't say why, but I expect it's because I fired Cameron for gross misconduct. I'm most upset about Leah, of course. She's a fine teacher. She'll be leaving at the end of May."

Summers nodded. "Sorry to hear that, Eric. Perhaps we could talk to Olivia Grainger now?"

"Yes, of course." Greenway made a phone call to Grainger, and after some persuasion, she agreed to come. It was another ten minutes before she arrived in Greenway's office, scowling at the officers.

"I am very busy," she said, dropping down hard into the chair.

"We appreciate that, Mrs Grainger," said Summers. "As are we."

"We've recently discovered you lived in Cotisham School as a child when it was known as Aversham College."

"What of it?"

"And your mother was the matron."

"Again, what of it?"

"You were here when Maisy Brady was here, as was your

partner, Archie Faulkner. He was known then as Simon Faulkner-Williams."

"Was that a question?" Grainger folded her arms.

"Not yet, just stating the facts. You seem very defensive, Mrs Grainger. We are investigating Maisy's rape and murder and talking to those who were here at the time."

"What do you mean, rape?" Grainger's face dropped like lead. Her voice shook. "What are you talking about?"

Summers looked over at Burgess. She must have seen Grainger's reaction, too. "Maisy was bound and sexually assaulted. Likely raped." Summers looked down at her notes, giving Grainger time to digest that information. "How well did you know Maisy Brady?"

"I... she was much older than me." Tears filled Grainger's eyes, and she put her hand to her chest. "I barely knew her."

"But you knew Charles back then?"

"Yes. I don't remember much about him. I didn't mix that much with the older students. He was quiet—not many friends."

"Do you know who Maisy's friends were at the time?"

"No. Like I said. She was older."

"Did your mother talk to you about Maisy?"

The blood drained from her face. "No. And I wouldn't tell you even if she did. It was between me and her."

"Your sister said she wrote you both a letter, but you wouldn't tell her what it said. Where is that letter?"

"I destroyed it. I didn't want the police to get their hands on it. You'd get the wrong idea."

"The wrong idea? What did the letter say about Maisy?"

"Sarge?" said Burgess, looking concerned.

Summers nodded. These questions could lead somewhere.

"Okay, Mrs Grainger," said Summers as she sat forward. "I'm aware that some of these questions could implicate you or others, so we need to do this properly. We would like you to attend a voluntary interview at the police station, where you will be interviewed under caution with a solicitor present if you so wish. Are you willing to do that?"

"A voluntary interview? No. Unless you've got something to arrest me for, I'm not going anywhere. Now, if you'd excuse me, Eric, I have reports to write and calls to worried parents to make."

Grainger stood and made to leave, but Summers stood in front of her.

"In that case, Mrs Grainger, as I suspect you either destroyed or hid that letter to hinder this investigation, I'm arresting you on suspicion of perverting the course of justice. You do not have to say anything, but it may harm your defence if you do not mention, when questioned, something that you later rely on in court. Anything you do say may be given in evidence. Your arrest is necessary for prompt and effective investigation through interview and to preserve evidence."

Greenway stood. "Is this *really* necessary, DS Summers? I want to talk to the Chief Inspector."

Grainger fumbled in her pocket and brought out a mobile phone. "I need to make a call first." Burgess snatched the phone out of her hand before she could hit the call button. "Hey! What are you doing? I get the right to make a bloody phone call!"

"You're mistaken, Mrs Grainger," said Summers. "This isn't a US cop show. When you get to Custody, you may be given the right to let someone know you've been arrested."

Grainger pushed Burgess, making her stumble back and crash against the bookcase. She lurched forward to take back her phone, but Summers grabbed her hand and yanked it behind her back. She ratcheted her handcuffs and pushed them onto Grainger's wrists, stacked on top of each other.

"This is bloody ridiculous!" she shouted. "Take them off. I can't let the students see me like this."

"No. You assaulted DC Burgess, and I'm further arresting you for resisting arrest and assaulting an emergency worker."

"Olivia!" shouted Greenway. "Just go with them and calm down! It will be okay."

~

Summers was sitting in front of Dinescu in his office. She had just returned from Custody after booking in Grainger. Dinescu looked glad for the interruption. He'd spent much of the day in meetings and writing a report that was overdue. He would have much rather been out with his team.

Dinescu's palms were together, his fingertips touching his lips. He was weighing up what Summers had just told him. "That was a strange reaction from Grainger."

"She went white as a sheet when she heard that Maisy had been raped. I thought she was going to break down or throw up."

"And she told you she had destroyed her mother's letter to keep it from the police?"

"Yes, boss. She could be lying. She may not have destroyed it."

"Who was she trying to call when she pushed Sarah?"

"Sarah said she saw *Archie* on the phone screen."

"Has she asked for a solicitor?"

"She has and wanted Archie Faulkner informed she'd been arrested. However, I requested that right be withheld until I'd spoken to you."

"You think she was trying to tip off Archie?"

"Judging from her behaviour, I believe she was. Perhaps to destroy the letter if she hasn't already, or maybe to give him the heads-up. If Archie is Simon Faulkner-Williams, then we know he was at the school when Maisy went missing. I asked DI Clegg to check if he was ever interviewed or gave a statement at the time. Clegg told me Simon's father had sent him abroad to visit a relative—probably to avoid answering questions."

"That's convenient."

Dinescu dropped his hands, slapping the desk. Summers jumped. "Emily, do you remember that note from Brady? At the bottom..."

"Sir?"

Dinescu pulled up a photograph he'd taken at Brady's flat. He zoomed into one section of the image and handed the phone to Summers.

Nurse - Juliet Butterworth (alive) "A, J, M were black. A. needed <u>compress.</u>"

"That was the nurse fired for raising concerns," said Summers.

"A, J, M. Archie, Jason and Mackenzie? We need to find her and get a statement."

"Yes, boss."

"I'll put a note on Grainger's custody record. We don't want anyone to be made aware she's been arrested just yet. I'll also authorise a Section 18 search of her home to look for the letter."

"And I'll update Ross and Chester. They're about to talk to Jason Hyde and Mackenzie Masterson."

"Yes. Get them to keep it low-key. Perhaps Gareth and Sarah can search Grainger's home. Hopefully, Archie Faulkner will be there. If we can find her, you and I will speak to the nurse, Juliet Butterworth."

Chapter Thirty-Three

By the time they reached Old Bosham, the tide was rising, cutting off Shore Road to traffic. The sun had risen high above Bosham Harbour, reflecting starry diamonds off the surface of the water. Boats bobbed, and seagulls called to one another. In the past, Dinescu remembered seeing a few vehicles close to being flooded on that road, and he had seen photographs in the local pub of submerged cars being dragged out.

Summers found a space in the car park instead. She looked over at Dinescu and smiled to herself.

"I never saw the SIO leave the office before I came here. They were glued behind their desks."

"I know it's unusual," said Dinescu. "I like to get out sometimes. When I went for promotion, I knew I wouldn't be doing so much of the fun, sexy part of the job. I enjoyed arresting and interviewing the bad guys. Now, I'm a project manager."

"I don't think of it as sexy," said Summers, laughing. "I think you're a very good project manager."

"Thank you. I'll take that."

They walked out onto Bosham Lane and passed the craft shops and cafes. It was more than tempting for Dinescu to sit and have a coffee there. Maybe they would if this visit to Juliet Butterworth's house turned into nothing. While Dinescu was busy thinking about the coffee, Summers had paused to talk in the lane.

"When we were in Brady's flat," she said, "you said your foster parents brought you to England. It's only just struck me that you were one of the Romanian orphans. That must have been terrifying for you."

Dinescu pursed his lips and thought. "I was nine when I came to England. I think we all knew it was coming, but I was too young to understand why. Things had changed in the orphanage in that last year I was there. We were getting many visitors from abroad, and children disappeared without notice. I didn't know it then, but Ceaușescu had been executed the previous Christmas, and the whole country was opening up."

"What was it like after that?"

Dinescu looked at Summers and then focused on something beyond. "It was like someone had switched on the lights. One day, June and Martin appeared. My foster parents were being shown around—I remember it well. We were like puppy dogs, jumping all over them, wanting to be noticed first. They spoke to me through an interpreter. All I knew then was that they were taking me to a new life."

"I had no idea, sir. You've been through more than most people in their lifetime."

"But look what I have now, Emily. I am very content."

They continued walking. Dinescu had noticed a change in Summers. Perhaps it was the spring in her step or a brighter disposition.

"Kieran said he enjoyed your company last night," he said, watching for her reaction.

"Did he? I haven't mentioned it because..."

"We're working?"

"Yes, boss. I wasn't sure if it was appropriate."

"That's okay... Well?"

"I had a brilliant time!" she gushed, looking around with a grin. "Your family is so lovely. Lisa, Sophia. She's amazing. Is that cerebral palsy she has? If you don't mind me asking?"

"It is. But she's as smart as a button. And she was very taken with you."

"Lisa is so beautiful. And clever, and kind, and—"

"Kieran?"

"He just... He's... He's nice."

"Nice?" Dinescu laughed out loud, even lifting his head.

"What?"

"I hear he asked you on a date."

"He told you?"

"He did. He panicked afterwards and called us. He thought he'd been too forward and didn't want you to be too embarrassed to say no."

"He was forward. But it was so funny, and..."

"Nice?"

"Yes, nice. He was the best company. Tell him I'm looking forward to seeing him on Saturday." She looked mortified. "When I say *seeing*... I mean..."

"You'll do that a lot, Emily. *Can't you see what I'm talking about? See you tomorrow. Do you like my dress?* Don't be embarrassed. He's not easily offended."

"Okay."

"He is the nicest person you'll meet on this earth. Apart from me, of course."

"That goes without saying, boss. And when did you tell him I liked cheese?"

Dinescu shrugged.

They took a right into High Street and found the cottage they were looking for. The homes there opened straight onto the narrow road and had flood boards in place, ready to catch very high tides. The cottage they wanted had a bright blue front door with matching blue shutters. The external walls were rendered and painted pale blue, looking more like the surface of a wedding cake. The name on the door said *The Rector's Cottage*.

Dinescu lifted a black iron knocker in the shape of a bulbous-eyed fish and rapped on the door. A woman in her mid-seventies opened the door to them and studied Dinescu and Summers. They lifted their warrant cards.

"Mrs Butterworth?" said Summers.

"You're the police officer I spoke to on the phone?"

"Yes. This is Detective Chief Inspector Dinescu, and I'm Detective Sergeant Summers."

"Right then," she said. Her voice was crisp and sharp, but she gave a welcoming smile. She looked up at Dinescu. "Don't bump your head when you come in. My husband was always effing and blinding when he bumped his head, and you're taller than he was."

She stood back while Summers and Dinescu climbed over the flood board and made their way into the cottage. The inside, indeed, had low ceilings and black oak beams. Dinescu had his head on a tilt as he stooped to look around. They had come into a spacious living room with a wood burner set into an open fireplace. Dinescu wondered for a moment if a priest hole might be behind it. The furnishings were soft and rich, with a thick beige carpet, many family photographs, and trinkets on shelves and in glass cabinets.

"If I had known you would be so handsome, I'd have done my hair, Chief Inspector."

Dinescu laughed. He liked this woman and her bare-faced cheek.

"Thank you, but I think you're pulling my leg."

"Dinescu. That's Romanian, isn't it?"

"Very good, Mrs Butterworth."

"I went over there in the late 1980s to help in the orphanages. Terrible places." Then she saw Dinescu's expression change. "And you were one of them, no doubt. Forgive me if I come across as coarse. It's the years in nursing."

"You are very astute, Mrs Butterworth."

"Call me Juliet. My solicitor calls me Mrs Butterworth, and I don't particularly like him."

Juliet Butterworth took orders for tea and coffee while Dinescu and Summers made themselves comfortable on her sofa. A few moments later, she appeared with the drinks on a silver tray and Jaffa Cakes on a side plate.

"This is about my time in Cotisham, isn't it?" she said, looking at Summers.

Summers took her coffee and grabbed a Jaffa cake. "Yes, Juliet. Have you seen the news recently?"

"I have. A teacher killed himself? Or is this about the babies?"

"Sort of. The teacher was murdered."

"Oh fuck! Please excuse my manners! Again, it's the nursing."

"No problem." Summers smiled. "And it's not about the babies found in the priest hole. Although, I think you were there during that time."

"I remember it well. I have a good memory. My husband, God rest his soul, used to call me an elephant. That's why he's dead... Ha! No. Just joking. Bloody stroke got him in the end."

"I'm sorry to hear that. This is also about Maisy Brady, the girl who went missing."

"Ah, yes. Maisy. You've found her, have you?"

"Yes, she was in the priest hole."

"Oh no! How could she have been? Faulkner-Williams had the fireplace bricked up."

"We are not certain. But there was another way in."

"That godforsaken tunnel?"

"You know about it?"

"All the staff knew about the steps under the folly. But old Faulkner-Williams didn't want us to tell anyone. He thought the press would go down there and cause havoc. So Maisy must have found her way into the tunnel. That teacher who died—was his name Charles, by any chance?"

"He was," said Summers, swallowing the last piece of Jaffa cake.

"I think he's the chap who phoned me a while ago. He asked me about a report I wrote. He was a bit... intense if you know what I mean. But I remembered him as a boy. He was Maisy's brother."

Dinescu put his cup on the tray. "What were the circumstances around you leaving Cotisham?" he asked.

"The place was a shambles. Faulkner-Williams was only interested in making a profit. Didn't care about the children. Bullying was rife—and more, might I add—but we shouldn't talk ill of the dead. Faulkner-Williams didn't give a shit, to be frank. His son ran riot, and he didn't care."

"Simon?" said Summers.

"Yes, Simon. He was a pest of the worst kind. I'd had enough of it and reported them to the local education authority. Faulkner-Williams found out and fired me. Wanker."

"What did you think had happened to Maisy Brady?" asked Dinescu.

"I thought she'd run off, to tell you the truth. But she loved that brother of hers. Couldn't work that one out."

"Charles Brady was convinced that Maisy was buried at the school. We believe there is a link between his search for her and his death. Let me show you a note he made."

Dinescu showed her a printed copy of Brady's note. He had highlighted the section about Juliet.

Nurse - Juliet Butterworth (alive) "A, J, M were black. A. needed <u>compress.</u>"

"Do you have any idea what that note may mean?" Dinescu handed the copy to Juliet.

A frown creased her forehead. She went to a side table and picked up a pair of reading glasses. "These look like notes from our conversation about my report. The compress... I don't know about that letter A, but the J was Jason, and the M was Mackenzie —Mac, they called him. It would make sense if it were S, not A."

"Simon Faulkner-Williams later changed his name to Archie Faulkner," said Summers.

"Well, that makes sense, then! Simon, Jason, and Mac were always hanging around together—inseparable pains in the arse. Simon came to me with a bloody mouth one afternoon. Said he got into a fight with a boy from outside the school. Knocked his tooth right out. I put a cold compress on his mouth." Summers's eyes were wide. "All three were covered in black stuff—all over their shirts and trousers. Had to get them to change, but the stuff wouldn't wash out."

"This is important, Juliet," said Dinescu. "Was this before, after, or around the time Maisy disappeared?"

Juliet thought for a moment. "That man on the phone asked something similar. I told him I wasn't sure, Chief Inspector. It was... No wait. It was the same day! I remember sending Simon to his father to tell him about the fight, and then later that day, Matron got all hysterical. Maisy was missing. I told her to calm down. She'd only been gone for a couple of hours. It was the same day, Chief Inspector."

"Would you mind putting that in a statement for us?" said Summers. "To make it official."

"Not at all."

"Even if it had to go to court?"

"Absolutely, young lady. I'd enjoy that."

Chapter Thirty-Four

Booker had just got off the phone with Dinescu. "There's a change of plan. We have enough suspicion to arrest Archie Faulkner."

Burgess turned in her seat and looked along the road. "His van's not here."

"That's unlucky. We'll still go in for the search."

"I don't believe in luck," said Burgess. She looked in her wing mirror and saw the marked police car parked behind them. "At least we won't need the muscle."

Booker rapped on the front door of the terraced house in Cotisham village. It was one in a row of ex-council houses, in dark red brick, with low, sloping roofs and long gardens, all cared for, and not a motorbike part in sight.

Behind Booker and Burgess were two uniformed PCs, both with Tasers. He knocked on the door again while Burgess peered through the windows to see through the net curtains.

"No movement. The place is in darkness," said Burgess. "Let's go in."

She brought out a set of keys seized from Grainger in Custody, and they all entered the house and made their presence known. The two uniformed officers went through each room, but there was no trace of Faulkner. They were stood down, leaving Booker and Burgess to resume plan *A* and carry out a Section 18 PACE search. Booker called Dinescu to update him.

"He's not here, boss," said Booker. "So we've entered the property to do the search. Just to clarify, you said it was a letter. Any description? In an envelope?"

"We don't know, Gareth. It's likely to be handwritten. Grainger said she destroyed it, but we can't be certain. I appreciate it's a little vague."

Booker heard Burgess calling him. "One minute, sir." He found her in a back room that was next to the kitchen. It had a large wooden dining table in the centre and a Welsh dresser against the wall. Burgess was pointing to a cabinet against the far wall.

"Shit!"

"Gareth?" said Dinescu.

"There's an empty gun cabinet here, boss. Space for one gun." Booker searched the cabinet one-handed with the phone against his ear. "No ammunition."

Dinescu didn't speak for a moment. "That changes things."

"I'll look around the rest of the house in case he's left it somewhere else."

Booker watched Burgess crouch down. She put on a pair of protective gloves from her pocket and pulled up threads from the carpet, putting them into an evidence bag.

"And boss, Sarah has spotted a greyish-blue carpet in the house. She's taking a few samples."

"Carpet? Okay. Thanks for the update, Gareth. Let me know if you find the letter."

While Burgess filled in the details on the evidence bag, Booker moved on to search the rest of the house. Apart from

Archie's apparent interest in sadomasochism, there was nothing of note in the bedrooms. In a wardrobe, he found leather masks and thongs, handcuffs, and a whip. Booker was glad he was wearing gloves.

He moved downstairs into the front room, which had a large TV and an oversize sofa. There was a cabinet full of old DVDs, most of which were porn and gruesome horror films. On a shelf was a photo of an elderly woman sitting in a high-backed chair with Olivia Grainger standing over her. There was a bookshelf where Booker found another photo. It was Archie, Jason, and Mac in their younger days. Mac had a cigarette hanging from his mouth, and Archie and Jason were in vest tops—taken in the early 2000s. Archie was carrying something bundled in a pink blanket. A small, pale thigh was exposed and the hem of a dress or skirt. The men looked cocksure of themselves, ready to take on the world.

Booker searched through the drawers below the bookshelf. It was full of invoices for Archie's business, scraps of paper, and quotations.

"Anything?" said Burgess from behind him.

"There's so much crap here. I can't see a handwritten letter anywhere."

Burgess pulled out the second drawer and joined Booker, sifting through anything that could be a handwritten letter. They didn't find what they were looking for.

Burgess sighed and rubbed the back of her wrist against her forehead. Her hands were sweating inside the protective gloves. "Did you try the spare room upstairs?"

"Yes," said Booker. "Doesn't look like anyone's been in there for a while. All the drawers are empty."

Burgess saw the photo of Archie, Jason, and Mac. "Is that a baby he's got there?"

"Could be a girl looking at the blanket and the clothes," said

Booker. "Though I'd say she was older than a baby. Difficult to tell. The photo's grainy."

"Is that Susan Grainger, do you think?"

Booker shrugged.

"Let's get back. I want to get those fibres analysed."

Booker left the Section 18 documentation on the dining table and looked again at the empty gun cabinet. "We're assuming it's his gun. Could be Grainger's."

"Why would she have a shotgun?"

"I hate to think."

Leah bit the bullet and called Andrew Winston.

"No, it wasn't Covid," she said.

"Talk to me, Leah. I'm listening."

"I've just screwed up big-time. My head's all over the place, Andrew, and now I'm scared of what Cameron will do."

"Look," said Winston. "What's happened has happened. If I'm honest, resigning was the right thing to do. I respect that. It could have got messy for you otherwise."

"Thank you."

"It sounds like Cameron's the biggest problem for you right now."

"I've been so stupid," she said. "Ethan was a mistake. I was in a bad place."

"I know. I get that."

"I don't want to be in the house in case Cameron turns up asking questions."

"So, what do you need?"

"I want to get away from him completely. I just don't know where to start. Can I come back into school—keep out of his way?"

"That's fine. You're not a risk to anyone, and no one here knows what's happened."

"Eric's not happy with me."

"He's not happy with me, either, so I wouldn't worry."

Leah laughed. "I'd like to work out my notice if I can."

"Well, the Board may decide otherwise, if I'm honest. They're meeting later, and they may ask you to attend. But I'm thinking of your best interests now. You should get out of that cottage as soon as possible. Can you go to a friend, a relative?"

"Maybe. I'll have to ask."

"Start getting your things together and come into school. At least here, you'll be safe when Cameron finds out."

After the phone call, Leah received a text message from Cameron.

We need to talk. I'll be home in an hour.

She checked her watch. An hour. She rushed through the cottage and packed up her things. She put everything she could in her car—a few boxes and a pile of clothes—and drove to the school. She would have to go back later to get Munchkin. She was wary of everyone she met, wondering if they knew what she had done. She felt sick with guilt and wasn't sure if she could last the day out.

It was the first morning break, and Leah had a free period afterwards. She moved her small blue Fiat over to the workshop. She had promised Cameron she would pick up his personal tools from the shed. It was a guilty peace offering of sorts, a prelude to telling him she was going to leave him. She knew it was over between them, but he didn't know it yet. He was still locked in his small, blinkered world. She wanted to get away from Cotisham, from Cameron, his controlling father, and from the guilt she felt over Ethan. She needed a new start and would leave before the fallout over Ethan caught up with her. She just needed to bide her time until the end of her notice period.

Cameron had a spare key to the workshop, but Leah was surprised she didn't need it. The door was unlocked. She stepped into the semi-darkness.

"Hello?" she called out as she opened the door. "Who's in here?"

Her ears rang in the silence until the sound of her heart pounded in her ears. This was Cameron's domain. It was like he was standing next to her.

She found Cameron's toolkit in a metal box under a workbench, as he'd described. It was heavy, and she had to use two hands and bend her knees to lift it. Something moved at the rear of the workshop, making her jump.

"Hello?" she called out to the shadows.

"Oh, Leah, it's you."

She put down the toolbox in case she had to run, but then she recognised the voice.

"Archie! You scared the life out of me. Didn't you hear me call out?"

"No, sorry. I had my head under the covers, looking for something." Archie's voice sounded different. Thicker and a little slurred.

"What are you doing in here?"

"I could ask you the same thing."

"I'm picking up Cam's tools. Did you know Greenway sacked him? Gross misconduct, he said."

Archie walked closer. Only the top of his head was lit by the perspex window overhead. The rest of him was in shadow.

"Poor Cam," said Archie. "He loved working here. All over that stupid shotgun."

"What are you looking for, Archie?"

"Just getting the feel of the place. Greenway asked me to take Cam's job."

Even though she wouldn't stay with Cameron, something grated inside her when she heard this.

"And you said yes?"

"At least it would keep it in the old family."

"What old family?"

"The boys. Cam's dad and me have known each other for years. Before it was Cam's job, Jason was the caretaker here. It went from father to son."

Archie stepped closer. She could see his face now and smell the alcohol on his breath. He looked dishevelled and pale. "Me, Jason, and Mac were family. We looked out for each other."

"You look awful, Archie. Have you been sleeping in here?" She felt a coldness creeping up her body.

"Did you see what they've been doing in the house? The girl in the priest hole. They reckon it was Brady's sister."

Leah took a step back. "His sister! Shit, that's terrible. Where did you hear that?"

"Shame he wasn't here to see it. After all this time, he got himself shot."

"It is sad. He really wanted to know what happened to her. He was talking about hiring a private detective to help him."

"It was a waste of money, and he wasted his life, Leah! Constantly looking for the dead, never looking at life. The living!"

"It must have been hard for him to move on. He loved his sister."

"Told you all that, did he? Close, were you? You and Charles?"

Leah stepped back. "What do you mean?"

"Was all that fuss at the party planned to throw us off the scent?"

253

She could hear the menace and violence in his voice. She glanced towards the door. Could she make it out?

"I have no idea what you're talking about, Archie. Why *are* you hiding in here?"

Archie laughed. "Hiding? No, sweetheart! I'm just waiting for Christmas. And you're the best Christmas present ever."

His hands moved to grab her, but the door opened, and two silhouetted figures walked in.

"Archie?" said Jason Hyde as he peered into the semi-darkness.

"What are you doing, mate?" asked Mac Masterson. "You okay, Leah?"

Leah nodded, and her breaths were shallow. "He's been drinking."

"Look who's here, fellas!" shouted Archie. "Fresh meat!" he laughed. "Come on. There's hot pussy all for the taking."

"Shit!" said Hyde. "He's been at my beer. Cam must have left it. It's okay, Leah—no one's going to hurt you. Archie's not great when he's had a drink. He doesn't mean it. Back away to the door. We only want to help Archie."

Leah nodded and took several steps back, still facing him.

"How did you know he was here?" asked Leah.

Hyde stood in between Archie and Leah. "We guessed he was. He's got something on his mind. Finding Maisy's set him off."

"What are you doing, Jase?" said Archie. "She's come to play. Don't let her get away!"

Hyde held out his hands to stop Archie. "No more, Archie, mate. Leave the poor girl alone. We know they've found Maisy, Archie. Is that why you're hiding in here?"

Leah stopped by the door to listen.

"We all know they found her, Jase."

"And we know what happened," said Mac Masterson. "We

know what you did now. We were waiting in the tunnel for you, remember?"

"What *I* did? But you were there, too." Archie stepped forward and gripped his head like he was in pain.

"No, Archie," said Hyde. "We stayed by the tower. When Maisy didn't come back with you, I spoke to your father."

"That's not what happened!"

"Your dad fixed everything. It wasn't right, though. It wasn't right at all. He covered it up."

Archie pointed at Hyde, spitting as he talked. "We told them it was an accident, Jason. She slipped over."

Jason shook his head. "That's what you told us, mate. But I'm sure you're right. We weren't there to see it. We were waiting for you to finish."

"You need to hand yourself in, Archie," said Masterson. "Tell them what happened. After all these years, you can clear your conscience. We'll back you up. We'll tell them you were sick. You *were* sick, Archie. Don't you remember?"

"Sick? No... We all agreed. She *slipped*. You were with me. You were at it, too! All of us!"

"That's in your head, mate," said Hyde. "You're not well. Why don't we ask Leah to talk to the police? Hand yourself in and set the record straight. Get it all out in the open?"

"No! What is this? You know they'll fucking crucify me!"

"They won't, Archie, not if it was an accident. Not if that's what you said it was. It was your old man's doing. He was head-master, and he persuaded you it would be okay. Don't you remember?"

"What about Susan, Archie?" said Masterson. "Doesn't she deserve to know the truth after all this time?"

"I told Liv and Susan that Maisy slipped. It's what we all—"

"No, Archie. No! That's not what we said." Hyde walked

towards him. "Your daughter only knows your version of what happened. Who knows what damage you've done to her?"

"Leah," said Masterson. "Get the police over here."

"Give myself up now?" said Archie. "Are you crazy?"

Hyde took Archie by the shoulders. "No. We'll all give ourselves up, but you tell them what really happened. Just like we will. Look at you, mate. You're a mess. They've got Liv. The police arrested her."

"Shit! They've nicked Liv? No! It's not her fault. She... This won't work now."

"But she *knew*, Archie. She knew what you did and said nothing. So give yourself up, and then Olivia will be let go."

"Olivia didn't know everything, fellas. Not *everything*!"

"Do it for Liv and Susan. Do it for them."

Archie's shoulders were hunched, and he sank to the floor until he was crouched down, rocking on the balls of his feet, whimpering like a tortured dog. "For Liv and Susan."

Chapter Thirty-Five

DC Taylor was in Cotisham village, outside the home of Jason Hyde. He had just tried knocking but only found an angry dog rattling the front door, trying to get to him. Taylor wasn't a dog fan. He and Bill, his husband, had two Blue Point Siamese cats: Una and Dos—Bill's idea for names, not his. The growling dog at Hyde's door wanted to rip his throat out.

Taylor stepped back and looked around at the windows and back gate. There was no sign of Hyde.

"Who are you then?" A face of a middle-aged woman appeared from behind a side gate of the house next door. "Are you Jehovah's?"

"No, I'm a police officer."

"You don't look like a police officer. Far too well dressed."

"Thanks, but I am." Taylor showed the woman his warrant card. "I'm DC Taylor from Chichester CID. I'm looking for Jason Hyde."

"Are you now? I see." She looked him up and down. "Probably at the Wild Goose. It's over in Lodsworth, about six miles from here."

"Thanks. How long have you known Mr Hyde?"

"About ten years. He was here when I moved in with my husband. He had his wife and son with him then. She died soon after, as did my Jack, and then his son moved out."

"Does Mr Hyde live alone here now?"

"Yes. Not that it's any of my business. Try the pub. He's bound to be there."

"Okay. Well, thanks for—"

A marked police car pulled up on the road behind him. It was Kirby and two other officers. Kirby got out and jogged over to Taylor.

"Did you get my message?" said Kirby.

Taylor shook his head and checked his mobile. It was on silent.

Kirby lowered his voice. "The boss said we're to bring in Jason Hyde and Mackenzie Masterson."

"Why?" said Taylor.

"Suspicion of murdering Maisy Brady. We're also arresting Archie Faulkner. I've just spoken to Masterson's wife. She said he was at a local pub."

"Don't tell me, The Wild Goose?"

"Yep. How did you know?"

"Come on. Let's try the school." Taylor looked at the woman over the fence and shook his head, and she scoffed at him.

"But the pub?"

"Come on, Chester! There's no bloody Wild Goose. Think about it.

Taylor, Kirby, and the two uniformed officers headed back in convoy to the school, which was only a few minutes away. Taylor updated DS Summers, who was coming to meet them at the school.

"What's the plan?" asked Kirby. He always deferred to Taylor.

"The Sarge is coming over now. We'll meet her here. I've

just heard her call up for a dog unit and tactical firearms. Archie may have a shotgun with him."

"Oh, shit! But we don't know for sure if they're here."

"No, but it's the first place to look. The Sarge said we're to do our best to locate them, but not to approach."

"Ask at the school office?" said Kirby.

"Could try. We need to let the headmaster know, anyway."

They walked through the school entrance with the two uniformed officers. They waited in the hallway while Taylor and Kirby went into Reception. Janice, the friendly receptionist, greeted them with a smile.

"Good afternoon," said Kirby. "Janice, isn't it?"

"It is DC Kirby. What a good memory you have!" She sat forward and grinned at him.

"Janice, do you know if Archie Faulkner is on the school grounds today?"

"You know, he signed in yesterday but never signed out again. That's unlike him."

"And how about Mackenzie Masterson and Jason Hyde?"

"Mac Masterson? Is that his name? All the years I've known him, I never knew—"

"Are they here, Janice?" interjected Taylor.

Janice sat up straight. "Yes, officer." She was curt, and the smile had gone. "I saw them together a little earlier. So, yes."

"Do you know where we can find them?" asked Kirby.

"Well, DC Kirby. They could be over in the workshop or cleaning up that awful mess your CSI people made in the library."

"Hello?" Leah Turnbull was standing behind them. She had lost all the colour in her face.

"Are you okay, Leah?" asked Taylor.

"DC Taylor, can you come over to the workshop? Archie

259

wants to hand himself in. He's with Jason and Mac. They said he killed that girl."

They all went back outside and met Summers as she pulled up in the car park. Taylor updated her, and Summers went over to Turnbull.

"Hello, Leah. Do you want to sit down in the car?"

"No, I'm fine."

Summers made her look into her eyes. "Has anyone hurt you or threatened you?"

"I think Archie was going to, but the others came in and talked to him. I'm okay. They asked me to talk to the police." She choked on her words.

"It's okay. Take your time."

"Mac and Jason persuaded Archie to hand himself in. They said Archie had killed the young girl, but they were there too, somewhere. I don't understand it. If you call them, then they'll come out."

"Is there a weapon, Leah?" said Summers. "A gun or anything else that could hurt us or themselves?"

"Not that I saw. Archie's not right in the head, and I think he's been drinking."

"Thank you, Leah. Stay right back here with DC Taylor. There's a shotgun unaccounted for, so these officers with guns will call them out. It's routine. No one will come to any harm."

"I really don't care if you shoot them all."

The six firearms officers approached the workshop, with everyone else kept out of harm's way. Two officers had heavy-duty shields in front of them, and they had trained their guns on the door.

"Armed police!" one of them shouted out. "Everyone inside the workshop, come out slowly, one at a time, with your hands on top of your head."

The door opened. "Don't shoot!" shouted Hyde. "We're coming out."

The lead officer pointed his weapon at him. "Listen only to me. Do exactly as I say, and you will not be harmed. Show me your hands."

Hyde obliged.

"Now put them on your head... Walk slowly towards me, and get down onto your knees."

Hyde obeyed the instructions and was handcuffed. Masterson followed, and he had a fixed grin on his face. But Archie took his time. He came out with slow, begrudging steps, wretched and filthy. Then he fell to his knees and wept.

Cameron Hyde had returned home after trying to find his father. He couldn't find anyone, and no one was answering their phones, not even Archie. He went into the cottage and noticed at once that something was wrong. All of Leah's things had gone —even Munchkin, her cat, was missing. It was almost as if Leah had never been there, except for the wooden love spoon hanging in the kitchen. They bought it in Wales together a year ago. That was all she had left behind.

He knew this was coming. He wished he had listened to his dad and put her in her place. Cameron tried his father's mobile again, but it was switched off.

There was a knock on the door, and Cameron found Leah standing there. She'd been crying, but her face was as hard as stone.

"Leah. I don't understand."

"I'm leaving you, Cam. I gave notice at work, but they now want me to leave immediately. I had to tell Greenway about something I'd done. I went to see him this afternoon, and they'd had a meeting about me... I'm going home to my parents—they're coming for me. You can have the car back. I can't afford to run it now, and as you paid for most of it..."

"What about us, Leah? After everything we've gone through." Cameron stood aside to let her in, but she stayed where she was.

"I've been sleeping with a student, Cam. He's eighteen. I've told the police and the school. I didn't mean to, but..."

"You did what!" His fists clenched. "Who?"

"I won't tell you! It's too late, anyway. It's all finished, and so am I, Cam. Goodbye."

"Who was it!" His voice screamed through the house, the reverberations shaking the glass.

But Leah was unmoved. She turned to leave. He grabbed her shoulder and raised his fist.

"Dad said I should have put you in your place, and he was fucking right!"

Andrew Winston appeared from the side of the door and grabbed Cameron's fist, smashing it into the glass of the front door. Shards sprayed everywhere, and Cameron's hand was streaming with blood.

"Come on, Leah," said Winston.

He led her away and looked at Cameron, who was grimacing in pain and holding his bloody hand.

"I'd get that looked at if I were you," he said. "Oh, and your dad's been arrested. Just so you know."

Chapter Thirty-Six

Olivia Grainger was sweating under her arms, and her eyes flitted around the interview room as she sat next to her solicitor. She was wringing her hands and jigging her knees, which made her feet tip-tap against the floor. This was Grainger's second interview. DC Sarah Burgess had already gone through the circumstances of her arrest and introduced the letter her sister had told them about.

Grainger's solicitor told Burgess that Grainger would give a full and frank confession after hearing the whole truth about what had happened to Maisy Brady, which would make the interview much more straightforward—in theory.

"Are you ready?" Burgess asked the young DC from Worthing sitting next to her.

He smiled and nodded. He was friendly, nervous, and looked very young. He let Burgess take the lead, which she was more than happy with. She hit the record button, and the long tone sounded.

"Interview resumed at 13:52 hours."

"You won't start shouting at me now, will you?" Grainger

said to Burgess. "I've seen the cop shows on TV. You're all nice to me, and then you shout and thump the table."

Burgess frowned and shook her head. "No, Olivia. I've already told you this interview is being recorded." Burgess pointed to the video camera on the wall. "That camera is recording everything. And you have your solicitor sitting next to you. We are governed by the Police and Criminal Evidence Act 1984. When you arrived, you were offered a copy of the PACE Code of Conduct. Don't believe everything you see on TV."

"I was wondering if you'd be getting your own back. I'm sorry I pushed you over. It was stupid of me."

Burgess gave a thin-lipped smile and glanced at the solicitor. "We were talking about the letter your mother gave you before you had a comfort break. Why did you destroy the letter, Olivia?"

"I tore it up and burned it. I was worried it would implicate her. In the letter, she said she had seen Maisy's body and told the headmaster, Faulkner-Williams, that Maisy was dead. She wrote it all down because she was becoming more and more frail and forgetful. It was like her last confession before it all left her. She never wrote that she killed Maisy. I want to make that clear! She was confused. She said she only *checked* Maisy, and she was dead. But as time passed, everything got mixed up in Mum's head. It was Faulkner-Williams who got her to go down there. He knew what had happened. The police would have got it all wrong."

"To clarify, you ripped up and burned your mother's letter. You did this to prevent the police from finding it, even though it could have helped them with their investigation?"

"Yes, but only because you would have got the wrong end of the stick."

"And when your mother wrote the letter, did she have mental capacity?"

"I don't know for sure. Some days she's as bright as a button, but others…"

"And as her mental state deteriorated, she believed she had been the one who had killed Maisy. She would tell other people she had. Is that right?"

"Yes. She was confessing to everyone she met. One day, according to my sister, Charles Brady was visiting his mother and overheard her. I felt I had to burn the letter to protect her. It showed that she knew what had happened to Maisy but didn't kill her." Tears rolled down Grainger's cheeks. "She carried that burden all her adult life. The poor woman."

"Did your mother know who had killed Maisy Brady?"

"Yes, I think she did, but she didn't tell anyone. After the inquest, she just walked away from it all."

"Do you know who killed Maisy?"

Grainger nodded, and she wiped away her tears with the backs of her hands. The young DC had a supply of tissues for her. "Thank you, young man… I didn't know she had been murdered until today. I didn't know—I believed him. He said it was just an accident. He was young, and they'd got carried away."

Grainger dried her eyes and wiped her nose on the tissues. Her hands shook, so she held them, clutching the tissues against the tabletop.

"Do you need more time or a drink?" offered Burgess.

"No. I just want to get on with it now." She cleared her throat and looked up again. "I've been in a relationship with Archie Faulkner for a long time. We had an affair that outlasted both of my marriages. I'm not proud of that. He was married, too, at one point. We had a daughter together. A timid thing—not like him at all. She's always been scared of him."

"Tell me about the doubts you had about Archie."

Grainger nodded. "Brady had been asking questions about Maisy."

"Asking who?"

"Archie. I overheard Archie shouting at him, saying he couldn't prove anything. I remember thinking at the time, who would say that if they were completely innocent? *Couldn't prove anything.* Even if it was an accident? No one. I confronted Archie about it. I got myself a bruised face for doing it. He said he had taken Maisy into the tunnel to have some fun with her. Those were his words. *Fun.* He told me she had slipped and cracked her head open. She died instantly, he said. He was broken about telling me. And I was stupid enough to believe him."

"Did Archie tell his father at the time Maisy was killed?"

"Yes, and Archie's father covered it up. He had to protect his reputation."

The solicitor stepped in. "Be aware, DC Burgess, you are asking my client for her opinion about something of which she does not have first-hand knowledge."

"I know. Thank you."

"Then today, when you said..." Grainger looked down at her hands. "You said Maisy had been raped! Raped, for God's sake! That wasn't what he told me. He never said he'd raped her."

"The pathologist is certain of it," said Burgess. "She was bound and gagged."

Grainger shook her head and sighed. She looked at her solicitor. "Archie must have murdered her."

"Do you know what Jason Hyde and Mackenzie Masterson were doing when Archie was with Maisy?"

"No, Archie didn't mention them."

"How did it make you feel when you discovered that Charles Brady was researching his sister's death?"

"I knew nothing about it until he confronted Archie."

"When was that, Olivia? Can you expand on that for me?"

"It was the Friday evening before Charles went missing. Jason and Mac had come over for a fish supper with my daughter, Susan. I went out to get the fish and chips, and by the time I got back, I could tell there had been a heated argument. Charles had turned up, shouting the odds. Susan was hiding upstairs, and there was a broken glass on the floor. That's when I heard Archie shouting at Charles, telling him he couldn't prove he'd killed Maisy. After Charles left, Archie was pacing the floor, cursing him, and Susan was crying. He kept saying Charles had nothing on him, telling Susan not to worry."

"Was it after that you had your argument?"

"Yes. We went out into the garden to have it out. Then Archie stormed off to the pub after thumping me. When I got back indoors, everyone had gone."

Burgess looked over her notes, giving Grainger a few minutes to recompose herself. She lifted herself in her chair, and Burgess took the opportunity to try a different tack. "Do you own or keep a shotgun in your home?"

"You know full well we do. It belongs to Archie. It's registered and licensed."

"Where is it?"

Grainger frowned and glanced at her solicitor. "At home, in the locker."

"When was the last time you saw it?"

"I don't know." She shook her head and thought. "A couple of months ago. I hate guns. I don't go near it."

"Have you ever fired it?"

"No! I said I hate guns."

"If it wasn't in your home, where else could it be?"

"What do you mean? It's in the locker."

"By locker, you mean the gun cabinet?"

"Yes, of course!"

"We've just been to search your house, Olivia. The shotgun isn't in the gun cabinet."

Grainger stared at Burgess and then looked at her solicitor again. "It's in the ruddy cabinet!"

"It isn't there, Olivia. Honestly. Where else could it be? Has Archie taken it somewhere?"

"He never told me."

"Perhaps you were worried that Brady would go to the police about Archie. Did you kill Charles Brady to stop him?"

"No."

"You didn't know Archie had allegedly raped and murdered Maisy then? Perhaps you felt you had to protect him from Charles?"

"No! I've never fired a gun in my life."

"Did you conspire with anyone else to kill Charles Brady?"

"No."

"It would have meant you didn't need to handle a gun and pull the trigger."

"I did not kill Charles. I did not get anyone else to kill Charles."

"Where were you on Monday, the 17th of April, from around three o'clock?"

"I've already given my statement. I was in my office at about three, and then I was doing my usual chores around the school."

"Did anyone see you?"

"Probably! Look, I can't remember."

Burgess looked back through her notes. "Do you think Archie murdered Charles Brady?"

"I hope to God he didn't. But I can't say if he did or not. He's obviously done it before."

"Is there anything you want to add or clarify? Anything you think I've misunderstood?"

Olivia Grainger shook her head. "No."

"Thank you, Olivia. This interview is ended at... 14:11 hours. You'll return to your cell, and we will consult with the CPS regarding a charging decision or whether there's a need for further investigation."

Chapter Thirty-Seven

The core team returned to the Major Crimes office after Masterson, Hyde, and Faulkner were booked into Custody and placed in cells out of earshot of each other. Burgess had just finished debriefing Dinescu and Summers on Olivia Grainger's interview. She sank into her chair afterwards, rubbed her eyes, and yawned.

"Let's just take stock here," said Dinescu, summoning the energy to continue in the afternoon slump. He spoke slowly, organising his thoughts out loud. "According to Grainger, we have Charles Brady confronting Archie in their home on the Friday before he was killed. Masterson and Hyde were also present to hear it. Archie told Grainger afterwards that Maisy was killed in an accident. But on hearing today that Maisy was also raped, Grainger now believes that Archie Faulkner murdered Maisy."

"That's about it, sir," said Burgess.

"According to Leah Turnbull in her statement, she heard Archie Faulkner admit to killing Maisy. But there was some doubt about the accident?"

"Yes, boss," said Summers.

Dinescu shrugged. "So he accidentally bound her, gagged her, and crushed her skull? Does he think we're fools?"

Summers ran her fingers through her hair and massaged her temples. "It was a long time ago, but he couldn't have forgotten what he did to her."

"What happens now with Hyde and Masterson?" asked Kirby, snacking on a packet of grapes. "They convinced Faulkner to hand himself in."

"We'll take it into consideration," said Summers, "but we can't assume anything yet."

Summers's mobile phone pinged. "Forensic results are in for Maisy Brady's body, sir." She scanned the main headlines, and her mouth dropped open. She passed her phone to Dinescu.

Dinescu smiled. "Emily, you and Ross will interview Archie Faulkner. Sarah, make sure you're refreshed. You and Chester have Jason Hyde waiting for you."

Archie Faulkner had a new set of clothes—spares from Custody, as his were soiled. He was sober now. His cheeky grin had gone, and his shoulders were slumped. Summers and Taylor were ready to interview him, and despite several appeals to his common sense, Archie had refused a solicitor. He had told the custody sergeant booking him in that he could speak for himself. So after Taylor had gone through the PACE prerequisites, Archie sat opposite the two detectives, ready to talk.

Summers began. "It's usual for someone arrested for a major crime to have a solicitor, Archie. Are you sure you don't want one?"

Archie folded his arms. "No."

"If you change your mind, let me know."

"I don't need one."

"Archie, you were arrested today on suspicion of the rape and murder of Maisy Brady on or around the 14th of May, 1987. Do you understand why you were arrested?"

"I think I may have killed her, but I didn't rape her. It was all an accident. So, yes. I gave myself up."

"Why did you do that?"

Archie looked up at the ceiling and took a deep breath. "I took advice from my mates. They told me to unburden my guilt, as it were. You found Maisy's body. It wouldn't take long before you would know we had sex."

"What happened, Archie, that led to Maisy's death?"

"I was seventeen, DS Summers. Seventeen. I was young and stupid. You must remember what it was like to be seventeen. Not that long ago, by the looks of you."

Summers looked down at her notes. She felt her skin crawl.

Archie smiled for a moment. "I'd seen Maisy at school. She was a stunner. She even got looks from some of the teachers. Pervs. She looked older than her age if you know what I mean. Anyway, me, Jase and Mac were always together. We were popular, you could say. All the girls wanted us. We were never in short supply. Maisy was always hanging around, flirting with us. She was a real prick teaser. She knew what she was doing—don't care what anyone says—she knew.

"The year before, they found the babies in the library chimney—that priest hole. It was a big thing. Police came and everything. Turned out to be something that happened eighty years or so previously. Some mad woman farmer or something. When it was all over, my dad got the fireplace sealed up, and that was that—or so he thought. But there was another way in. We knew about it, and so did a few others. The escape tunnel, as we called it, came out at the tower. We used to dare each other to go down to the priest hole and come back. Scared the shit out of us. But then Matron found out and tried to stop us."

"That was Olivia Grainger and Celia Lambert's mother?"

"Yep. The mad cow didn't stop us. It made it more... you know. Well, that May, Maisy kept coming on to me. She wanted it badly. I know she did. So. Me and the others—"

"Mackenzie Masterson and Jason Hyde?"

"Yes, who else? We took Maisy down into the tunnel and into the priest hole. She got a bit freaked out, and I held her to calm her down. One thing led to another, and..." Archie smirked with a shrug.

"And what, Archie? Shrugging doesn't tell me anything."

Archie rolled his eyes. "We had sex. Her first time, too."

"Did she tell you that?"

"No. But it was obvious."

"Did you all have torches?"

"Yes. Everyone had a torch or a lantern in that place."

"Where were Jason and Mackenzie?"

"They were there, too."

"You had sex in front of your friends?"

"Yes. Well. They joined in afterwards."

"Excuse me?"

Archie sat forwards. "I said they joined in afterwards."

"You all had sex with Maisy, a fourteen-year-old girl?"

"Yes. She wanted it. She really did."

"Did she ever tell you to stop?"

"Not that I remember."

"So, are you telling me she agreed to have sex with all three of you?"

"Yes, I am. That's what she wanted. It does happen."

Summers took a sip of her water and cleared her throat. "How did Maisy die, Archie?"

"It was slippery in there, and when we were leaving, she slipped and hit her head."

"And that was it?"

"Well, no. We couldn't wake her. So, we went to my dad, who got Matron. She went down there, and when she came out, she said that Maisy was dead."

"What happened then?"

"Dad didn't want this to ruin the school's reputation, and he didn't want an accident to ruin my life. That's all it was—an accident. So, he helped us brick up the priest hole."

"So, you entombed Maisy?"

"All of us bricked it up together. I'm not proud of it. But that's what Dad wanted. He reported her missing, and we all felt terrible and everything, but I couldn't go against Dad. You didn't know him."

Summers sighed louder than she meant to.

"Okay. Let me see if I've got this right. You, Jason, and Mackenzie took Maisy into the tunnel below the folly tower, up the steps, and into the priest hole. There, all three of you had sex with her with Maisy's full consent, even though this was her first time and she was only fourteen years old. She was a virgin. *Unfortunately*, Maisy slipped, fell, and hit her head. You all went and spoke to your father. He got the matron to check on her, and Maisy was pronounced dead. So far, okay?"

Archie smiled and nodded. "Perfect."

"You, Jason and Mackenzie helped your father cover up what had happened by sealing the priest hole with Maisy in it, and your father claimed Maisy had gone missing."

"That's it exactly. All to save his reputation."

"And yours, by the sounds of it."

"Yes. He was a proud man."

"Did he send you abroad afterwards?"

"He knew I was upset by everything that had happened. He sent me to France for twelve weeks. I had a cousin who lived there."

Summers brought out some notes she had in a folder and studied them.

"The thing is, Archie, your friends have said something a little different to you." Summers looked up into Archie's eyes.

"No, no, they didn't. They wouldn't do that."

"We've already interviewed Jason and Mackenzie. They've given us very similar accounts to each other. They told us you had made them wait by the tower entrance to the tunnel while you and Maisy walked along into the priest hole."

"No... That's not what happened."

"They said they heard Maisy screaming for you to get off her."

"You're lying! They wouldn't say that."

"And about ten minutes later, Maisy went quiet, and you appeared on your own in a state of shock. Are their accounts true?"

"No."

"Do you want that solicitor yet, Archie?"

"I don't fucking need one! They were with me the whole time."

"The rest of their accounts were similar to yours. You spoke to your father, and Mrs Lambert, the matron, arrived and checked on Maisy."

"They were with me, DS Summers."

"Now, DC Taylor here, and I have a big problem with *all* of your accounts." Taylor nodded, and Summers looked into Archie's flickering eyes. "Are you sure you don't want to change your account? Is there anything you may have missed?"

"No. It happened as I said it happened."

"Because I think, after all this time, you have forgotten something else you did to Maisy Brady. Can you remember anything else you did to her?"

Archie flared his nostrils. "It happened *exactly* as I said."

"When we found Maisy, her hands were bound behind her back with her bra, and her knickers were stuffed deep into her mouth as a gag. And it would have made her gag, Archie. There were the remains of her stomach contents found on them."

Just then, Summers saw something in his eyes. He had remembered.

Taylor brought out two photographs.

"These photographs we're showing you now are exhibits ER/09 and ER/10. They were taken at the scene of the priest hole, and that mummified corpse is how you left Maisy Brady."

Archie looked away, swaying in his chair.

"Look at it, Archie! You can clearly see the remains of the bra and the underwire around her wrists. And that rag in the remains of her mouth is her knickers... No, Archie. I put it to you that you forced Maisy into that priest hole, that you bound her, gagged her, and raped her. And we know she was brutally raped, Archie—the tearing is still visible. Then, with a brick, we found very close to her body, you smashed her skull, hitting her three times and killing her. What is your response to that, Archie?"

"You people are sick! No comment."

"No comment? Okay. Suits me fine." Summers looked at Taylor, who produced another set of notes.

"These are the forensic results from tests done on Maisy's clothing, hot off the press this afternoon. On Maisy's skirt, which she was still wearing, various stains were found and tested. To cut a long story short, we've got your DNA in that semen, Mackenzie's DNA in another patch of semen, and finally, we have Jason's too. So, some of what you said was true. You all raped her. By the way, we've put that to your friends, and they have admitted it. They were as stunned as you are. Oh, yes! One more thing. We've recovered your lost tooth, Archie. The one Maisy knocked out in your struggle to remove her underwear, no doubt. It's loaded with your DNA. Remember the school nurse?" Archie had turned away. "She remembers you and your mates. And crucially, she remembers giving you a compress for your mouth that day. Anything to say to that?"

Archie shook his head.

"The video should have picked up that you shook your head. No comment, was that?"

"No comment."

"Want that solicitor yet?"

"Yes."

"Interview suspended at 16:35 hours."

Chapter Thirty-Eight

"Interview resumed at 18:30 hours," said Summers. "Now present is?"

A woman in a black trouser suit sitting beside Archie Faulkner looked up. "Margaret Wright, duty solicitor."

"DC Taylor has left the interview, and now present is..."

"Detective Chief Inspector Dinescu, warrant number ND3265."

"Aren't you the senior investigating officer in this case?" asked Ms Wright.

"I am."

"We don't get many of those in interviews."

Dinescu smiled. "I need the practice."

The solicitor held a statement in her hand and was eager to show it to Summers and Dinescu.

Summers looked at the paper. "Ms Wright, have you had the opportunity to speak with your client?"

"I have."

"Mr Faulkner," said Summers, "as discussed with your solicitor, we consulted with the CPS regarding charging you for the rape and murder of Maisy Brady, along with Mackenzie

Masterson and Jason Hyde. We would now like to ask you questions regarding the murder of Charles Brady on Monday, the 17th of April. You have been further arrested on suspicion of his murder. I see your solicitor has a prepared statement for us."

"I have," said Wright. "It's a shame I wasn't here for the earlier interview."

"Mr Faulkner was given repeated opportunities to request a solicitor."

"Hmm. Mr Faulkner will not be answering your questions regarding Mr Charles Brady. However, he would like to say that on the day in question, the 17th of April 2023, he was at home until ten o'clock in the morning. He then travelled to Bognor Regis to visit his daughter. On the way to Bognor, at about 10:30, Mr Brady went to the petrol station on Chichester Road and filled up his car. Then he drove to his daughter's house and stayed with her for about two hours. At about 1:30 in the afternoon, he drove to Worthing, where he attended the Magistrates' Court regarding a speeding ticket he had contested. He was in Worthing until about four o'clock when he paid for parking in the Civic Centre car park using his bank card. He then returned to his daughter's house at about 4:30 and had dinner with her, leaving Bognor Regis at 6:30 that evening. Once you have made your inquiries, you will find the evidence supporting Mr Faulkner's alibi. Mr Faulkner would like to say although he had had disagreements with Charles Brady, he would never have hurt him. He did not kill Charles Brady. That is all he is going to say on the matter."

"Thank you, Archie," said Dinescu. "That is extremely helpful. I want to show you an email that Charles Brady sent to Celia Lambert, dated Monday morning, the 17th of April, 2023. This is exhibit ES/17."

Dinescu read out some text from the email printout in front of them. *"Your mother, Olivia, and Archie know something.*

There's Mac and Jason, too. Do you want Maisy's blood on your hands?" He looked into Archie's eyes. "What did Brady think you knew, Archie?"

"No comment."

"No comment? Okay. After we arrested Olivia, we completed a Section 18 PACE search of your home. I am specifically interested in something we didn't find there."

Wright raised an eyebrow. "Something you *didn't* find?"

"Yes, Ms Wright. Archie, do you own a shotgun?"

He looked at his solicitor. "No comment."

"We have on our records that you have a shotgun licence. You have a shotgun cabinet in your house. It didn't contain a shotgun. Where is your shotgun?"

"No comment."

"Did you lend it to someone?"

"No comment."

"Your partner, Olivia, told us she thought it was still in the cabinet. Do you think Olivia borrowed it?"

"No. She hates it."

"That's what she said. So where is it?"

"No comment."

"Who else could have had access to the gun?"

"No comment."

"How about Jason or Mackenzie?"

Faulkner looked up and gave him a filthy look. "No comment."

"How about Cameron?"

"No comment."

"No, wait. He had access to the gun in his workshop, so he didn't need to borrow yours."

Archie Faulkner sighed and glanced at the solicitor.

"Cameron mislaid that shotgun for a week. What do you think happened to it?"

Wright looked up. "My client can't possibly know what happened to property in someone else's possession."

"But we think he does, Ms Wright," said Dinescu. "We believe Archie found the gun in Cameron's workshop and hid it for a while."

"I assume you have evidence to support that statement."

"You assume correctly, Ms Wright. Forensics found carpet fibres stuck to the heel of the shotgun. I'm told that's the end part of the butt. The carpet fibres are an exact match for the carpet in your house, Archie. The one by the gun cabinet. How did the fibres get on the gun that Cameron Hyde had, Archie?"

Dinescu could see the slight shake of Wright's head.

Archie's breathing had become shallow, and he shrugged. "No comment."

"There must be a perfectly reasonable explanation, mustn't there?"

"I didn't kill Brady!"

"Archie, I believe you took the shotgun from the workshop to incriminate Cameron. That gun wasn't used to kill Brady, but trying to incriminate him with it tells us that you know who did. Do you know who killed Charles Brady?"

"No."

"I believe that you hiding that gun points to you conspiring with someone to kill Brady. Why else would you do it? Am I right, Archie?"

"No comment."

"Who were you conspiring with?"

"No comment."

"Olivia told us Charles had come to your house and challenged you about Maisy. Was it Mackenzie, Jason? They were there, weren't they?"

"No fucking comment."

Dinescu looked at the notes from Olivia's interview. Then

he felt like something was crawling up the back of his neck. He had seen something, and that sparked another memory. He reread Olivia's account of Brady at their house. Then a thought made its way to his lips, forcing a smile.

"Interview suspended. I need to confer with DS Summers. One minute."

Summers followed Dinescu out into the corridor, and Dinescu pointed to the notes she had taken.

"What is it, boss?"

"Archie couldn't have killed Brady if his alibi checks out. And it will be easy to check."

"True, sir. But as you said, the fibres on the gun returned to the workshop show he was trying to frame Cameron. He must have been conspiring with someone to kill Brady."

"Who else was there when Brady went to their house to confront Archie?"

Dinescu handed Summers Olivia Grainger's interview notes. She reread it twice, and then she saw it. "Susan? We know nothing about Grainger's daughter. Archie said he visited her on the way to Worthing. He could have brought the gun to her in Bognor."

"But suppose we've got this wrong, Emily. What if it wasn't Archie who Ethan saw returning the gun to the workshop? If it wasn't Archie returning the gun, then he wasn't conspiring to kill Charles Brady."

"Who? Olivia Grainger?"

"She was worried Brady was getting too close to the truth. She was at the school already and had access to Archie's gun. If framing Cameron didn't work, then it would fall back on Archie. And she suspected Archie had lied to her about Maisy. Grainger didn't want to be seen carrying the shotgun, so Susan could have helped her by dealing with the gun for her. She may even still have possession of it. I'll get Archie put back in his cell, and then you and I can visit his daughter right now."

It was dark, and Dinescu was driving. The wipers on the silver Ford Focus were sweeping the windows, trying to clear the torrential rain. Traffic was crawling along the road to Bognor.

"Jeepers!" said Summers. "We'll have to call out a rescue boat if we get stuck in this."

Dinescu was fixed on the road ahead, sitting forward in his seat.

"Sorry to make you work late. It's been a long day, but I think we're nearly there with this."

"It's been an eventful day."

"You can tell Kieran all about it when you see him at the weekend."

Summers felt herself blush like a schoolgirl, and she was glad it was dark.

After another twenty minutes, they had made it into Bognor Regis, and the satnav took them to a house on Rowan Way. After they had pulled up outside, they waited for a few minutes, but it didn't look like the rain would ease up anytime soon.

"There's a light on," said Summers. "How are we going to do this?"

"I don't know." Dinescu laughed. "Play it by ear."

Dinescu put on his waterproof flat cap, and Summers pulled up her hood. She updated control with their location, and then they hurried to take cover under the porch. Dinescu rang the doorbell.

A blonde woman in her thirties opened the door. "Hello?" She had a medium build, large blue eyes, and high cheekbones. On the right side of her nose was a silver stud.

Dinescu and Summers held out their warrant cards.

"Hello, Susan. I'm DS Summers, and this is DCI Dinescu from Chichester CID. You spoke to one of our colleagues recently regarding Charles Brady. I have a couple more questions if you don't mind."

She looked wary of them and then glanced behind her. "I'm about to go out."

"It won't take a minute. And the roads are flooded around Bognor. Awful weather, isn't it? We're getting drenched."

Susan Grainger let the detectives in, and they walked into her front room. It was in low light, but Dinescu could see the packages of sex toys and lubricants on the dining room table.

"Not embarrassed, are you?" she asked Dinescu.

"Not at all, Miss Grainger. You are hosting a party tonight?"

"Yes. Local, thank God! What do you want?"

Dinescu studied her face. "You're Olivia Grainger's daughter?"

"Yes."

"Seeing you in the light, I see you take after your father, Archie."

"I know. Why?"

"You'll know we are investigating the murder of Charles Brady. Did you ever meet Charles?"

"In passing. I sometimes visit my mum at the school and give her a hand."

Dinescu looked at Summers and nodded. She brought out folded sheets of A4 paper with printed writing on them. She handed one of them to Susan.

"This is a search warrant signed by a magistrate. We suspect you have your father's shotgun. He's been arrested on suspicion of the rape and murder of Maisy Brady, along with his friends. Your mother's been arrested for perverting the course of justice."

Susan Grainger dropped onto the sofa behind her. Her legs and knees were shaking, and she retched.

"Do you need a glass of water, Miss Grainger?" asked Dinescu.

A red rash swept down her neck, and she looked up at Summers and Dinescu. "No... It's under the stairs."

"The gun?"

"Yes."

Dinescu clipped on a body-worn video camera, put on a pair of gloves, and returned to the hallway. The cupboard under the stairs had a light inside. He cleared away a spider's web and pulled out a vacuum cleaner and some old coats. On the floor lay a shotgun. It was streaked and peppered with something that had dried on the barrel and stock.

When he walked back into the lounge, he saw Susan had been sick on the sofa, and she was weeping. Dinescu nodded at Summers.

"Susan," he said, "listen carefully. I am arresting you on suspicion of conspiracy to murder Charles Brady. You do not have to say anything, but it may harm your defence if you do not mention, when questioned, something that you later rely on in court. Anything you do say may be given in evidence. Your arrest is necessary for prompt and effective investigation, to prevent loss or destruction of evidence, and to prevent you from causing harm to yourself or others."

Summers moved over to Susan and handcuffed her, avoiding the vomit on the chair. Dinescu called the control room and requested SOCO to come and deal with the gun.

"Come on, Susan," said Summers.

"Charles was going to ruin us. You don't know what he was like."

"We can't talk about it now, Susan. Wait until the interview." Summers looked at her watch. "That will be tomorrow morning."

Chapter Thirty-Nine

It was early on Saturday morning. David Roberts and Andrew Winston were covering for the lack of a matron. Winston had heard that Grainger was still in custody, but Greenway couldn't see that she had done anything wrong and wanted her to return to work as soon as she was released. It was Winston who objected. He'd had enough of trying to bury news and short-cutting procedures. So Greenway told him he had to cover for Matron himself.

The morning light through the visitor's bedroom window had woken him before the knock on his door. Winston took a while to find his bearings and realise where he was.

"Who is it?" he shouted.

"Harry Price, sir," said a voice behind the door.

"What is it, Harry? It's Saturday morning! Why are you up so early?"

"It's Dan, sir. I'm worried about him."

Winston sighed. "Really? Go back to your room, Harry. I'll be with you in a few minutes."

After dressing, Winston left the room and walked along the

corridor, smelling the beginnings of breakfast. He went down one floor and found Room One-Alpha. He knocked and entered. Harry was sitting on his own, looking out of the window. Ethan Bishop's old bed was bare, as was his table, and Daniel Curtis's bed didn't look like it had been slept in. Harry turned around, and his eyes were wide open.

"What is it, Harry? Where's Daniel?"

"He didn't come in last night. I haven't seen him since after dinner. He's been acting strangely. Rocking, mumbling to himself. That twitch of his has got worse. Then he said he wanted to go home."

"I know, but his parents told us they wanted us to keep him here."

"I don't understand why he wants to go. He hates it there."

"I don't know, Harry."

"None of you lot ever listen. Greenway doesn't care about us. He's just out to make money. You don't know half of what's going on around here."

Winston sat on Ethan's bed and rubbed his eyes. He felt defeated. "I think you're right, Harry. Too many heads buried in the sand. Where do you think he is?"

"I don't know. His stuff's still here."

Winston groaned. "God, not another one gone. Is there something in the water? Give me a clue where he'd be?"

"He spends all his time by himself. He spies on people, watching everything that goes on."

"Is that how he got the New Year's party photos in the dining hall?"

Harry nodded. "There are hidden passages all over the place. He knows them all."

"Do you know where they are?"

"One of them. Above the dining hall."

"Show me."

Harry grabbed a torch and led Winston into the corridor and to the top of the main staircase. He stopped beside some oak panelling and looked at Winston.

"What? Why have we stopped?"

"It's here, sir." Harry pointed to the panel. "You have to get your fingers into the crack and pull."

Harry showed him, and Winston helped him pull. The panel was a narrow door that opened outward, revealing the cavity behind it.

"Just follow the passage." Harry handed Winston the torch, and Winston checked he had his mobile phone with him. He didn't want to be the victim of a prank and be left shut in.

"Wait here and keep the door open." He gave Harry a look that ensured he understood he wasn't in the mood to be messed with.

Winston slipped behind the door and saw the passage lying straight ahead. He walked on and saw the gaps in an iron grate. He looked through and saw the dining room below him. He turned on the torch and walked further. There was something black on the floor. At first, he thought someone had left an old coat there. He shone the torch onto the coat and saw a pair of white hands clasped together over bent knees. The hood was covering the face. Winston felt his heart racing as the thought came to him that Daniel Curtis could be dead.

"Dan?" he said.

The hood moved, and Daniel looked up into the light. He held his hand in front of him.

"Who is it?" he said. "Don't kill me! Please!"

"Dan, it's Mr Winston. Why are you here?"

"Leave me alone! I won't let you kill me."

"I won't hurt you, Daniel. I want to help you."

But Daniel sprung to his feet, and Winston saw the terror on his face.

"Dan. Come on. Let's get out of here. We'll get some breakfast. I don't know about you, but I'm starving."

There was a sudden swoosh of Daniel's coat, and he ran past Winston, knocking him to the ground.

"Dan!"

But he had gone through the door. Winston got to his feet and ran after him. When he returned to the top of the staircase, he saw Harry looking confused.

"Which way, Harry!"

"He went towards the other staircase."

"Harry, get Mr Roberts!"

Winston ran towards another set of stairs and heard footsteps above him. He ran up, two steps at a time, but Daniel was leaving him behind. He had reached the top floor, but there was another set of stairs that led into the attic. A light appeared from above him. Daniel had gone into the roof space. Winston continued up, now out of breath, and found the door into the attic was open. He ran in. Windows were looking out onto the roof. Spare mattresses were stored in piles, along with old pieces of furniture. Winston stood still and listened. All he could hear was his own rapid heartbeat.

"Dan! Come on. It's okay. You're not in trouble. Come and talk to me. I want to help you."

Nothing.

Winston walked along the boards that creaked under his feet. The dust was hitting the back of his throat, and he stifled a cough.

"Dan? Come on. It's okay. I want to—"

There was a clatter from across the attic. A window flew open, and he saw Daniel climbing through.

"Oh, shit! Dan!"

He ran over and climbed onto a heap of mattresses. Looking out the window, Winston saw the slope of the roof tiles that dropped onto a ledge covered with lead flashing. Daniel was standing on it, looking down at the drop below him onto the driveway.

Winston stopped. He felt helpless. Daniel was out of reach, and he'd most likely fall himself if he tried.

Daniel glanced at Winston. "They said it would be dangerous for me here."

"Dangerous? What do you mean, Dan?"

"They said the school would hurt me if I told anyone about the blonde woman. I knew who she was, though. I've seen her before."

"I don't understand, Daniel. Who told you that?"

"They said I couldn't tell anyone. I know it's the right thing to do, Mr Winston, but if I do..."

"Can you come in and talk about it with me, Dan? It's not very safe up here. I don't want you to fall. What would your parents say?"

"They don't give a shit about me, Mr Winston. No one does. Everyone thinks I'm a joke. A bloody joke. Soon everyone will be gone. First, it was Ethan, and then... Harry."

"You can't stay at school forever, Dan. You're eighteen now. Harry's eighteen."

"He doesn't even notice me, Mr Winston."

"Who, Harry?"

"Yes, I do, Dan." Harry was there behind Winston. "You're my mate. Of course I notice you. You are a bit quiet sometimes, though."

"Harry?" Daniel looked around and saw Winston holding out his hand. "No! They're going to kill me. The Grey Friar is going to kill me! They got to Ethan, too, and now he's gone."

"I know what he's talking about, sir," said Harry. "Ethan told us someone had threatened him. He reckoned he saw someone by Cam's workshop the night before that gun reappeared."

"Who was it?" said Winston.

"I don't know. Dan's all confused. He keeps saying Archie's going to kill him. Then it's the Grey Friar who's after him."

Winston nodded at Harry and then stretched down further towards Daniel. "Dan? Please take my hand. Archie's been arrested. He can't hurt you now." Daniel went still and took half a step towards the ledge. "Please, Dan! Don't."

"Arrested?"

"Yes! Archie, Jason, and Mac. They're all in police cells. Did they threaten you?"

"They said something bad would happen if I told anyone about the blonde woman."

"Dan!" shouted Harry. "I promise you. I won't let anyone hurt you. Mr Winston really is here to help you. That shit, Archie, is never coming out again. Police with guns arrested him."

"Isn't he, Harry?"

"Archie's gone, mate. I know I mess with you sometimes, but I was following Ethan. I'm sorry—I won't do it again. I promise."

Daniel turned around and looked past Winston to see Harry's face. He nodded and gave a gentle smile. Winston opened and closed his hand, and Daniel stepped towards him. There was a scuff of a shoe. Daniel slipped and dropped. He was on his side, sliding towards the edge. Winston leaned out and grabbed the hood of Daniel's coat, but it was slipping off him, and Daniel cried out.

"Your hand, Dan!"

Daniel stuck out his hand, and Winston had the tips of his fingers. He couldn't grip them, and they slipped out of his grasp. For an eternity, there was nothing but horror as Daniel slipped away. Winston was knocked out of the way by a flash of blue.

Roberts and Harry both reached out, hanging out of the window. Roberts had a sleeve, but Harry had Daniel's forearm. They both heaved, and Daniel came back from over the edge and in through the window, where they all fell back onto the mattresses.

Chapter Forty

DS Summers was happy to come in on a Saturday morning when needed. The same was true for the rest of the team. She knew they would be tired, but the rush from being so close to the end drove them on.

Summers and Burgess would interview Susan Grainger that morning. Summers had lost some sleep thinking about it, and she was also nervous about her date with Kieran later. She would be stepping out into unknown territory with Kieran. She had already decided what she would wear. She still had that dress she'd bought for a wedding that never happened. She loved it and was sad she'd never had the opportunity to wear it. It was short, like most of her dresses, but still classy. She knew Kieran wouldn't know what she looked like, but she hoped he would pick up on what she felt like wearing it.

Summers gathered herself together. She was working now and had to focus—even if her excitement didn't want her to.

Fewer staff and officers were around on a Saturday, so it was easier to find somewhere to park. She had found a space next to Dinescu's car and saw him ahead. She jogged to catch up with him.

"Good morning, boss." Her legs had to work twice as hard to keep up with him.

"Good morning, Emily. The sun has blessed us again this morning."

Summers looked up. Her mind was so preoccupied she hadn't noticed the golden morning light.

"Yes, sir."

"I requested the forensic testing for the shotgun be expedited. It's a shame it's the weekend, though. We may need an extension to keep Susan Grainger in custody. I'm sure the CPS will agree to charge her father, Hyde, and Masterson today with Maisy Brady's murder." Dinescu swiped his warrant card to enter the building. "What do you think Susan's defence will be?"

"She was looking after the gun for her mother, or Archie even? Or someone else?"

"That is what I was thinking. We need to place her at the school. That's the only thing we're missing. I have requested ANPR checks on the road to Midhurst. We have her vehicle details."

The two detectives walked into Major Crimes. Burgess was already there and met them both with coffee.

"Thanks, Sarah," said Summers. "You're in early."

"I had trouble sleeping. My cat didn't help when it jumped onto my stomach, either."

"Any updates?" said Dinescu.

"DNA results are in," said Burgess. "They confirm for certain it was Maisy Brady's body in the priest hole—well, a biological sister of Charles."

"That's good, especially with the name tags sewn into the clothing."

"And they've already started work on that gun you seized last night."

"Excellent," said Dinescu. "The CSI Manager expedited them."

Burgess nodded. "When we were searching Grainger's home, we saw a photo of Archie carrying a young girl. I didn't know Grainger and Faulkner had a child together."

"Poor girl," said Summers.

"Susan Grainger is consulting with a solicitor as we speak," continued Burgess. "The CPS wouldn't go with the perverting the course of justice charge for Olivia Grainger. They thought there was too much of a risk with her mother's lack of mental capacity when she wrote the letter. Shall I get her released?"

"No," said Dinescu. He sipped his coffee. "But there is something you can do. We have some suspicion now that she shot Brady. She also had access to the gun that was returned to the workshop. She could have tried to frame Cameron Hyde. There is enough to further arrest her on suspicion of conspiracy to murder Brady."

"Certainly is, boss. You want me to do that?"

"Yes, please, Sarah. Emily and I were asking, what evidence was there to put Susan Grainger at the school at the time of the murder?"

"Nothing so far, sir."

"We can hold off the interview, boss?" said Summers.

"No. We will make a start. Further arrest Olivia Grainger, then you and Sarah can start your preparation. I'll look over the notes and watch the interview."

"Yes, sir."

Summers hadn't met Susan Grainger's duty solicitor before. She had an implacable look in her eye and a sour face, but Summers knew it was her professional disposition, and it wasn't personal.

Burgess was with Summers for the interview, and she entered the room with her usual smiling confidence that reassured Summers.

Summers was calm and had everything ready to go—just how she liked it. There was no point in stirring anyone up at this point. Susan Grainger didn't look so relaxed. She kept glancing up at the video camera as if she were sending messages to it.

"Apologies for keeping you both. We had a last-minute matter to deal with."

"That's okay," said Susan. "As long as I'm out by lunchtime. I have an appointment with a client."

Burgess flashed her a smile.

"Susan," said Summers, "when we arrested you last night, we have on the body-worn video that you said, and I quote, *Charles was going to ruin us. You don't know what he was like.* Explain to me what you meant by that. Unpack it for me."

"I don't know what I meant," Susan replied. "I was upset. I was just thinking out loud. Charles Brady didn't like Dad. He made loads of threats against him."

"What sort of threats?"

"You need to ask my dad about that, not me."

"When we searched your home last night, we found a double-barrelled shotgun in a cupboard under your stairs. It was covered with coats and other clothes. Whose gun is it?"

"It isn't mine."

"Okay. Whose gun *is* it? It's not hard for us to find out, but it would be helpful if you could tell us."

"My dad's."

"Archie Faulkner?"

"Yes."

"What circumstances led to the gun being under the stairs of your house?"

"My dad asked me to look after it for him."

"Did he bring it to you?"

"Yes."

Summers nodded and made a note. "What reason did he give you?"

"He was worried that someone was trying to frame him for Charles Brady's murder. He gave it to me last week to look after."

"Did you ask him why he thought that?"

"Yes. He thought Cameron was trying to set him up."

"What day did he bring the gun to you?"

"Monday, the 24th."

"The day we discovered Charles Brady's body."

"That's it."

"Did you handle the gun yourself?"

Susan Grainger nodded. "I touched it, yes. I put it under the stairs."

"Did you touch the trigger mechanism?"

"God, no!"

"Can you describe the appearance of the gun when your father brought it to you?"

"I don't know! It was a shotgun."

"Had you seen your father's gun before?"

"Yes. It just looked the same as it always did."

"When we seized the weapon, I noticed it was soiled with dried matter. Smeared with blood to my untrained eye. The weapon has been sent to our forensics teams for analysis. It may take a few days."

"Shame."

"However, they could immediately confirm the smear marks were blood. A lot of blood. They also found debris in some of the grooves and crevasses on the external surfaces of the barrel and the stock. Where do you think that material is from?"

Susan's head jerked as she shuddered. "Rabbits?"

"A close-range kill, perhaps?"

"Must have been if there was blowback on the gun."

Summers nodded and smiled. "Must have been."

"Have you fired that shotgun in the last two weeks?"

"No. About a year ago. But not recently."

Summers sat back and nodded at Burgess.

Burgess took over. "Tell us about your relationship with Charles Brady."

"I didn't know him. I knew who he was, but we weren't friends or anything. We barely spoke."

"Did Charles Brady know you were Archie Faulkner's daughter?"

"No, but I think he knew Olivia was my mum."

"Would you have any reason to meet with Charles at all?"

"No. I had nothing to do with him."

"So, you have only said a few words to each other since you've known him?"

"Maybe hello or goodbye."

"Did your mother talk about Charles at all?"

"Sometimes gossip."

"Have you ever been to his flat?"

"No! I didn't know him."

"Someone told us they visited Charles on the evening of the last Saturday in March. That was the 25th. They described a blonde woman matching your description in his flat. Charles and the woman were arguing together. He even described a nose stud like the one you took out when you were booked into custody. How can you explain that?"

"I can't. I've never been to his flat. I'm not the only woman who wears a nose stud."

"I suppose we could get his flat forensically examined. Would we find your fingerprints in there?"

"I doubt it."

Summers smiled. "What did you know about Charles's sister?"

"Just random stuff I'd heard from Mum. When she was little, she went missing, and Charles thought she was buried in the school. He thought my dad had killed her. Bollocks, most of it."

"Charles thought your dad killed Maisy? Did your dad tell you that?"

"Mum."

"Do you believe your dad killed Maisy, Charles's sister?"

"No! Mum said Charles was a fantasist. Mum was living in the school when he was a kid. She knew Dad then, too. Dad wouldn't have hurt anyone."

Summers held her gaze for a moment. "Your mum was only seven, Susan. I'd be surprised if she could remember all of that. Charles wasn't a fantasist, though. Did you hear we found Maisy's body?"

"I heard something, but the body could have belonged to anyone."

"No. It's Maisy Brady. We've had DNA results through that confirm it."

Susan Grainger looked at both of them and sighed, trying to look bored. "Fair enough."

"So, Charles was right about Maisy being buried in the school. Did your mother believe Archie killed Maisy?"

"I'm not going to answer questions about my mum."

The solicitor looked up from writing her notes. "Sounds reasonable to me, DS Summers."

There was a knock on the door, and the interview was suspended. It was DCI Dinescu, and he had some new information for Summers. They went out into the corridor and closed the door.

Dinescu was smiling. "I have some news. Ask Sarah to put her back in the cell briefly."

～

Dinescu and Summers left the custody building and walked over to the police station. Summers was glad for the break. Dinescu led the way to a witness interview room.

"She's lying when she said she'd never spoken to Charles Brady before," said Summers. "She's pretty much an exact description given by Ricky Brady. What was she doing there? Trying to warn Brady off?"

"We don't need it," said Dinescu. "We have something, and Chester has pulled together a video ID parade for us."

"Intriguing, boss."

Summers and Dinescu entered the interview room. Daniel Curtis and Andrew Winston were on one side of the table, and DC Chester Kirby was on the other. Daniel wasn't in uniform and looked relaxed while signing a statement. He looked up at Summers and Dinescu.

"All done, sir," said Kirby.

"Hello," said Daniel. "I've seen you around the school."

"Hi, Daniel," said Summers with a smile. "It's really brave of you to come in. I'm Detective Sergeant Emily Summers, and this is Detective Chief Inspector Dinescu."

"Chief inspector? Gosh! That's a high rank, isn't it?"

"It is," said Summers.

Daniel studied Dinescu's face for a moment. "That mark on your face—did you get it from rescuing someone?"

"I did," said Dinescu. "And he rescued me, too."

Daniel nodded. "You can be proud of that, sir."

"I am, thank you. That was a brave thing you did today,

Daniel," said Dinescu. "You identified the woman you saw talking to Mr Brady in his office."

"I did. I've seen her before in the school with Matron. I hope it's helpful."

"Extremely. What day was it you saw her?"

"The Monday before last. The 17th."

"What time was that?"

"About three o'clock."

Dinescu picked up Daniel's statement. "And you overheard her say this to Mr Brady?"

"Yes. Definitely."

"Archie and his cronies threatened Daniel," said Winston. "He's put that in a statement, too. Daniel needs to know Archie's not coming out."

"Oh, yes," said Summers. "Archie Faulkner is unlikely to be free ever again."

Chapter Forty-One

Dinescu stepped into the interview room, and the solicitor went a little pale. The scar on his face had unsettled her.

"Yes, I know," Dinescu said to her, smiling. "You don't often get the SIO in interviews. Some days are like that around here."

"Interview recommenced," said Summers. "DC Sarah Burgess has left the interview room, and with us now is…"

"Detective Chief Inspector Dinescu, warrant number ND3265. I appreciate your patience."

Susan examined her fingernails, and Summers sat forward. "How tall are you, Susan?"

"How tall am I? Five-eight. Same height as Mum."

"Do you own a blue fleece? Like the Cotisham School fleeces?"

"No."

"What were you doing in the afternoon of Monday, the 17th of April 2023?"

"I was with my dad. He came to see me and then went to Worthing for a court case. I stayed in and waited for him, making tea. He had tea with me and then went off. I stayed at home."

"So you never went to the school that afternoon, around three o'clock?"

"No. I was at home."

"You said you had seen Charles Brady a few times before but had never spoken more than a few words to him. Have you ever sat with him in his office for a private meeting? Face-to-face?"

"Ha! Never. Why would I? He didn't know me."

"Not once."

"No!"

"And not on the 17th of April?"

"Are you deaf or something? No!" Susan Grainger sat back in her chair. There was something about her attitude that reminded Summers of Susan's father.

"It's just that we have someone who said he saw you at the school at about three o'clock on the 17th."

"No, you haven't!"

"In Brady's office. With the door closed. Talking face-to-face with him."

The corner of Grainger's mouth twitched as she tried to smile. "Bollocks you have!"

"I'm not playing with you, Susan." Summers sat forward and met Susan's dark stare. "We have a student witness who has identified you. He knows who you are. He knows you are the matron's daughter. We also used an approved video identification parade method, including a video of you in Custody. The student told us he heard you telling Brady to meet someone at the folly tower."

Susan Grainger's head twitched. "He's lying! The little shit!"

"Why would he lie? He doesn't know you personally. He's seen you with your mother before."

The solicitor gave a polite cough. "Forgive me if I'm being

dense here, but how could anyone have witnessed my client meeting with Brady if the door was closed and they were alone together?"

"Of course," said Dinescu. "You wouldn't know. Nor would you, Susan. There are cavities behind many of the walls in the school. I recently learned the Tudors designed them to listen into secret conversations. They even gave an early warning in case the priest hunters came calling. This particular student had the unfortunate habit of spying on people. He's known for it. He saw you, Susan, walking with Brady to his office and followed you. He stepped into the cavity and listened to your conversation."

Susan Grainger looked down at the table. "Weasel!"

"Is that your only response?"

"Can I see the statement?" said the solicitor.

Dinescu shook his head. "No, you can't—not until we've fully redacted his details."

"My advice to my client is for her not to answer any more of your questions."

Dinescu shrugged. "Susan, you were seen in Charles Brady's office shortly before his murder. What is your response to that?"

Susan looked at her solicitor. "No comment."

Dinescu sat forward and produced a printout of numbers and times. "I am showing you exhibit SB/05, Susan. It is a copy of ANPR records for the date of Charles Brady's murder. ANPR stands for Automatic Number Plate Recognition. They are cameras that read the registration plates of cars that pass by. Susan, do you own a red Renault Clio with this registration?" Dinescu pointed to the printout.

"No comment."

"We have checked with the DVLA, and you are the vehicle's registered owner. We also know you have insurance on that vehicle as the only driver."

"No comment."

"Your vehicle passed an ANPR camera heading towards Midhurst on the A286 at 14:32 hours on the 17th of April. That camera is one mile from Cotisham School. I put it to you that you weren't at home making your dad's tea at that time. I believe that was a lie. So, we are now wondering what else you are lying about. What is your response to these allegations, Susan?"

"No comment."

"Susan? I am listening. Is there something I have misunderstood here? What is your explanation? We know you were at the school. You were seen, and you were in the area according to ANPR—"

"Fucking Curtis!" She exploded, thumping the table.

Dinescu looked unimpressed. "So, you know it was Mr Curtis who saw you."

"Dad told me."

"Your dad and his so-called friends put two and two together. They thought you'd met with Charles Brady to kill him, probably to silence his accusations. He's very protective of you, so he threatened young Mr Curtis to keep him quiet. A foolish thing to do."

The solicitor held up her hands. "I need to talk to my client alone!"

"Not at the moment," said Summers, ignoring the solicitor.

Susan Grainger's eyes were flitting between Dinescu and Summers. "Mum said she'd—"

The solicitor sat forward. "Now, please, DS Summers."

"In a moment," said Summers. "Susan was going to tell us something. Your mum said what?"

"Nothing."

"So," said Dinescu, "I put it to you that you met with Charles Brady around three o'clock on the Monday he died, within the time window he was shot. What is your response?"

"No comment."

"I also put it to you that you asked Charles Brady to go with you to the tower. You were overheard saying you would be meeting someone there. Who were you meeting? Or were you actually on your own?"

"No comment."

"Perhaps you didn't meet anyone. Perhaps you led Charles Brady to the tower and shot him yourself. Perhaps you hated what he said about your father or even your mother. Is any of that true, Susan?"

Susan Grainger trembled. "No!"

Dinescu pressed on. "You know as well as I do that the material deposited on the shotgun was, as you put it crudely, *blowback*. But it was from Charles Brady's body. Will we find your DNA and fingerprints on the gun, Susan?"

"I only had to get rid of it for her. That's all. I didn't kill him!"

The solicitor tapped Susan Grainger's shoulder. "Susan, I advise you to shut up and speak to me in private."

"Shit! I can't do this anymore." Her face was red, and her eyes were bloodshot. "I didn't kill Charles Brady. I just had to put the gun in the tower. Later, I delivered Charles to her and took the gun away."

"Delivered Charles Brady to who?"

"Mum."

"Olivia Grainger?"

"Yes."

"Did you see your mother shoot Charles Brady?"

Susan shook as she sobbed. "Yes!" She buried her face in her hands. "It was horrible!"

They gave her a moment, and Summers passed her some tissues. The solicitor shrugged and closed her notepad.

"Did she tell you why?" asked Summers.

"She knew Dad lied to her, but she still protected him. Everything changed when she got a letter from Gran. It all went wrong from then on. You'll have to talk to Mum."

"Why did you offer to help your mother?"

"She was desperate. She thought Brady was going to ruin us. She said something about Gran, too. I didn't understand it. I was terrified, but I had to help. Mum hates guns, but Brady threatened to call the police on her and Dad. I didn't care so much about Dad. Mum and I found a way to blame it on that tosser, Cameron. But it didn't work. Look, I tried to stop Brady myself. I went to his flat. But Brady wouldn't listen to me. That's when I saw his son at the door—he just messed everything up."

"Did you know Brady had hired a private detective to help him?"

"Yes, and she looked a lot like me. She was getting too close to discovering the tunnel under the tower. Dad said he put the frighteners on her, and it worked."

Dinescu looked at Summers and nodded.

"You need to know the truth, Susan," said Summers. "I believe your dad lied to a lot of people. This afternoon, the CPS has agreed to charge Archie, Mackenzie and Jason for the rape and murder of Maisy Brady."

"I hope Dad burns in hell."

"We'll also be putting forward our evidence concerning you. Anything else to add? Anything you want to clarify?"

She shook her head.

"Interview terminated."

Dinescu was watching the video feed of the interview alongside Taylor, Booker, and Kirby. Summers and Burgess were in the interview room and looked weary now. It had been a hard day for them both.

"She always looks fresh," said Kirby out of nowhere.

"Who?" said Booker. "The DS?"

"I meant Sarah. She's like always chilled. Like she's stepped out of the shower."

"Steady, Chester!" laughed Booker.

"I didn't mean it like that."

"Shush, guys," said Taylor. "I can't hear."

Olivia Grainger stared in front of her as Summers put to her the evidence from her daughter. She told her about Daniel Curtis's statement and the details about the shotgun. Finally, she revealed what Archie Faulkner had said in his interviews.

Ross Taylor turned up the volume on the screen to hear Grainger's reaction.

"Brady was going to ruin me and my family," she said to Summers. "He could have hurt my mother."

Summers ran her fingers through her hair. "Susan said things changed when you got the letter from your mother. Is there anything else you want to say about that letter, Olivia? Is there anything you may have missed?"

"No. I said what I said. Mother was probably in the land of the fairies when she wrote it, anyway. She was and is a good woman. She'd put up with much heartache in her life. When Gerald Faulkner-Williams made her go down and check the girl was dead, it nearly broke her. She was a different woman after that."

"How could Charles Brady have hurt your mother?"

"He would have dragged it all up again. He would have told everyone what he had heard her say in the nursing home. I wasn't going to let him bring her name into disrepute. I would not let him slander my mother. She couldn't defend herself."

"How did you convince Brady to meet with you in the folly tower?"

"I told Susan to tell him I could show him where Maisy was buried. He had a thing about that bloody tower. He was convinced Maisy was buried beneath it or entombed in its walls. He spent hours up there, thinking and drinking. I could see him from my office in the school some days, even when it was raining. Idiot. I told him I had something I could show him. That was all it needed. Susan came first, and he followed. Susan had put the gun in the tower earlier for me. She'd do anything for me. He came up to meet me and... I did it. I pulled the trigger. I had to get close to him, or I'd miss him. I killed Charles. Detestable things, guns."

"Did you try to put suspicion on Cameron Hyde by taking the shotgun from his workshop?"

"Yes," said Grainger. "I returned it after Charles's body was found, but one of the students saw me—Ethan. I tried scaring him with the Grey Friar by chasing him away with a hammer." She shook her head and smirked. "My mother invented him to keep the boys from poking their noses where they shouldn't. I just carried it on."

Burgess and Summers looked at each other, and then Summers straightened her notes.

"Is there anything you think I've misunderstood or anything you want to clarify?"

"No."

"The time is now 16:30 hours. Interview terminated."

Dinescu switched off the monitor.

"I don't get it," said Booker. "Charles Brady just wanted to know what happened. He wasn't being a dick about it. He didn't deserve what they did to him."

"I think it's something about the house," said Taylor. "It's like it's built around secrets. Secret passages, snooping on people, hiding dead babies and children. Hiding people away. Maybe it's all the curse of this Grey Friar."

"We deal with people hiding the truth all the time," said Dinescu. "It's human nature, sadly."

"Never seen it before like this place," said Taylor.

"Agree with you there, Ross," said Booker.

"Lots of writing to do now," said Dinescu. "But most of that can wait until Monday. Thank you all for your extra hours today."

Chapter Forty-Two

"You know this is a bizarre thing to do," said Beniamin to Lisa.

It was Saturday night, and the bar was busy, but they had found stools with a good view over the restaurant dining area.

"I can't help it if I'm overprotective of my little brother," said Lisa, ducking down behind Dinescu's large frame. They were sitting a safe distance away from Emily and Kieran, and Emily had her back to them. She looked stunning in a short blue sleeveless dress and heels, with her hair tied up.

Beniamin could hear Kieran's loud laughter, and Emily was gesticulating as she did when she was excited and telling a story.

"We should leave them alone now. They are both happy. Emily isn't going to make him do anything he doesn't want to."

"That's a shame." Lisa laughed as she said it, and Kieran turned his head. "Bugger. I think we've been rumbled."

"Rumbled?" said Beniamin, looking at Lisa's embarrassed grimace. "What is *rumbled*?"

"This is," said Emily, standing behind Beniamin with Kieran.

"Emily! Fancy that!" said Lisa, who had turned bright pink. "There's no point in pretending, is there."

"No," said Kieran. "You are a hopeless liar."

"How do you know I'm lying?"

"Are her lips moving, Emily?"

"They are."

"I'm sorry," said Beniamin. "We just wanted to spy on you because we are very nosy."

"I thought you'd taken a reconnaissance course, sir," said Emily. "Not very secretive today, are you."

Beniamin laughed. "Perhaps I wanted to be discovered. You both look very happy, so we're going back to Lisa's parents to pick up Sophia. We'll leave you alone."

Emily smiled. "I don't mind. It's sweet."

"Sickly sweet," said Kieran.

"You did amazing today, Emily," said Beniamin. "I've just heard from the CPS—all charged and remanded as expected."

"Of course."

"Now, we're going."

Beniamin and Lisa Dinescu left the restaurant and made their way back into West Street, towards their car. They were about to pass Doctor Siobhan Maguire's offices when Beniamin stopped outside and looked at the door.

"Going down that tunnel in the school has fixed something inside me," he said to Lisa.

"You're still going to continue with Doctor Maguire? I want my shopping trip and the stay in the hotel you promised."

"Did I promise that?"

"Yes, sort of."

Beniamin laughed. "Yes. I will see Siobhan, as agreed. Even if it's just to get some closure."

Lisa stretched up and kissed him on the cheek. "You did well today, too. And you came home again to me."

Epilogue

Monday, 1st May.

The front room of the nursing home felt the lift of the morning sun. The light was glinting off the sea, and the kite surfers were being thrown up into the air by the fresh breeze.

The staff were all in, talking about their weekends while they were clearing away the breakfast things and wiping down the table tops.

Sitting in her favourite chair, Ruth Lambert felt satisfied after having her porridge that morning. Toast for breakfast made her grumpy. Her mother had always burned hers when she was a child. Her father liked it burnt, and he wore a blue tie at the breakfast table most days. Gerald had a blue tie.

"Finish your toast!" Ruth said to a memory of herself. "We can't afford to waste it. Starving children in Africa would eat it."

But now she wasn't in her kitchen at home. She remembered her father was dead. She looked up, and there was Clare, the pretty nail girl.

"Hello, Ruth. It's time to do your nails again. It's a beautiful morning! The sun's shining—windy, though."

The nail girl was pregnant, and Ruth remembered that she had been pregnant once or twice. The babies were born at home, and Father had removed his tie and waited in the kitchen.

"I'm going to call her Liv," she said to Clare, but Clare just smiled. "Olivia. It's such a pretty name, don't you think?"

"It's a lovely name, Ruth. I'm trying to think of names. We already know it's a boy. I'm thinking Leo."

Ruth gave her right hand to Clare. She watched her paint the varnish the same way her mother used to do her own. Was her mother's name Clare, she wondered?

"Thank you, Clare," said Ruth, smiling.

"I bet you've had your porridge today."

"Yes."

"I had toast and marmalade. I love marmalade."

Ruth remembered Liv loved marmalade. She must get some more from the shops. That other girl hated it.

"Are you going out into the sunlight today, Ruth? Sit in the garden? You don't want to be stuck in the dark on a day like this."

Stuck in the dark. Sweet Maisy's stuck in the dark. Then she remembered.

"She's a whore!"

Clare patted her hand. "Now, now, Ruth. Not on such a lovely day."

There was something she had to tell Liv. There was a letter. She had put it in the letter.

"Simon needed little persuading—simple Simon, easily led."

"Who's Simon?"

"Tell Liv to read the letter. Maisy was a flirt, you see."

"Okay, Ruth."

"Tell Liv I killed her. The little bitch was trussed up like a chicken. Flaunting herself at Gerald. Tramp! My Gerald."

"A chicken!" Clare laughed and swapped hands. "Who was?"

"Maisy! Simple Simon did what I knew he'd do, and I found her in the dark. Her pretty blonde hair was all bloody. The boys had hit her, but not hard enough."

"Ruth? What are you saying?"

"She was still moving, you see. Still wriggling. I put her out of her misery, and I hit her again. And she stopped. It's in the letter. Tell Liv I killed her."

Acknowledgments

Firstly, I'd like to thank my editor, Val Evans, for her determined enthusiasm for my work and for seeing me through this project. Not only is she a brilliant editor, but she has also put up with me for twenty-five years of marriage.

Again, my heartfelt thanks go to my family and friends for your continued love and support, read-throughs, and suggestions, including Bob Lock, Beth Leeworthy-Evans, and Caitlin Gale. I'd also like to thank Darren Triggs for his more technical police procedural support. Any mistakes in this book are entirely my own.

To the Reader

I'm truly grateful for your support as a reader, and it would mean a lot to me if you could share your thoughts by leaving a review on Amazon. Your feedback is invaluable, helping both me and fellow readers. Thank you for being part of my writing journey.

London Bombings

I had recently started my police training in Ashford, Kent, when the news broke of the terror attacks in London on the 7th of July 2005. I still remember how I felt watching the unfolding horror on TV with other student officers and the feeling of helplessness we felt at the time.

Although I have fictionalised an account of one of the terrorist bombings that day, I do not wish to trivialise its terrible effect on the real victims and their families. I pay tribute to the bravery of the emergency workers who fought hard to save lives and the detective and forensic work that brought the murderers to justice.

About the Author

Matthew Evans lives in Chichester, West Sussex, UK. He is married, has three children and one grandchild. He served as a police officer for 18 years. He's a folk musician and the proud owner of 'Betty', his 1962 Morris Minor.

Email: matt@matthewjevans.co.uk
Website: www.matthewjevans.co.uk

Visit my website to subscribe to my newsletter, where you can read my latest updates, find out about new releases, and get exclusive inside information on my creative processes.

Also by Matthew J. Evans

The DI Angelis Crime Thriller Trilogy

You've never met a detective like DI Angelis before.

Chasing Shadows

Detective Inspector David Angelis investigates a gruesome murder that hits close to home. As he digs deeper, he uncovers a conspiracy with him in the centre, revealing unexpected abilities he can't explain. Angelis uncovers a dark underworld and a deadly psychopath fuelled by designer drugs. "Chasing Shadows" is the first instalment of a gripping crime thriller series with a supernatural twist like no other, where reality and the supernatural collide in a relentless chase through the shadows.

Hide Her Away

She thought she would be safe here, but how wrong could she be...

Alice is alone and terrified. He's hidden her away, and no one can find her. Can her strength of will, forged in an abusive marriage, bring her through this terrifying ordeal?

DI David Angelis, hit hard by personal tragedy and self-doubt, must solve the puzzle of Alice's disappearance and the trail of murder that ensues.

Hide Her Away is a gripping supernatural crime thriller and the next instalment in the Detective Inspector Angelis series, following the first novel, Chasing Shadows.

Take You Home

Unquestioning trust can be dangerous.

Detective Inspector David Angelis is thrown headlong into a mystery that links the tragic death of a mother over 12 years ago to the evil killer of two young women.

Angelis, enveloped in personal tragedy, finds solace and strength from his team and leads them in search of this perverted murderer. But a shadow looms over them from within the rank-and-file that sours the investigation and challenges Angelis's determination. Can he overcome personal bitterness and find his way to solve this mystery?

Take You Home is the third book in a police procedural crime thriller series with a supernatural edge. It has dark themes throughout.

The Max Fortis Thrillers

Heel of Achilles

Private detective **Max Fortis** is a former Met Police protection officer and MI5 agent. When a mysterious woman comes to Fortis for help, he becomes embroiled in a ruthless vendetta against him. Partnering with reporter **Ella Munro**, he takes on an investigation the police won't touch and uncovers a sordid underworld of murder, sex trafficking, and modern-day slavery.

Fortis must confront the demons from his secret past and form an unexpected alliance to bring down a ghost—a forgotten enemy bent on revenge—before it destroys him.

In this dark and fast-paced crime thriller, will the secrets and lies of the past exact their chilling revenge on Fortis, or will he overcome and serve justice on his enemy?

Made in United States
Orlando, FL
06 September 2024

51207426R00200